Dead Set:

A Zombie

Anthology

Edited by

Michelle McCrary

and

Joe McKinney

ISBN
0-9801850-9-2 (10 digit)
978-0-9801850-9-6 (13 digit)

Library of Congress Control Number: 2010902487

First Edition

Printed in the United States of America

Published by
23 House Publishing
405 Moseley St.
Jefferson, TX 75657
SAN 299-8084
www.23house.com

Cover illustration by George Cotronis
www.ravenkult.com

Table of Contents

THE CHILDREN'S HOUR

by Marge Simon

"You've a whole life ahead of you,"
That's what gramps said
at my birthday party this year.
He gave me a ten dollar bill,
& Momma wouldn't let me
spend it, so it's in the bank.
It's for college, Momma says.

We talk about the good things.
It's Anna's need, not mine,
& she keeps squeezing my hand.

Momma went out for food.
She came back so strange.
Now her face is gray,
& there's blood on her mouth.
It's my fault for crying.

Momma pounds on our door,
but Anna says we can't let her in,
now that she's one of them.

Dad's gone, don't know where.
Maybe he'll be home tomorrow,
but Anna doesn't think so.
It was so dark last night,
we couldn't see the moon.

I wonder if there is a moon in the sky
anymore.

INTRODUCTION

We've been up in this second floor motel room for three days now, waiting for the river of walking dead people out in the street to run its course. There's enough food and water for the four of us to last another week, maybe, as long as we ration it out. Hopefully, this particular flood of zombies will have moved on by then. But as the days bleed together, I'm getting less and less sure of that.

I remember reading the journals of pioneers out in the American West. They wrote of huge flocks of passenger pigeons that could blacken the sky over three states at a time. Those birds would decimate everything in their path And what they didn't eat, they left covered in their filth.

Well, it seems the zombie is the new passenger pigeon. They form huge carnivorous rivers of fingernails and teeth, eating anything they can catch. And when they leave a place, it's a ruin, streaked with their rotted gore.

My companions are all youngsters, not a one of them over twenty-five. To them, this is the world as it has always been. They've lived with zombies all their lives. But me... I remember the time before. I remember eating a meal without having to glance over my shoulder. I remember not having to sleep in shifts, a weapon ever at the ready. I remember the comfortably warm glow of ignorance.

Living in this world has made my young friends pragmatists. When we find a library, they rush for the books on surgical procedure, water distillation, botany. I go to the old newspapers and magazines and lose myself in the world that

1

once was.

That's where I found these stories.

I've chosen them because each represents a benchmark in our dark descent into the apocalypse.

Perhaps, if you're an oldster like me, they'll give you a few nights of uneasy remembrance.

But maybe, if you're young and determined and pragmatic, like my companions, they'll offer you a slideshow history of how your world got so screwed up.

I hope you're the latter. The world doesn't need another daydreaming old fool like me. What it needs – even more than bullets and bread – is a sense of continuity. This is your past, people. This tells you why the present is the way it is. And I hope it will guide you to a better tomorrow.

And hope, really, is the most important thing. Man cannot live on food and water alone. There must always be hope.

ORIGIN

RESURGAM

by Lisa Mannetti

" 'You can't buy human flesh and blood in this country, sir, not alive, you can't,' says Wegg, shaking his head. 'Then query, bone?'"
– Our Mutual Friend –
Charles Dickens

"For most of the 19th century, anatomy professors and students could secure bodies only on surreptitious nocturnal visits to a church cemetery or, more likely, a potters field."

– Dissection –
John Harley Warner
James M. Edmonson

It had happened before and Auden Strothers knew it. So now on an uncharacteristically snowy March night he was in Yale's Cushing Whitney medical library looking for answers that stubbornly evaded him.

This morning at approximately 2 a.m. the cadaver (nicknamed Molly until today) he shared with three other fledgling doctors suddenly sat up, hemostats clinging to her open mid-section like long silver leeches, widened her jaws and took a chunk out of Sheri Trent's right shoulder.

Sheri hissed – as much from surprise as pain, Auden guessed – and clamped her left hand against the wound. Auden's own breathing became rapid behind his paper mask,

5

and he found himself staring at the blood that seeped between the fingers of his teammate's pale yellowish latex glove. Sheri's gaze followed his and, for a second (a second too goddamn long, Auden thought), she watched the blood that dripped from her glove and pattered on to the naked woman's waxy thighs.

"Christ, I'm bitten. She bit me!"

At the same time Auden's mind declared *You've gone crazy! I told you a thousand times to stay the hell away from Gronsky's stupid meth lab...* his right hand which held the scalpel that had been so recently and delicately buried inside Molly's exposed liver came up and plunged the knife straight into the corpse's nearest eye.

There was a soft drawn out pffft – as if he'd let the air out of a mostly deflated party balloon – and Molly collapsed backward against the steel table. *God, they'd only recently unwrapped the woman's head and face (the better to preserve her, my dear) and now he'd absolutely ruined her eye and their other teammates – not to mention Professor Sriskandarajah – were going to have a fit –*

"Help me, Strothers – what should I do?" Sheri pivoted her wrist and peeled her cupped hand back from the wound a few times tentatively, wielding the lunate and scaphoid bones at the bottom of her palm like a hinge.

The bite was a ragged open mouth at the juncture where the fleshy part of her upper arm began. He blinked under the glare of the brilliant overheads and automatically recited as if his professor called on him to evaluate the case and answer up quickly: "Size 4-0 absorbable suture..."

"What the *fuck* is wrong with you?" she said. "I'm bleeding!"

Ordinarily on a Thursday night, even this late, there'd be five or six students bent over the semi-flayed bodies on the metal slabs, but the spring holidays were coming and they were the only ones in the dissecting room. Trent was as much a

6

grind as he was.

She couldn't go to the university clinic or the emergency room or the local doc in the box – that much was clear – because how could she explain who had bitten her? The medicos would want to know whose teeth sank into her flesh, would want to set police officers on the trail of the perpetrator. She could use a mirror and stitch herself – awkward, of course, utilizing just the one, left hand – but not impossible.

Sheri started toward him, moving out from her side of the table.

But all that Auden Strothers could think about was how the first day that his hands probed and dived inside Molly, the skin beneath his gloves had gone numb from contact with the eight gallons of formaldehyde that had been pumped into her – that had been unsettling and nasty – and now Trent expected him to risk... *infection.*

He shot out from the aisle created by the tables, intent on hustling his skinny ass through the nearest door at the rear of the lab.

Still holding her hand against the wound, Sheri closed in on him. Even then Auden realized she might want no more than a brief comforting touch, a friend and colleague's hand laid gently on her good shoulder, but the combination of the crystal he'd snorted two hours earlier and the spectacle of the uprising cadaver rocketed his mind to panic. He meant only to fend her off with outthrust elbows (less chance of contagion, he gibbered inwardly). Instead, he got his back into it and, with his arms extended and his palms upraised, gave her chest a hard shove: Sheri crashed against Team 22's table which lay perpendicular to their own.

Maybe someone on that team planned to come back after a break but fell asleep over a textbook in the lounge, or a Red Bull in the cafeteria; or maybe Sheri Trent had unzipped the black body bag halfway to get a look at her competitors' handiwork. Arms flailing, her hands skittered wetly under the

7

rectangular skin flaps tessellating the corpse's chest and pushed them back like doors on a bulkhead. Auden caught a brief glimpse of both the layer of bright yellow fat and the reddish striated muscle that reminded him of very old skirt steak.

"Strothers!" She sounded shocked and disappointed more than physically hurt.

A few drops of Sheri's blood – no more than a scattering, really – flicked onto the cadaver's pallid torso and blatted against the heavy plastic. The noise seemed preternaturally loud to Auden. He saw the corpse's feet twitch inside the bag.

The last thought he had before he fled the room stripping off his gloves and cramming them into his lab coat pocket was that Team 22's cadaver had been tagged with a blue cloth – which meant the family, if there was any family, didn't want the remains. Instead, when the first year medical students were finished with it, the body would go into a common grave.

* * * * *

Auden sat at one of the heavy wooden reading tables in Cushing Whitney, one hand resting on the opened pages of the 19th century facsimile text before him, absently mulling over which disease or condition might hold the key he so desperately needed now. Cholera? Tuberculosis – known as consumption for hundreds of years prior to the 20th century? Glanders? Leprosy? No, none of them had the right feel; he had no sense of that click he experienced that was part frisson, part lightning-shot inspiration that told him he was dead on. But there had to be something that would help him understand the seemingly spontaneous resurrection of the dead, because he was certain it wasn't a new phenomenon.

He looked past the shaded table lamp, his gaze wandering from the tall arched windows that framed pelting snow, the elegant mahogany paneling, the balcony with its tiered ranks of books, to the canopy-shaped ceiling two stories overhead.

After he'd fled the lab last night leaving Sheri Trent bleeding he'd gone back to his tiny apartment in North Haven, snorted two thick lines of meth, then decided what he really needed was sleep. He rummaged the medicine cabinet and came up with three Percocet – the remains of a battle with an aching molar last summer.

He stayed away from the lab all day, but he'd come to the medical library after darkfall to try and puzzle his way through what precisely had happened to the cadaver inked with identification number C 390160 and what might happen to Sheri Trent.

He'd pored over incunabula, drawings, and historic pamphlets; he'd downloaded digital images and manuscripts. After three frustrating hours and two more lines of meth he snuffled quietly and surreptitiously in the maze of stacks, it occurred to him to hunt through the library's journal resources.

Journals, he knew, could often be highly personal documents...

※ ※ ※ ※ ※

Auden scavenged both printed and online materials for a long time; the library would be closing soon, but he wasn't overly worried – even if Yale had increased security since that kid at NYU suicided the previous November when he clambered up and over plexiglass shields and plummeted ten stories to the floor of the atrium.

All the grinds had ways and means to access the lab or the library after hours and to hide out from patrolling guards.

It was getting on for 1 am – nearly 24 hours since the Sheri Trent disaster – and he was about to give up. He toked vapor from a black, electronic cigarette, and the thought crossed his mind that it was ironic that the library addition had been built in the classic Y shape of an autopsy incision.

Auden fingered the thin leaves of the journal (not an

original, but a bound reproduction, he thought) written by a 19th century medical student named John Sykes. Glancing at the neatly lettered pages, it occurred to him that the whole thing might be a fabrication... dissection humor concocted to amuse fraternity brothers during long winter nights. On the other hand, as he thumbed and scanned and read – not passively, but with verve – his own excitement grew.

Maybe the nicotine jolted the precise synapses he needed to make the mental connections, or maybe it was the result of his hours-long research, or pure dumb luck on a snowy March night; maybe Sykes' journal *was* nothing more than a series of monstrous notations by a man hoping to write a harrowing novel someday.

Whatever it was, it didn't matter; because Auden Strothers realized he'd just found exactly what he needed.

* * * * *

February 26th, 1873

Until tonight I thought I was inured to providing the college with medical specimens... I'd even overcome the resentment I felt about being a "scholarship boy." The sons of Dunham, Wister, Parkerton – those giants of commerce and industry – aren't expected to grub in dirt or hacksaw through metal and marble to produce cadavers the future doctors desperately need to perfect skills they'll use when they treat their patients. Strictly speaking it's not illegal; the law looks the other way in hopes that one of us or our counterparts here or across the pond or in Europe will save his life down the line. Books are nothing to bodies.

Each time we go out, we meet by pre-arrangement in front of the lecture hall and shuffle our feet in nervous anticipation and blow on our hands to ward off the chill while Dr. Perry stands on the steps of the lecture hall and gives a little pep talk – part lecture, part plea, part innuendo. "Men," he says, "our

10

duty – unpleasant as it may be – is of the utmost importance. Never forget that for an instant."

Twice the professor slipped up during his standard speech; once last autumn he accidentally inserted the phrase "of gravest importance," and a second time, around the Christmas holidays when brandy-toddies and rum-shrub were abundant, he made reference to "the task that lies ahead." Only a second year student we call "Cruncher" laughed out loud – he was overly familiar with digging down over the head and yanking out a corpse cranium-first.

But tonight's task was supposed to be simpler. After all, the ground is still frozen hard in New England, so we were going to nearby Blue Haven to raid a 'receiving vault,' where they stack up the dead until the spring thaw permits gravediggers to shovel deeply into the thin stony soil.

There were just four of us and – quelle luxe – Dr. Perry brought along his own Miller landau for us to ride in and collect the bodies we'd carry back, instead of sending us off to the dark, wide-scattered cemeteries in groups of two and three.

I was glad for once that more of my fellow resurrection men had not shown up. It's only now that I'm writing these pages that I wonder if they knew what was afoot or if their intuition – or some yet unknown, unmapped sense, or even angel guardians – warned them.

* * * * *

We were seated inside the coach; Perry was upfront alongside his driver. Cruncher sat facing me. "Here, Sykes. You look like you could use a bolt." He extended a flask, and more for the sake of politeness than anything else, I took a swig.

"Have another and pass it around." He nodded toward Freddie O'Rourke and Tom Winterbourne who were both first year students and had only been on one or two other midnight

11

raids. "There's wild work ahead, laddies."

Winterbourne looked uncomfortable and shifted in his seat.

"I've got armlets, you bet," O'Rourke said. "and they're vulcanized, to boot."

Cruncher tilted his head back against the upholstery and laughed. "You're going to need more than a couple of rubber sleeves to grope amongst this lot," he said. "And more than those flimsy cotton butcher aprons, Perry's toted along."

The carriage lights were swaying as the horses jigged along and Cruncher studied my face. "Sykes doesn't know."

"Sykes doesn't know what," I said.

"Liked it better when to work off your scholarship, you only had to wait tables or sweep out the lab or set out the gear for the rich boys, Sykes?"

"You're drunk, Cruncher." I turned away. It had been bad when I had to don black tie and serve meals, or clean up blood and vomit in the lab, or lay out everything from yachting togs to surgical notes for the sons of senators and kingmakers. I had actually begged the professor for some job, *any* job where – away from the tonier crowd – I thought it would be easier for me to maintain my dignity, my sense of self.

"Fourth year students – even those with straight A's who have to unbury the dead – think they know everything."

"I know you're an ass, and for the moment, that's enough for me," I said under my breath.

He passed the flask to O'Rourke who drank and handed it to Winterbourne.

"Maybe you imagine you'll be in practice some day," Cruncher said. " 'Mrs. Smythe, it seems poor little Teddy has contracted influenza,'" he said in a stricken voice; then paused. "Only you *won't* be treating the swells on Park Avenue like the rest of your class, *you'll* be seeing a bunch of immigrants and rotters and drunks and ignorant women who haven't gotten their monthlies and are shocked to learn they're expecting another 'blessed event' for the seventh time."

I didn't say a word; there wasn't any point to arguing with Cruncher. He wasn't on scholarship, but it was clear he drank too much and there were rumors he was well-acquainted with opium dens in the city. He wasn't like the swells, but his family had money. He must have wanted to get his medical degree or please a demanding father: why else would he be out after midnight scrabbling in cemeteries?

"No answer, eh, Sykes? Well, here's one for you." Show 'im, Tommy."

Winterbourne reached inside his coat and pulled out a folded sheet of paper and handed it to me.

There wasn't enough light to read it carefully, but it didn't matter because I knew the page from the Communicable Diseases text book very well:

Small pox *(variola, qv.) Causative organism, not definitely known. More common during the colder seasons. No age exempt. May occur in utero. No preference as to sex. Acquired chiefly by direct contact with patient.*

Symptoms: Onset abrupt with chills. Headache (usually frontal), intense lumbar pains, elevation of temperature which may rise to 104 or higher, nausea, or more frequently, vomiting. Fever remains high until evening of 3rd or morning of 4th day, when it falls sharply, often to normal.

With the drop in temperature, the eruption makes its appearance, coming out as a rule about the face, and soon afterward on extremities and to a lesser extent, the trunk. These lesions pass through a series of well-documented phases: macules, papules (which are raised and filled with fluid), vesicles, pustules (which feel to the touch as if bird shot pellets have been embedded under the skin) and finally, crusts.

About the 2nd day of eruption, the macules become papular (raised and filled with fluid) which increase in size and become vesicles. The vesicles increase in size and from the 7th to 8th

13

day well-developed pustules are present, having the appearance of drop-seated or inverted areolae. In some cases, the blisters overlap and merge almost entirely producing a confluent rash, which detaches the outer layer of skin from the flesh beneath it and renders the sufferer more likely to succumb to death. From the 8th to the 11th day, desiccation occurs and by the end of the 21st day, scabs have formed over the lesions and flaked off, leaving permanent, pitted etiolated scars if the patient survives.

There is no disease so repulsive, so dirty, so foul smelling, so hard to manage, so infectious as smallpox may be and is...

I felt my face blanch and I suddenly felt light-headed.

"Ho, Winterbourne, hand over the flask. Feeling a trifle peaked, Sykes?"

I was livid all right – with rage. But I made myself sound calm: "The joke's over. How much are you paying them for this little stunt, Crunch–?"

"The name's Van Dyson, Sykes, and you damn well know it–"

Now he was turning red; he wasn't as drunk as I thought, this time he'd caught my sarcasm.

"–and it's no joke."

In the flicker-glow of the carriage lantern his dark eyes met mine. For a second, I thought they were lit with greed – but it was a peculiar kind of avarice: it had nothing to do with money. He was after something and he wanted it badly, but I suddenly knew it wasn't anything as unimportant as recompense or stipends – we really did come from different worlds. But I wouldn't back down. "And I'm no fool," I said. "The nearest outbreak's in Provincetown – 80 miles from here."

"Ever been in a pest house, Sykes? No, I didn't think so." He groped for the flask and drank, wiping his mouth with his sleeve. "The one in Provincetown is fourteen by fourteen feet.

14

Plenty of room for the stricken *and* the nurse – if they can get one." He smirked.

"And your point is?"

"With less than a third of the population vaccinated, why do you think they build pest houses smaller than gazebos?"

"Well, I hardly–"

"You hardly *what*? You hardly know anything but what you've read in books or heard from fringe academics like *Professor* Perry." He leaned forward. "Let me tell you something. People are so afraid of the pox – so afraid of being isolated like lepers and sent to pest houses to rot and die alone – that it helps spread the disease."

"The bodies of the dead are supposed to be *burned*," O' Rourke said. "Jesus and Saint Mary." He crossed himself quickly.

"People have been put to death for burning bodies – except during plague times – but Brunetti of Padua is going to unveil a cremation chamber at the Vienna world exposition this summer, Sykes," Cruncher said. "Not that you've seen the piece in the *New York Times*, I'm sure – considering the cost of the subscription these days."

"Being poor doesn't make people stupid, Van Dyson," I said.

"No, but it can send them to a pest house."

"Are you saying the rich don't get reported?"

Cruncher threw back his head and laughed. "Not only do they fail to be reported when they're alive and raging with smallpox and shedding scabs like noxious red confetti, when they're dead their doctors put down the cause to 'heart disease' or 'paralysis of the diaphragm' or 'puerpal – that is, childbed – fever.'" He nodded toward Winterbourne and O'Rourke. "Dirty, ugly way to die – but not as ugly or dirty as smallpox."

"Of course," Winterbourne said.

"Nor does the ego-bloated mayor of Provincetown want his wife burned like a Salem witch or buried in a common grave or consigned for eternity to Pox Acres – which during the winter is merely a hole in the ground in the pest house cellar and, during the rest of the year, some raggedy ground a few hundred yards north. No, the mayor wants to visit his wife's tombstone after church on Sunday mornings wearing his top hat, and ready to shake the hands of the recently bereaved."

"She died from small pox," I said.

"Yes," Cruncher said. "And as long as you brought up Provincetown, Sykes, you might as well know that only eight names out of 27 of people who had small pox were reported in the newspaper–"

"Enough, Cruncher–"

"–and according to the 1870 census, the average income of *those* eight was $547.50; but the average income of the *other* nineteen was $2,300."

"Christ, I said *shut up!*"

"All of the headstones in pox cemeteries face east. Isn't that curious?"

I started to lunge for him, but O'Rourke threw his arm between us and Winterbourne hissed. "Stop it both of you, right now, we're here."

The landau slowed and out the window I saw the curved stony embrasure of the receiving vault.

* * * * *

Dr. Perry's driver had hitched a small cart-like wagon – long enough to accommodate bodies – to the landau, and now he rolled back the canvas tarp and pulled out tools while the rest of us stood just outside the metal door. Winterbourne twirled a hooded lantern and its single ray sparkled against the gravel drive and played over gleaming saw blades and pry bars.

"Lots of medical men eschew protection," Perry began while Winterbourne held the light and the driver worked at picking the lock. "In my day, surgeons operated in blood-stiffened frock coats – the stiffer the coat, the more it conveyed the expertise of the practitioner. Some still believe there's no object in being clean, that cleanliness is out of place and they consider it finicky and affected – that pus is as inseparable from surgery as blood. An executioner might as well manicure his nails before chopping off a head," he said. "But we've got gloves and armlets and heavy rubber aprons," he glanced at Cruncher. "And we're going to be very careful. We're only going to take the bodies toward the back of the vault – no one's going to miss them, because no one is going to check very closely. Not with a dozen pox victims stashed in the crypt, too." He paused. The lock clattered onto the gravel and Perry's driver stooped to retrieve it and loop it in the staple of the hasp. "All right, we're in," Perry said.

The Blue Haven receiving vault was built into the side of a steep hill. Its façade was typically ornamental: heavy bronze doors fancied with grille-work and set in bricks that rose above the rounded snow-covered hill like crenellated castle walls.

Inside, the ceiling was arched and the bricks were skim-coated with flaking white wash, but moss grew on the damp walls and the air was dank. Even in this cold weather, you could detect the subtle scent of decay. Perry tied his handkerchief over his mouth and nose, and the others followed his lead. I was too embarrassed to fumble mine out – it was dotted with tiny holes and its edges were badly frayed.

"Let's be quick, gents. Get the lids pried off and hustle the bodies out to the cart. My man will get the coffins nailed shut again."

Either there'd been a hell of a lot of typical deaths that winter in Blue Haven or small pox was more rampant than anyone who lived in the area had been led to believe: There must have been a hundred caskets. Someone (probably the sexton from St. Bartholomew's parish and his crew of gravediggers) had started off packing the coffins onto the heavy wooden shelves that lined three walls, then given up and crammed them in upright like matchsticks. Indeed, one shelf on the western side of the crypt had collapsed under the weight, and the coffins lay helter-skelter, tipped onto their sides and crowding the narrow space between them and their vertical neighbors.

"Standing room only, eh, Sykes?" Cruncher said.

I inserted my crowbar under the wooden lid of a cheap toe-pincher model and put my weight into it.

"C'mon, you're not seriously mad at me, are you?"

The body fell out and smacked headfirst into the back of another coffin. It sounded like a frozen side of beef being hit with a cook's rolling pin. Cruncher steadied the upright casket, so it wouldn't domino the rest.

"I'll help you carry her out to the wagon," Cruncher said, taking the corpse by the shoulders.

I picked up her feet. She was face down and her long brown hair swung against Cruncher's knees. "She must have been young," I said.

Her skirt hung wire-straight and stiff. It creaked like a sail in an ice storm, and a pair of glass beads she'd been decorated with rattled against the brick floor. Her leather shoes chilled my hands even through my gloves.

"Yes, too young to pin up her hair," Cruncher agreed, looking over his shoulder to navigate the maze of coffins and move us toward one of the lanterns resting on a casket near the door.

* * * * *

The moon was barely visible behind heavy cloud cover. Still there was enough light to see the wagon and swing the dead girl into the pile of corpses.

"Christ, I could feel the crystals of ice melting in her hair where my hands touched," Cruncher said. "Here, warm up. Have some brandy."

18

When I weighed the flask in my hand and hesitated, he said: "Finish it and don't worry. I've got a bottle stashed under the seat in Perry's hearse."

That made me laugh and I snorted and coughed, spraying brandy onto the bodies.

"Hey, don't waste it on the stiffs – they've already been baptized."

That made me laugh harder and bending over, cough more. Cruncher pounded my back.

"All right now, Sykes?"

"Yes," I said, straightening up and giggle-coughing into my fist.

"Good," he said, and gave my shoulder a light squeeze that had, I thought, all the camaraderie in the world behind it.

* * * * *

"We might as well get a good haul," Perry was saying to Winterbourne and O'Rourke as I re-entered the crypt. "We've got the wagon and I know of another medical institution that will pay good money for any left-overs. If there are any..."

"Sure, Professor," Winterbourne said. "As many as you like. Me and Freddie are as strong as oxes."

" 'Freddie and I'" Perry automatically corrected. "And it's not oxes," he paused, catching sight of me. "Never mind. Oh, Sykes, perhaps you could start opening a few crates on the east side of the vault? Where's Van Dyson got to?"

"Right here, Professor," Cruncher said from behind a coffin near the door. He caught my eye and mimed refilling his flask.

"Excellent. Hard as hell to keep track of things with all these caskets lying chockablock about. Well, I was just saying to young Winterbourne and O'Malley here–"

"O'Rourke, sir." Winterbourne took a step sideways and tromped on Freddie's foot.

"What's that?"

"Nothing, sir," O'Rourke said.

"Good. Please don't interrupt. First year students have that habit and it's a bad one. Never learn a damn thing that way. What was I saying?"

"About the haul, Professor," Cruncher said.

"Yes. You partner up with Sykes and get to work on the caskets on my left here. It's better to take a few from each area – less likely the gravediggers will notice. They won't, anyhow – morons, the lot of them."

We snaked toward the eastern wall.

From across the vault, Perry was saying, "Now, even if we pick up too many for our own students, we can always render bodies down to bone. There are medical schools in the Midwest just crying for skeletons. And I can show you how to articulate a specimen. It's quite an art,"

"Yes, Professor," O'Rourke said.

"Like to learn that skill, O'Malley?"

"You bet."

"Good lad, you never know if you'll get through all four years and it's good to have a trade – a lucrative trade – to fall back on..."

* * * * *

"Did Perry make you learn how to articulate a skeleton?" Cruncher said in a low voice, as we started to pry open the first lid.

"No. What about you?"

"No, but I watched – from a distance... I guess he figures 'O'Malley' doesn't have much chance making it through the program." He dropped a coffin nail in the pocket of his leather apron.

"Or if he does get a degree, Perry thinks he's only going to treat shanty Irish, anyhow," I said.

20

"God save the Queen," Cruncher said, winking. "Dyson is strictly English. The Van in my name is from my mother's family." Cruncher tilted the flask and took a long swallow; then he passed the brandy across the coffin to me. I had a drink and handed it back.

"Ready?"

He nodded and we lifted the lid away.

"Aaugh!" I stepped back, pressing my sleeve against my nose and mouth. The stench rising out of the casket was unbelievable.

"Not quite frozen yet," Cruncher said.

I felt myself beginning to retch.

"Here, sit down a minute."

I sat on the cold floor and lowered my chin between my knees.

"Put some of this under your nose."

He handed me a small round tin.

"It's camphor ointment with a little peppermint and lavender." He pulled aside his makeshift mask and I saw it gleaming above his upper lip. "Keeps the reek safely at bay."

"She has the pox," I said.

"No question there; her dancing days are done."

I laughed weakly.

"And for godssake, take this handkerchief and tie it on."

Maybe he saw me blush, or maybe it was because I didn't immediately put my hand out for it when he took it from his pocket. "Go on, use it. I don't give a good goddamn if you don't have a handkerchief, Sykes. You're smart. I like intelligent people."

I smeared on a thick dollop of the waxy cream. *He has magic pockets*, I thought irrationally. *What's next? A white rabbit, a flock of parrots?*

"That's right, cover your mustache hole," he said.

I took the handkerchief – heavy linen – and monogrammed JVD, and began to fold it.

"Thanks, Jerry."

"Don't let the monogram show, a gentleman never does." Above the makeshift mask, his eyes were merry.

"I know," I said, tying it on, then standing up again and looking down at the woman's hideously scarred face. "Terrible. Even her eyelids."

"Maybe her eyes, too. She might have died blind." He leaned over and lifted the scabrous flap of flesh and I saw that the sclera of her right eye had gone red from hemorrhage. He whispered, "Let's take her Sykes... think of what we could learn dissecting her."

I realized that avarice I'd seen in his eyes earlier was for knowledge, even forbidden knowledge; but it didn't stop me from interjecting. "Are you mad?"

He held up his gloved hands and waggled his fingers. "Nothing to worry about, Sykes. Seriously."

I put my face up to his until we met like a bridge over the body and were nearly nose-to-nose. "The scabs... she'll contaminate all the other bodies..."

"Chuck her to one side at the bottom of the wagon, once we're in the lab we can spray 'er and any of the others in proximity with phenol – no one's going to get sick."

"The professor–"

"It's dark, he's old and tired, he won't see a thing. And a little judiciously dispensed cash will keep O'Rourke and Winterbourne shut up if they do notice her; and we make sure we're the ones to haul our specimen out of the cart."

"But in the lab – the others are bound to notice tomorrow when it's daylight..."

"We'll start tonight, we'll hide her till we're done... Sykes, this could be the making of our careers."

He didn't say, 'Especially yours.' We both knew that medical school scholarship boys were lucky to eke out a living – and they had to compete with midwives and barber-surgeons and even dentists. "What about afterward, Van Dyson?"

I saw the corners of his eyes crinkle and tilt upward and knew he'd smiled behind his mask. "That's pie, Sykes... pure-d pie. We cut her up, flense and boil her to get rid of the grease; then we can articulate the skeleton."

"And?"

"Keep it for a souvenir in your office or sell it. But I'm betting that when we're done dissecting, neither of us will have to concern ourselves with anything more than where we're going to display our Copley Medals. We'll be in the company of Franklin and Gauss and Ohm..."

* * * * *

We had to shift a few bodies, but we wedged the pox victim on the bottom and against the wagon's sideboards. I started to push a corpse on top of her but Van Dyson caught my arm. "One more, Sykes," he pleaded "A male. It will make our research more complete. And after tonight, neither one of us will have to play at being resurrection men ever again "

I nodded.

He was whistling as we walked back into the crypt for the last time. Cruncher really was an apt nickname, I thought – he wanted knowledge and, like his fictional counterpart, he was going to renounce grave robbing.

* * * * *

I heard the tower clock strike 2 a.m. We'd unloaded most of the corpses and dragged them to the lab. There was an oversized dumb waiter to hoist them to the second floor, but it took two men to pull its ropes – especially if there were two bodies on its platform.

"I must be getting old, lads... Can you handle the rest of these?"

"Sure, Professor."

23

"No problem."

"Certainly."

"Absolutely. Good night Dr. Perry," I said.

"All right, I'll take the landau and one of the horses, and my man can stay behind till you're done, then drive the wagon back."

"We can handle it, sir, no need for your man to hang about. Winterbourne can drive the wagon back."

"Thanks, Van Dyson. Thank you all. It's been a magnificent catch: An even dozen new specimens."

"G'night, sir."

* * * * *

Winterbourne had hooded the lantern again, and in the semi-dark, Jerry and I loaded the pox victims onto the dumb waiter.

"You go upstairs; shout down when the bodies are level with the floor, and I'll tie off the ropes down here and I'll send O'Rourke up." His hands were clumsy with the thick gloves; he fumbled under his apron, then handed me a five dollar gold piece. "But don't let him hang around. Give him this. I'll come up and we'll move the bodies into the lab ourselves. All right?"

We shook hands briefly, then he pulled out the silver flask for the last time. "To Van Dyson and Sykes," he said. "To our success."

* * * * *

The anatomy lab was on situated on the second floor to take advantage of the sun that poured in through its skylight. Adjacent and behind a heavy, metal-clad door, was a kind of cold storage unit (also completely lined with metal) stacked with huge blocks of ice procured from the river and where we'd trundled most of the bodies we collected. But

Winterbourne and O'Rourke had laid out three or four on vacant tables in the dissection room.

"Even a top-notch school like Yale has a dearth of specimens," I said when we wrestled the male smallpox victim onto the last dissecting table.

"Well, these two won't be occupying valuable space for long," Jerry said. "Get some phenol, alcohol, whatever you can find." He'd pulled down all the dark green shades and lit the room like Christmas – candles and lamps, even a crackling fire.

I went to the glassed cabinets. My hand was on the knob and I turned and said, "Let's just spray them down and cover them up, I'm whipped."

"Not on your life." He was rifling a drawer in the dissection table he normally used and pulled out a syringe and a vial. "Seven percent solution, cocaine. Nobody will be here before noon, they'll be in the lecture hall."

I swallowed uneasily.

"Are you sure?"

"Of course I'm sure. How do you think I have the best grades in my class?"

* * * * *

Nightmares come to life. They really do. No one's going to believe this – believe *anything* in these pages, but I'm going to leave them in my room after I flee. For all I know, they'll be thrown away, but at least I'll have written down what happened. Was it something in the disease itself that initiated the transition? I keep thinking about what Van Dyson said about the segregated pox cemeteries when I'd been about to punch him in Dr. Perry's landau: *All the headstones face east.* And these victims were from the eastern wall of the crypt. It wasn't *folie a deux*, it wasn't the cocaine. *It wasn't.*

* * * * *

25

We'd sprayed the bodies; perhaps unwittingly we tracked scabs, carried them on our cuffs from one corpse to the next. I was chattering away a mile a minute, my mind seemed filled with an exultance that bordered on ecstasy: there was nothing I or Van Dyson couldn't do. He smiled. "Really clears the brain, doesn't it? Let's inject one more hypo each, then get started."

We undressed the body. He lowered the lamp over the male. "Excellent. He's thawing. That will make things easier for us." He handed me the scalpel. "You may have the honor of the first cut, Dr. Sykes."

"I'll start with the classic Y, so we can look at how the organs might have been affected."

He nodded. "I've got a stack of slides ready next to the microscope." He stood opposite me, leaned in.

I pushed down, concentrating on making a straight line, keeping the depth even, and drew the knife upwards toward the sternum.

The man suddenly gave out a groan and his body convulsed.

I stepped back, scalpel in hand.

The corpse lurched upright and before I could react, its hands were around Van Dyson's throat and its mouth... dear God, its mouth... was buried in the flesh of Van Dyson's cheek. Van Dyson screamed. The thing broke his neck as easily as you'd snap a wishbone. His head hung at peculiar cant, his tongue rolled out between his slack lips and his eyes dulled. The corpse gnawed mouth, nose, the tender skin beneath the chin, grunting. Blood poured down its throat and chest.

I shrieked.

It raised its eyes to look at me and what I saw in them was malice beyond any evil I could ever have imagined. Then it grinned.

Behind me, the female was stirring.

Half-flensed bodies began to tremble on their tables beneath the sheets.

26

I lunged at the male creature with my scalpel upraised and plunged it into his ear.

The blade snapped off and he fell in a heap onto the wooden boards.

Be quick now, Sykes, aim true, I told myself. *There are knives by the drawer-ful here.*

* * * * *

I stabbed eyes, ears, heads. I dismembered as many of the bodies as I could, boiled the parts in a huge black kettle I hung inside the fireplace. I could scarcely keep myself from vomiting a hundred times. It wasn't doctoring, it was butchery.

Then I heard a rattle from behind the metal-clad door. As their bodies thawed – just enough – the time of the others we'd collected had come.

It was already near daylight.

I looked around helplessly at the carnage of the dissection room, then toward the knocking from behind the heavy metal door.

I'd never get all of them rendered quickly enough.

Besides, I mourned inwardly, it was Sykes who knew how to articulate them, how to give a corpse a purpose even when its flesh was gone. They'd be harmless when the meat of their brains was gone, I thought; and fire would have to see to the rest.

I raked the logs from the fire, turned over the kerosene lamps.

I heard the wild scream of the rising flames mingling with the guttural cries of the resurrected ones from behind the metal-clad door, and I fled.

* * * * *

Auden Strothers crept stealthily into the darkened anatomy

27

lab. *Not a soul in sight – just whatever's left of their wrecked bodies.*

There was no time to worry about what might have happened to Sheri Trent, he reminded himself. Their cadaver – C 390160 – lay under its blue sheet, its punctured eye hanging slightly askew on its cheekbone. *Impossible to think they ever nicknamed the foul thing, Molly.* The autopsy students were always roving from table to table, watching a group prepare a slice of pancreas for histology, observing one of the professors work on a delicate area like the tongue and larynx... and people got their hands in – even if the cadaver technically belonged to another team.

He carefully unzipped the body bag embracing Team 22's cadaver – the one that Sheri Trent had spattered with her own blood after she'd been bitten. Trent must've gotten her shit together when she saw the thing twitch – it too, had a deflated eye.

But, there were all those daily casual exchanges from table to table... and... he counted two more blue sheets tagging corpses in the room... *and* the common graves where, Strothers had no doubt, the 'disease' spread quietly underground and from place to place to place.

He snorted three lines of meth and joked inwardly that dismembering the bodies he was *sure* were infected, was essentially hackwork.

In his mind's eye he saw the dead woman sit up and lunge, yellowed teeth bared. He saw the bloody pocket of the wound in Sheri's arm. He cut and flensed, retching over his shoulder. Strothers picked up a surgical power saw, intent on wresting the femur from the pelvis. "For Christ's sake," he said aloud. He was trained to work carefully, what he was about to do was a waste. Besides, he hated the whine of the saw. If he proceeded cautiously – with precision – the bones could be articulated and used in schools and labs and hospitals.

There was a kitchen off the lounge where he could boil up

the remains. Hell, if it came to it, he could cart them home in plastic garbage bags and fire up his own stove.

It was going very well, he was whistling when the lab door suddenly burst open.

He started; sure for a brief second that a mindless, shambling corpse that had once been Sheri Trent had come to gnaw his flesh.

"Security!" A female officer with blonde hair advanced on him.

More cops piled into the room.

Strothers followed their gaze from the flensed bodies to the baggie spilling white powder cheerily across an empty chrome table.

"You're under arrest!"

"You don't understand – they're infected!" he shouted.

He felt his arms jerked backwards, cold metal handcuffs bit into his wrists.

Outside, through the windows, Strothers could see the flashing red lights of town and state police cars.

He watched the crimson glow play over the pale skin and ruined muscles of the cadavers, giving them an unearthly vibrancy – a warmth, he was certain, that would soon return them to life.

THE PLAGUE BEGINS

JAILBREAK

by *Steven W. Booth and Harry Shannon*

"Say again?" Sheriff Miller slid worn boots from the edge of the desk, slammed them down on the messy floor. The antique office and jail were both in the middle of yet another round of remodeling. Paint cloth whispered. Dust rose, spread and slowly settled. The old style radio crackled with static. Outside, night was spreading like a dark blanket over the little town that crouched further down the road.

"I said, he killed Miss Barbara by the library, Sheriff," Deputy Bob Wells said. He spoke rapidly, baritone voice thick with panic. "He killed her with his bare hands, so I shot him."

"Slow down. Shot who, damn it?"

A long pause. More static. "It was old man Grabowski, Sheriff. Sure as shit."

"Lazlo Grabowski is dead, Bob."

"I know."

Sheriff Penny Miller blinked and straightened her long legs. She leaned forward over the desk, stomach tingling. "You okay, Bob? You been drinking?"

"I ain't had a drop, Sheriff, I swear. It was the strangest damned thing I ever saw. Old Grabowski came out of the bushes while I was talking to Miss Barbara. Looked like shit, some sort of zombie. He tackled her and started... biting. I tried to pull him off her, but his arm came right out of his shoulder. Jesus, blood come out of her quick as a double-dicked bull pissing on a flat rock. Miss Barbara was screaming. He wouldn't stop, so I shot him. He kept on biting anyway. I shot

33

him again, in the head this time, and then he quit."

"And Miss Barbara?"

"Bled out like a pig. Then I saw some more of 'em coming and I ran."

"Some more of what?"

"Of them," he repeated, as if that explained everything.

I've got a lunatic in uniform out on the township streets with a loaded gun, the Sheriff thought to herself. Great.

"Deputy Wells, where the hell are you?"

"I'm in the car, on the way back. Sheriff, this gets worse. All kinds of people are out on the street tonight, kind of stumbling around all drunk-looking. They look like... well, zombies. And, yeah, I do know how this sounds. I wouldn't believe it either if I hadn't seen it with my own eyes."

"Zombies?" Sheriff Miller said. She sighed into the radio. "Come on, Wells, what's really going on?" She stretched the microphone cord, went around her desk and stepped over some lumber to get her gun belt. She fastened it on as she spoke.

"I'm serious as liver cancer, Sheriff," came the static-clouded voice through the speakers. "Dozens, maybe a hundred of them. A handful attacked Mrs. McCormick's store, clawing and chewing. They flat-out ate her alive. I shot two or three with the Remington, but they just kept coming, so I had to light out for base."

The sheriff heard Wells sounding panicked as hell, so she knew that whatever was happening, the deputy thought it was real enough. "What's your position?"

"Like I said, in the cruiser. I'll be back at the station in two minutes tops. Leave the prisoners locked up. We got to get out of here. Shit!" The radio popped. Wells stopped transmitting.

Miller wasn't sure she bought the story. Maybe it was a prank, but that wasn't like Wells at all. Big old serious redneck sonofabitch like him wasn't prone to joking around. So something was going on out there, but freaking zombies? Whatever it was, Miller knew she had only a few minutes to prepare. She was the Sheriff and had her duty. She rounded the desk and grabbed her broad-brimmed hat off the rack. She jogged out of her office, past the construction mess and into the small, old-fashioned western jail. The big key turned smoothly in the brand new lock, the barred door swung open with a creak. The two prisoners looked up as she approached the cells.

"Get up," Miller said.

"Time for my strip search, darlin'?" The closest prisoner swung his feet off the edge of his cot. Bowen was busily tattooed; a large biker with long, stringy hair, a scraggly beard and a darkened bandage on his head. He hefted his sweaty bulk off the cot and approached the steel bars. "I'm sure I've got something in here you'd like," he said. He leered and began to paw at his crotch.

"Shut up." Miller produced a pair of handcuffs. "That little thing wouldn't scare a gnat into buying a diaphragm. Now get over here and put your hands through the slot." She indicated the large rectangular hole in the barred door. "Move it. We got us somewhere to go."

"Where?" the second prisoner, Stillman, asked. He was a tall, wiry, foul smelling man with a tattooed head and surprisingly delicate hands. He approached the door of his cell. If it weren't for his weirdly tatted head, Stillman could have passed for an accountant, rather than a Hell's Angel. How he wound up in a motorcycle gang, Miller didn't care to know.

"Sheriff, where we going?" he asked again.

Miller paused. She hadn't yet considered that part of it. "We're moving you to another facility," she said. The lie didn't come easy. She usually preferred to play it straight, even with the cons. "Come on, I don't have all day."

Bowen smelled trouble. "What's the rush?"

Before the Sheriff could answer, Wells burst through the door. "They're fucking everywhere, Sheriff!" The former high school athlete was out of breath, uniform dark with sweat; clearly sorry he had let his gut get the better of him. "I saw more coming out of the woods as I was pulling up. We ain't got much time."

"Who's coming, a lynch mob? Are they coming for me?" demanded Stillman. He gripped the bars of the cell door, a sudden nervous tic making his face twitch. Sheriff Miller could smell the guilty sweat from two yards off. Stillman was accused of drugging and sodomizing a minor. His wide eyes gave him away.

"Never mind. Put your hands through the slot," Miller commanded again. She was surprised by the strength in her voice. She didn't feel very strong. Zombies? The hell?

"What's going on, Sheriff?" Bowen spoke calmly. He stepped away from the door and crossed his arms. Stillman stepped back, a reluctant imitation of his leader. "We ain't going nowhere 'less you tell us the truth."

Wells huffed with frustration and fear. "Sheriff, leave them. They'll be safe in there."

She stared at him.

"Probably," he shrugged.

"I'm not leaving my prisoners," Miller said bluntly. "We have our duty."

"We don't have time for this." Wells turned his attention to the big motorcyclist and drew his club. "Okay, do what the Sheriff says, asshole, or I'll come in there and crack your skull again. Then the zombies won't have a problem getting at your shit-for-brains."

"Zombies?" Bowen released a sharp laugh. "Oh, bullshit! What's really going on? Some family members coming for my friend here?"

In his cell, Stillman wilted.

"What is going on," Sheriff Miller said, "is that we need to get you two to safety. We don't have time for any macho posturing. Now, present your hands."

"Holy bat shit, Scratch." Stillman muttered, peering out his small, high cell window. "You really got to check this out."

Wells and Miller exchanged glances. "Get the shotguns ready," she barked. Wells ran for the gun cabinet.

Meanwhile, Bowen stood on his own cot and looked through the barred window. "Whoa, what the fuck is that?"

"I told you," said Wells, from across the room. He was loading two shotguns as fast as possible. "Zombies."

"Damn." Bowen hopped down from his cot immediately. He slid his hands through the slot. "Move," he ordered Stillman. "We gotta go." Miller snapped the cuffs around each of their wrists. She opened the cell doors, ushering the two prisoners out. As they headed down the hallway, Wells jabbed Bowen with his stick. Bowen stumbled a bit.

"Watch it, dickhead, or I'll turn around and break you in two," snapped Bowen.

Wells raised his stick, ready to strike. The convict glared back like a pit bull.

"Wells!" The deputy turned to see Miller with genuine rage in her eyes. "They are our prisoners. Knock it off."

Wells opened the door to the parking lot and stopped short. The last sunlight was fading out, a yellow ball dipping down into a huge pond of black ink.

"My God," Wells gasped.

Miller swallowed. "We ain't gonna make it to the cars."

Bowen and Stillman stepped forward to look. It was a living nightmare. The things were everywhere, covering the black top around the isolated sheriff's station. Feet shuffling, throats moaning. Features were distorted, clothing ripped. They could have been anybody; townspeople, tourists passing through, distant relatives. Tattered clothing, gaping wounds and blood splatters covered their bodies. Dozens of zombies with missing limbs staggered forward in broken formation. The moaning sound floated on a low breeze that carried the stench of rotting meat. The three men stared. Miller looked down at her hands. They were not trembling. Her mind plotted strategy. She looked up again. The closest zombies were perhaps twenty yards away.

Wells leveled the shotgun at a man in a dark suit. He fired, the noise making Stillman jump. The zombie fell heavily to the ground.

"Now, watch this," said Wells. "It ain't dead for real, not yet."

Bowen snorted. "Hell he ain't."

After a moment, the creature picked itself up and began lumbering toward the station, dark intestines sliding from its gut.

"See what I mean, Sheriff?" Deputy Wells said, terror in his eyes. "I do believe we are in some pretty deep shit."

"All right!" snapped Sheriff Miller. "Everyone back inside. Lock the door, Wells. I think we're staying put."

They locked up. She turned the lights on outside to give them better vision. Peering out through the window, Miller didn't like what she saw. The army of creatures approached relentlessly from all sides, groaning with a terrible hunger. Miller rallied her deputy. They fired through windows and doors as best they could. Soon Miller wished she had put in earplugs when she'd had the chance. The steady gunfire hurt like hell.

"Aim for the head," called Bowen. "It's the only thing that works."

"I am aiming for their heads, smartass," shouted Wells.

They fired and fired. Meanwhile, Stillman sat handcuffed to a chair at Wells' desk in the lobby, the receiver stuck between his ear and his shoulder. He dialed furiously. Prisoner Bowen had gone back into his cell for security. He was visibly shaking. His eyes were wide and white.

"They're getting closer," Wells hollered. "This keeps up, these motherfuckers might be yanking our zippers down pretty soon." The bodies of several of the seemingly endless stream of undead were piled in a rough semicircle around his position at the barred back window. Wells paused for a moment to reload.

"Shit fire!" Bowen jumped back as a rotting, three-fingered hand appeared at the barred window, grasping at his head. "Holy damned Jesus Christ on a jet ski!" He stumbled backward off his cot, tripped on the toilet and banged his already bandaged head on the cinderblock walls of the small cell. "Ow!"

"Shut up," said Miller. She peered though the smoke in Bowen's general direction. "Bob, how are you holding up?"

Wells fired the shotgun again. Steel balls ripped the head off another zombie. A wide cloud of blood, brains and skull resulted. The zombie, a little girl in a puffy white dress, went over backwards, tumbling over other bodies. A moment later, an old man began clambering over the rapidly growing wall of undead. They kept coming. The floodlights threw long shadows past them, like long black ribbons running off into the desert.

"Not good, Sheriff." Wells looked over his shoulder at Miller, then down at the growing pile of empty ammo boxes and shell casings. "Running low, here. Fact, I'm down to about three boxes of ammo, and there are more coming. Maybe we been et by a bitch wolf and shat over a thousand foot cliff."

Miller began to worry, something she hadn't done in a long time. She was doing only slightly better on ammo, but just because they had stocked more 30.06 than shotgun shells last month. Miller sighted another zombie, a decaying Mrs. McCormick, and fired. The right eye imploded, a reddish-grey cloud blooming at the back of its head. The woman fell forward, only to be replaced by another female limping behind her. Miller called to Stillman. "Any luck with the phones?"

"There's a ring, but no one picks up. I've tried every number in your book, and a few of my own. I get a machine or one of those God-damned automatic messages every time." He slammed his fist on the dusty drop cloth. Dust rose from Wells' desk. "Whole world must be screwed up. Bet those

Goddamned A-rab terrorists done this."

"Man, we're running out of time," said Bowen. He paced to and fro in his cell, fondling the bandage on his head.

"If you have any brilliant ideas," Miller said coolly, targeting the next zombie, "now's the time to share."

"Sure I got one. Let me and Stillman loose and give us a couple of them scatter guns."

"Not a fucking chance!" Wells, reloading again, turned his weapon on Bowen. "We ain't letting you anywhere near those weapons."

"Bob," said Miller quietly, without looking up, "cover your position and shut up."

"You ain't seriously thinking of arming this piece of shit, are you, Penny?"

Miller looked, turned her Remington rifle on him and screamed, "Duck!"

Wells dropped to the floor, scattering red plastic shells. Miller fired at the huge zombie, a tourist in Bermuda shorts, hitting it in the fat belly. The thing didn't even notice it had been shot. It reached down to Wells and grabbed him by the shoulder. Wells brought the muzzle of his pump-action shotgun under the zombie's chin and fired. The resulting boom was deafening. The zombie's head exploded and the escaping shot shattered the window above. Glass fragments, splinters and vaporized brains showered down on Wells. On the edge of sanity, he giggled. His broad-rimmed hat protected his face from the fallout, but his uniform was red and soaking wet. Wells pushed the zombie out the window, out of sight.

Stillman suddenly shifted. "Behind you, Sheriff!"

In one smooth movement, Miller drew her pistol and stuck it in the mouth of a child zombie coming in through the window. She winced but pulled the trigger, and the dead boy – one she didn't know, thankfully – slid below the windowsill with a hole in his brainstem.

Wells resumed his first position, firing madly to keep up

with the ground he had lost.

"There are still more coming," said Bowen, peering out his little cell window. His voice was high and tight with panic.

"We aren't going to make it, are we?" Stillman looked ready to piss in his pants. A crashing sound erupted from Sheriff Miller's office area. "What the fuck was that?"

Miller didn't know if she should keep firing through the window or shift to deal with the new threat. Torn, the Sheriff tried to keep her eye on the window and her office simultaneously. "Fuck a duck!" she mumbled under her breath.

Suddenly the door to Miller's office burst open. A zombie in full football gear emerged through the door, cleats clacking on the tile. The foul smell of decomposition flooded the room. Wells swung around and blasted at it, but only took off one shoulder pad. The shot came close enough to Stillman to cause him to jump. He was still handcuffed to the chair, and went over backwards. The zombie wore the number 12 and looked like a quarterback. It turned to Stillman. It was just shy of two yards away and moving closer. It fell on Stillman, biting off large chunks of the small man's face. Stillman shrieked like a girl. Blood spouted and pooled around him.

Miller struggled to get a clean shot. Before she could fire, Wells made his own decision. He shot the quarterback, exploding his helmet and shearing off the top of the boy's head. Sadly, half of Stillman's face vanished as well.

Stillman lay still, mouth gaping wide. Blood pooled red around him.

"Needles!" Bowen stood at the cell door, gripping the bars. "Wells, you miserable fuck. You killed him."

Wells shrugged. "Sucker was toast anyway."

Another zombie in a filthy business suit emerged from the office. Miller fired, hitting the thing in the right arm to no effect. She shot it through the face and it dropped like something made of sticks and rags.

"Fall back!" Miller grabbed a box of ammo as she

41

retreated. Wells scooped up two boxes of shells and followed the sheriff.

Miller dashed into the old cinderblock jailhouse, motioned Wells in and closed the door after him. She turned the key in the lock, and stepped back from the barred door. "At least that will keep them out for a while."

"A while?" Bowen's voice cracked. "That's your master plan?"

Miller turned to confront Bowen, but she was cut off by a blast from Wells' shotgun. The new zombie went down, but several of the shot ricocheted off the iron bars, some fragments narrowly missing Miller's head.

"Knock that shit off," Miller said. "They can't get in here. And, yes, that's my plan. Find a way to stay alive."

"How are we supposed to get out?" whined Bowen. He seemed afraid, alone in his own little cell.

"Why don't you shut the fuck up and let the lady think?" Wells raised his shotgun to his hip, aimed at Bowen.

Miller put her hand on the warm barrel. She shoved it down, hard. "Bob, we've got enough to worry about as it is. Besides, he's my responsibility."

"Give me two reasons not to blow his ass to hamburger," snapped Wells, jerking the weapon out of her grasp.

Miller ignored Wells' insubordination. A gore-splattered housewife was reaching through the jailhouse door. The moaning of the creatures outside the jailhouse door was constant and piteous, impossibly loud. Wells drew his sidearm and shot one, two, three times. They fell, piling in front of the barred door. The others tugged them aside and struggled to get in. The entrance was blocked for the time being. Those outside began to eat at the ones in the way. The beasts turned upon one another, biting and clawing.

She stood between Wells and the temporarily blocked door. "Listen up. We're in deep shit. The rest of the guns and nearly all of the ammo are out there with them," she said. "We have no food in here – it's all in the galley. No one knows we're here. That means we're on our own. If we're going to get through this, I can't have you two at each other's throats. We need to work together."

Miller stepped up to the cell door where Bowen waited. She hesitated, reading his eyes, and then unlocked the door.

"Wait!" Deputy Wells put his hand on Miller's. He had a look of real terror on his face. "You ain't actually gonna trust that scum-sucking bastard, are you?"

"I don't see we have any choice," she replied. She turned the key in the lock, swung the door open. It squealed. "Come on out."

Bowen stepped forward, bloody from the cut on his head. He smiled for the first time. Seeing that grin, Wells brought his shotgun up to his shoulder, aiming at Bowen's head. Bowen stopped short and looked at the sheriff.

"Bob," she said quietly, "until this shit storm is all over, he's with us. Got it?"

Wells glared at Miller. He could see that she meant it. He lowered the shotgun.

"Scratch," she said, using the prisoner's gang name, "don't make me regret this." Miller unbuckled her gun belt and handed it over to Bowen. Disgusted, Wells turned away and spat on the floor.

"Thank you, Sheriff. That's mighty decent of you." Bowen buckled the belt around his hips like an old-style gunslinger. He quietly drew the handgun. Expertly, Bowen pulled the slide halfway back to make certain it was loaded. In one smooth movement, he raised the pistol and fired. Wells' face collapsed into itself. His thick neck gushed; the lifeless body dropped heavily to the floor.

Instantly, Miller and Bowen both raised their weapons. They aimed at each other. Mexican standoff. The mob of creatures outside kept trying to push and shove their way into the jail.

"Drop it," said Miller from the other end of her rifle. She was stunned to see her hands were still not trembling. They stared at one another in silence. On the floor, what was left of Wells farted noisily.

"Sorry, Sheriff," said Bowen. He grinned. "That prick has been looking for a way to get shot since he cracked my skull. I was just, you know, helping out."

"You're still my prisoner, Scratch. Put down your weapon!"

"What, so you can lock me in that cell again to get eaten alive by them things?" He gestured toward the door behind her. "You saw what that son of a bitch did to Needles a minute ago. He flat out had that coming. Like you said, we got to work together. Now come on, they'll be on us again soon enough."

Miller applied a small amount of pressure to the trigger. The Remington seemed to vibrate. She was about to fire when she saw a hulking creature appear behind Bowen. Miller rapidly shifted her aim and shot the tall, thin zombie just before it bit down on Bowen's neck. It flew backwards.

Bowen's gun discharged. His shot was a half second behind hers. Miller found herself spinning; a pain in her left shoulder that bordered on unbearable. She went down hard, hitting the tiles. Her small body slid through slimy gore and entrails. She ended up several feet away, face down. She passed out.

Miller woke up to a buzzing sound. Her right eye wouldn't open; it was crusted shut and covered with blood. Her left shoulder hurt like blazes. Someone was talking to her, but she couldn't understand – the shooting had damaged her ears. She could feel pressure on her shoulder. She looked up to see Bowen kneeling over her.

"You awake, Sheriff?" she heard Bowen saying from a distance. "You're one tough bitch, I'll tell you that."

"What happened?" she managed. Her voice sounded far away.

"We made it," he announced. "I shored up the hole in the wall with some of the lumber, pumped a few rounds into some of those miserable fucks, and then they just kinda went away. Thought you died a couple of times, but sure as shit, you made it."

He finished tying the bandage around her arm, stood, and picked up a shotgun.

"Now here's the way this is going to work. I'm gonna get you outside, into your truck, and put the keys in your hand. Then I'm gonna hop on my ride and get the ever-lovin' fuck out of here. After that, you're on your own. Deal?"

"You killed Wells," she protested, without much conviction.

"Come on, Sheriff. Let's let bygones be bygones. He had it coming and you know it. Besides, what are you gonna do, arrest me?" He held the shotgun casually, and smiled.

"I saved your life."

"Yes you did, much obliged. So now I'm gonna save yours, and we'll be even." He hefted her off the floor "God, you are a sight, Sheriff. If I didn't know better, I'd think you was one of them zombies." Bowen slung a shotgun over his shoulder and carried her past the decomposing bodies. It was early morning outside. They went out the back door.

The dead lay everywhere. Wells had a hell of an aim, that was sure, because hardly one had its head anymore. The stench was unbearable, but Miller was too weak to vomit. The first hint of the sun peaked out over pines to the east, bringing a bone-chilling wind. She felt cold, colder than she'd ever been before. It was the loss of blood, she knew it, but she couldn't do much of anything about it. Miller shivered.

Bowen opened the door to her cruiser, a worn brown-and-white Ford Blazer, and shoved Miller inside. He got her feet and hands situated on the pedals and wheel, took the keys from her gun belt. He inserted them into the ignition, started it up.

"There, I done what I promised. Good luck, and thanks for

saving my ass."

"Scratch," she began, "I could die without your help."

"Oh, quit bitchin', Sheriff."

He closed the door with a slam, strolled over to his impounded Harley. Her ears were still ringing. She watched Bowen through the windshield as he stepped on the starter, saw him gun the engine and shake a bit when it roared into life. A hulking zombie came out of nowhere. It jumped up behind Bowen, kind of like it was going for a joy ride, and then chomped down on his neck. Bowen's eyes popped open, all funny and wide. Blood sprayed his face. The motorcycle went over sideways, taking Bowen and the huge zombie with it. His boots kicked. The motor kept roaring. She couldn't hear if he screamed.

Moments later the zombie reappeared. It looked up at her, Bowen's blood dripping from yellow, broken teeth. It rose up, lumbered towards her. Miller had a moment of clarity. Her adrenaline kicked in. She let her hand fall on the gearshift, slammed it into drive. The Blazer surged forward. The zombie didn't flinch. It went 'thump thump' as she drove clean over it.

Swerving like a drunken teen on prom night, she made her way roughly out onto the open highway. Sheriff Miller didn't know what she would find out there in what was left of the world, but she knew that she had a job to do.

And no fucking zombies were gonna stand in her way.

RECESS

by Rob Fox

"Today is going to be a good day," Sam said to himself as he sat quietly looking over his fellow classmates and wondering who he could beat up during recess. He scoped out the room for possible targets. First on the list was Robbie; he was a short plump kid who had just moved to the school. Samantha, Kate, and Kylee were all girls, so they were easy targets. Teddy was taller than him, but from previous encounters, Sam knew he could take him; and finally there was William and John, the class clowns.

Every day at recess, Sam and the other kids would go outside and pretend to be pirates or spacemen, and every day Sam would win whatever game they chose to play. Today would be no exception; Sam just had to make it through Mr. Donaldson's fourth grade Math class. Every Friday was the weekly pop quiz day and as usual he was not prepared.

Sam unexpectedly breezed through the test; sure that he had answered every problem correctly, even the tricky extra-credit question. When the bell rang for recess, Sam jumped out of his chair and headed outside. Just as he got to the door, his English teacher Mrs. Foshee stopped him to ask about his book report that was due later that day. By the time Sam finally made it outside, the other kids were already playing.

A bright red ball slammed into Sam's face as he stepped out the door.

"You're it!" Somebody yelled from across the playground.

Sam was not happy.

"Who threw that?" He asked aloud.

No one answered.

Across the yard Teddy stood staring at something in the woods. "Don't try to pretend you're innocent Ted, I know you did it." Sam shouted as he made his way through the crowd of third and fourth graders. Anger boiled inside of him. "Who does he think he is hitting me with that ball; I'm going to beat his face in," Sam mumbled as he approached.

Sam reached out to grab Teddy by the back of the shirt, but was surprised when Teddy turned around to reveal a pale white, blood smeared face with grey eyes. Lying on the ground in a pool of blood and intestines was Robbie. Teddy lunged forward, snapping his teeth towards Sam's face. Sam, startled, fell backwards and landed hard on his back, hitting his head. Without missing a beat, he jumped back up on his feet and was now face to face with Teddy. Behind him, Robbie began to slowly rise up off the ground.

"I don't know what you think you're doing, but it's not funny and I am telling," Sam said matter-of-factly. As he turned to walk back to the school, he was met by a group of children, all pale white and covered in blood.

"I said this is not funny, now stop it or I am going to punch you."

Ignoring his warning, the group of children began walking slowly towards him, their arms stretched out in his direction as if they were going to grab him. Sam drew back and punched one of the kids directly in the nose. The boys' nose broke with a snap and blood began flowing like a river over his lips and down his sweatshirt; he did not even flinch.

Sam was completely surrounded. With nowhere to run, he began swinging wildly, hitting anyone that got near him. His arms began to ache from the constant punching and swinging, however, the children kept coming. Just as Sam's arms began to fail, he saw a group of kids running his way; they were carrying bats, slingshots, and rocks. As they approached the group of pale-faced kids, they too began swinging wildly; their makeshift weapons sending kids flying.

William and Samantha led the charge, followed by John, Kylee and Kate.

"Come on you idiot," William yelled to Sam, "Let's get out of here!"

Sam wasted no time, he quickly ran to hide behind the kids with weapons. Samantha handed him a red aluminum baseball bat and a metal garbage can lid to use as a shield. Together with the other children, they ran back towards the school doors.

"Wha... what are those things?" Sam asked.

A small voice came from somewhere behind him. "They're zombies."

Samantha ran ahead of the pack, desperate to get inside the building. As she reached the doors, she instantly stopped and turned back to the others. "They're inside too" she yelled. The children stopped where they were. Everyone turned to Sam for guidance. "What do you want me to do?" Sam asked, wildly looking around; "My mom doesn't let me watch horror movies, I don't know what to do."

"Does anyone have a cross?" Kylee asked.

"That's for vampires." Kate responded, sounding a little more irritated than she had wanted to be.

"Well, how do you kill a zombie then?" Sam asked aloud.

A small voice came from the back of the group, "You kill the brain; once the brain is dead, so is the zombie."

Everyone turned to see who had given the information and was surprised to see William.

"We have a friend of the family that writes books about zombies and he taught me everything I know." William exclaimed proudly.

"OK, then zombie boy, what do we do now?" Sam asked.

"We run; they're getting closer to us." William yelled as he began to move. "Head for the Jungle Gym, it will give us a place to gather, and give us the higher ground for now."

The Jungle Gym was a state of the art play place that the local board of education had argued about getting for two years. It had two twisty yellow slides located on each end, a rope craw-through, monkey bars connecting two sections, three sets of swings, and at the very top, was a fort, big enough to fit at least eight kids inside easily. "We can rest here for a little bit, until our parents come for us." Sam huffed. "If we can each take a section, maybe we can hold them off until then."

"I think we will be alright," William reassured the others as he made his way up the metal steps leading to the fort.

As the words passed his lips, a decaying hand grabbed him by the foot, causing him to fall backwards onto the ground. Before any of the other kids could get to him, three zombies began ripping him apart. Samantha pulled back her slingshot and nailed one of the zombies in the head, however, the shot was not hard enough to do any real damage, so the zombie, unaffected, continued to rip the flesh off Williams little body.

Without thinking, Sam jumped over the rail and began swinging the baseball bat at the zombies and screaming for them to get off William. Sam closed his eyes and imagined he was on the baseball field with his dad. "Keep your eye on the ball, son, and swing the bat like you mean it" his dad would always say to him. Sam opened his eyes, pulled the bat back over his shoulder, stepped forward, and smacked the first zombie directly across the temple. The bat made a squishing sound as it crushed through the young skull. He immediately pulled the bat back and finished the other two off in the same manner. Blood soaked and crying wildly, Sam ran up the stairs to meet everyone back at the fort.

Kylee and Kate were huddled in a corner, holding each other and crying for their parents. John stood watch over the yellow slide connected to the fort, while Samantha stood watch by the monkey bars. Sam climbed up on top of the fort, as he had done so many times before, so he could get a good look around the playground. Zombie students and teachers began slowly making their way out of the school, while from every direction on the playground, other zombie students began making their way towards the survivors. Sam jumped down and went inside the fort to talk to everyone.

"We are outnumbered and completely surrounded," Sam began, "but I think we can hold them off if everyone does their part; I know you guys are scared, I'm scared too, but we do what we have to do to survive." "Now who is with me? Who will survive with me?"

Sam began to raise his voice, until all the children were cheering with him.

Wave after wave of zombies attempted to get to the students, and repeatedly they were knocked back, with their heads busted wide open. Sam was tired, but he knew he had to survive and he would stop at nothing to do so. He could not show any weakness; after all, he ruled this playground.

"Help, they got me!" Kate yelled out of both panic and pain. Sam turned around just in time to see her being pulled down the slide, a blood streak smeared on the sides around in circles all the way to the bottom. Sam turned back as three zombies had made their way up the steps. He pushed them back with his metal garbage can lid, and then swung his bat, successfully hitting all three, one right after the other like in the "Three Stooges" movies his grandfather used to make him watch. From behind him, another group of zombies crawled up the winding slide and made their way inside. Sam dropped down to one knee, pulled back the trashcan lid and hurled it at the approaching ghouls. The lid severed the jugular vein in the first zombie, spewing blood in all directions like a bloody sprinkler system; however, it continued making its way slowly in his direction. Sam ran towards the zombie, with the bat pulled back, ready to strike, when he slipped in a pool of blood. He slid across the floor of the fort, knocking the approaching zombie back down the slide.

John had moved over to the other slide and was fighting

alongside Samantha, who now held a bloody brick in her hand. As new zombies would come up the stairs, John would smack them with his broomstick and Samantha would hit them with a brick. Kylee stood in the fort, looking out the windows, too afraid to go outside into the action. She was so engrossed by what she saw outside the window, she forgot to watch the slide. Before she knew what had happened, Kylee was grabbed by her ponytail and yanked backwards down the slide into the arms of hungry zombies.

With only three survivors left alive, Sam, John and Samantha pressed their backs against each other, swinging bats and bricks, smashing skull after skull of the advancing zombie horde. Sam ran around John and Samantha and climbed up on top of the fort, narrowly escaping the bite of one of the zombies. Samantha tried to climb up with Sam, but was pulled down to the ground and eaten alive.

"Help me up Sam," John begged.

Sam reluctantly reached down to pull him up, but was too late. A now zombie Kylee was able to bite a chunk out of John's neck. Sam jumped back, dropping his bat to the ground with a clank as it bounced off the metal Jungle Gym. He could not move; he was frozen in horror as all his classmates were eaten and returned as zombies and he stood, over looking everything completely unarmed.

The pale-faced zombies climbed onto the jungle gym and completely surrounded the fort. Sam had nowhere to run. He looked around the playground that was now completely covered in the undead children and teachers. As the sun slowly began to sink below the horizon, the moans of the zombies grew louder in Sam's ears, drowning out the ringing bell that would on a normal day let the children know their parents could take them home for the day. On this day though, the normal long line of yellow and black busses were not waiting outside the school; parents were not waiting in the car-pool lane, the children were not running around playing tag and

52

throwing rocks at the stop signs. Today the children were slowly making their way up the sides of the jungle gym, towards him.

Sam sat down, legs crossed one over the other; he could hear the sound of someone or something behind him. He could feel and smell the rancid breath on the back of his neck. "This was supposed to be a good day."

BITING THE HAND THAT FEEDS YOU

by Calie Voorhis

Mary pulled open the louvered pantry doors. As usual, the one on the left jammed. She kicked it out of the way, bent down, and pulled out two large cans of fire-roasted tomatoes and a green Tupperware bin full of brown sugar. A box of diet cola followed, then forgotten cans of green peas, bought on a whim while stocking up one year for a hurricane. She shoved three cans of potted meat to the right. A bottle of vinegar crashed on the Tuscan tile floor and spilled out.

Her stomach growled and she burped. A quick rush of acid burned her throat.

The television from in the living room blathered with the voice of a talking head. "Stay inside, don't open the door to anyone," the announcer said. "Not even your family. Trust only those you've been in constant contact with for the last four days. Use protection. Examine your loved ones for signs." Mary rubbed at the mark on the nape of her neck, a souvenir hickey from Friday's date with Donald from the office. It was now Monday.

The box of thin mints lay hidden in the back, stashed. She

hadn't had the will power to throw the box away when she'd started the diet.

A gunshot blasted the air. Mary paused, one hand on the Girl Scout cookies. Next door, from the sound of it. Probably the parents taking care of their kids. She'd never met the next-door neighbors, just seen the mom unloading groceries from a minivan, and nodded at the children on their way home from school.

That would be the son, she knew. Mary wondered if he'd fought. He'd been big enough; she'd seen him swaggering home from football practice, his helmet in his hand, wearing a battered orange jersey. Dark grass stains on his faded jeans and a cocky smile on his face as he waved to her while she watered her azaleas.

No matter what, Mary wasn't going outside. No others would end up like her. Or at least if they did, it wouldn't be her fault.

Bingo barked from the back room and Ms. Kitty hissed. "Shut up," Mary yelled. She'd locked the animals in there to keep them away from her and her appetite. A quick vision of her dog – short, chubby legs and sleek brown body – made her mouth salivate. She straightened, knees popping, and ripped open the flap of the box. Her fingers grabbed the cellophane and pulled. The cookies spilled out onto the floor and the smell of mint and chocolate mixed with cider vinegar drifted up.

Mary moaned.

Another shot. Mary remembered the daughter had liked pink and always wore a Hello Kitty backpack.

Her hands fumbled on the floor for the cookies, even though the smell of the sweet chocolate roiled her stomach. An acrid tang of gunpowder seeped in through the kitchen window above the sink, along with the smell of fresh grass and an alluring odor Mary couldn't identify. It overpowered the smell of the vinegar with something both sweet and rotten. Her mouth watered again and she had to gulp to clear it. She rubbed her stomach. Her hand pressed deep. The hunger pangs felt like the onset of cramps, tight and kicking at her insistently. The aroma drifted in on another breeze.

She stood, the thin mints forgotten at her feet, and shuffled to the window. Her oversized jeans caught on her bare feet, and Mary pulled up the loose waistband with one hand as she walked. The bright yellow cabinets reflected the sun streaming in from the skylight over the butcher-block island. So strange, she thought, to have something like this happen during the day. In the movies it always happened at night.

She leaned over the sink and pulled daisy curtains out of the way so she could see out the bay window. The bright grass of her neighbor's side yard gleamed. A discarded pink Big Wheel lay forlorn in the concrete driveway and their garage door gaped open.

She sniffed the screen for a whiff of the tantalizing aroma. The mesh rubbed against her cheeks.

Bingo barked again from the spare bedroom. His claws clattered against the door.

Mary closed her eyes to better concentrate on the scent. Ah, there it was, just a wisp. The sound of Bingo's barking and the television faded. Her hands strained against the window screen. An image of a rare steak filled her mind. She could see the meat pulse.

That's what she needed, something bloody. Mary forced herself away from the window with a last glance at the body of the girl sprawled in the garage. The pool of blood seeped into the concrete and oozed outward, past three forgotten Barbies and down the driveway. The girl didn't move. The parents must have gotten her before the virus took hold.

Mary averted her gaze from her warped reflection on the stainless steel refrigerator door, distorted shades and ovals. It took her a few tries to open the fridge side, her hands grown clumsy, unwilling to respond.

The meat drawer contained lean chicken breasts and a

plastic-wrapped slab of seasoned tofu. She pulled the chicken out and ripped off the plastic. She forced herself to take a bite.

Not bad, she thought. Her teeth chewed, ground, over and over. She could taste the hint of blood in the still raw meat, the satisfaction of chewing through the firm breast.

Still, her stomach wanted more. It gurgled at her. The craving spread outward. Mary could feel the virus in her cells, multiplying one by one, turning each cell into a ravenous mouth, red and gaping. A slave to her appetite. She crammed the chicken into her mouth.

Ms. Kitty howled again. Mary knew she wanted outside, wanted to stalk and attack blades of grass and dust motes. Or perhaps she just wanted more of her kibble. Mary hadn't remembered to put their food or water in there with them. She found herself walking towards the door. How good the cat would taste, so plump and furry and struggling. How the bones would snap! Her feet stepped, one past another. Bright pink toenails smiled up at her. She grabbed the counter at the end of the kitchen. Mary impelled her feet back around.

Two more blasts from the rifle, a scream, then silence, except for the voice of the television. Probably the dad had killed the mother, then himself. She'd thought about suicide herself, but it was too late. All she could do was delay.

She forced herself to eat the second breast slower. Each bite lessened the craving, but it wasn't enough. Her body screamed at her for more, insistent. Her stomach throbbed.

At least she wouldn't gain any weight from this gluttony. The thought almost made her cry. Years of dieting, trying to get her weight down to the point where she wasn't pudgy, daily jogging to slim her thighs. Weight-lifting and aerobics classes, yoga, Pilates, and kick-boxing. And after all that, finally, a date with Donald, the cute guy in the cubicle next to hers. The date had gone terribly wrong.

And now she could eat anything she wanted, except it all tasted off. Even the chicken breast wasn't right, wasn't fresh enough. She thought of the body of the girl outside on the concrete. If only her parents didn't have guns – Mary knew if they saw her they'd shoot her. She chewed harder.

Ah, there was the taste, tangy and tart. Her throat gulped as Mary swallowed. The cramps eased. The chicken worked! She waddled back to the fridge and opened it again. She froze. Blood dripped from her hand. It trickled down the cool white plastic, a red stream on the refrigerator door. In her haste to eat the breast, she'd gnawed her hand, ripped a chunk of flesh from her thumb.

Two more gunshots echoed from outside the house.

Mary sat down on the golden tiles, laid her head on the cool floor, and closed her eyes. Her thumb throbbed, her stomach spasmed, and the taste of her own blood lingered in her throat. Bingo barked once and then began to whine. Perhaps she should kill herself before this went any further.

The doorbell rang.

Bingo whined louder and scratched at the door. Mary propped herself up and struggled to her feet. She might as well answer the summons, it didn't matter anymore. Her thumb found its way into her mouth and she sucked on it as she shuffled through the living room to the front foyer. Sunlight from the glass side panels of the door pooled in even squares on the wood floor.

A shadow drifted into the box of light and Mary looked up. Donald stood in front of the glass.

So this is what she would come to, Mary thought as she sucked her thumb harder. Pain from the bite nagged at her, but the taste of her own blood soothed her stomach.

Donald's hands pressed against the glass. Mary could see traces of dried blood on them, worn into the creases and whorls of his fingertips. His mouth worked, but no words came out. Inarticulate groans shook his body, still dressed in the suit he'd had on Friday night. Traces of her lipstick dotted his collar.

"You infected me," she said, around the thumb in her

59

mouth.

He disappeared from view. A pounding started at the door, heavy and meaty. Mary stumbled forward and turned the deadbolt.

The thumping stopped. She sighed in relief and turned to head back to the kitchen. Perhaps she had a roast in the freezer.

Glass crashed to the floor. Mary swiveled around. A hand reached through the broken window and turned the lock on the door. Donald didn't seem to care that the shards lacerated his skin and sent rivulets running. The smell threatened to overpower her self-control. Food.

The door opened. Donald stepped inside, arms outstretched. Again Mary thought how strange to see zombies lurching, exactly like old horror movies, only during the day and in color. He reached for her. Blood oozed from a graze in his arm and he smelled like gunpowder. He'd been shot, at least once, possibly twice from his limp, but he still moved.

Mary backed up. She had to fight her own feet, force them to move. She needed a weapon; there would be no reasoning with the creature in front of her, driven by appetite. Her thumb throbbed.

Donald's hands grabbed again. Mary spun and stumbled into the kitchen. She dragged open her utensil drawer. Serving spoons were no good to her. She hesitated for a moment over a meat tenderizer, but put it back in favor of her meat cleaver. She hefted it in her right hand and faced Donald.

He'd been so cute. She supposed for a Zombie he wasn't half bad. Perhaps when she was fully turned she'd find him attractive again, but right now the light of desire in his brown eyes, the moans from his lips, showed Mary her future. She'd be just like him. She'd eat her pets, her neighbors, and move on, consumed and consuming. The only thing she could do was stall.

Donald's hand closed on the counter. His body and the smell of ripe flesh trapped her. Mary swung the knife. She didn't have the leverage of distance, so it only opened a small gash on his right arm. Donald shifted and Mary slid past him.

She could smell his blood. Mary's mouth watered. Saliva gushed and she swallowed, again and again. Unlike the faint aroma of the little girl next door, this smell raged through the air. Like the smell of her own blood had. Her nostrils twitched.

This was his fault, after all, she thought. He'd infected her. Well, she was partly to blame; she'd known the virus was spreading. Donald had to have known he was tainted. The bite marks on her neck, breasts, and thighs told her he had. He'd been trying to fend off the famishment. Instead of a stash of cookies, he'd tried with sex. And though she'd known something was wrong when he asked her out, she'd gone anyways. The normal Donald never would have had time for her.

He lunged forward again. His eyes met hers without recognition. Mary steadied herself. She had no choice; he was her chance for another few hours of sanity. Her hand lifted and swung. She watched the knife arc through the air. The stainless steel of the refrigerator door reflected a warped image of herself, elongated like a praying mantis.

His head jerked from the impact. Blood spurted from his neck. She hadn't expected that, had thought it would pool, or maybe drip, but not gush in such an appalling manner.

Her stomach growled and Bingo yelped. She spared a moment of pity for the poor dog, scared and trapped, then hit Donald again. His shirt turned red. Donald staggered forward. She sliced him one last time. He fell to the floor, twitched.

She noted with the part of her brain still capable of thought and not wanting to scream that his white dress shirt was tattered and stained, his tie loose around his neck. Donald never would have permitted himself the luxury of a loosened tie. If any remnant of him had been in the creature at her door, it was gone now.

She had her dinner. Mary slid down to the floor beside him

and watched his brown eyes glaze. So this was death, she thought. Anticlimactic and still in the end. She licked the blood from her fingers and ran her hand through sticky hair.

The cells of her body propelled her. She dipped her hand in the pool of congealing blood, still warm, and brought it to her mouth. She licked. The taste burst over her tongue, salty and sweet.

But something was wrong. Although the taste was right, Mary's stomach ached. The more she licked, chewed, and gnawed, the less it sated.

Yet her own blood had filled her, had stopped the terrible throb. Why did Donald not satisfy her? She sniffed back the revulsion rising up from her center. Gorge and acid swirled in her stomach. She had to fight the urge to vomit, fearing what she would see in the splatter.

"Damn it," she said. Ms. Kitty mewed. Was it because he was infected? Or because the magic faded as the body died?

Either way, the taste of him revolted her. Mary leaned against her cabinet with her throat tight and blinked her eyes to clear them from the cloud forming as tears threatened. She dropped Donald's hand.

The open door beckoned her from the front room. She could walk out of the house, into the suburban green and miniature mansions, lurch from door to door, waiting to be shot and dismembered by the healthy and wise, or feast on the old or silly. Mary grabbed her hair and tugged. She didn't want to go, she wanted to stay here and die in her own house, penned in as she preferred.

Mary thought of the closed guest room and the animals, her friends, trapped in there. Bingo would give her no problems; he would gaze at her with the same deep look he gave her whenever she looked at him. Ms. Kitty would be harder to catch, but... She could do it. She craved it, needed the flesh to sustain her own.

Her hand fumbled for the meat cleaver. It lay on the floor

next to her, by her feet. Pink toenails and blood.

A hand closed over hers, pressed tight against her gnawed thumb. She screamed and scrabbled away.

Donald levered himself up, his back against the green cabinets. His head lolled to the left, the wound gaped at Mary. It looked like killing herself wouldn't work. After all, she couldn't both kill and then dismember herself, not when consciousness and whatever soul fled at death, even if the body went on, mindless and full of gluttony.

She forced herself to go back for the knife. Donald fought to grab her, to pull her down to him. His mouth worked, open and chewing as though he could taste her already, his eyes dim and vacant.

The handle slid in her hands. She hacked down at Donald. The knife glanced off his neck. Over and over she swung. He didn't fight her, just reached for her over and over. His hands grabbed at her ankles, her hair. She kicked him off and sawed at his neck again.

Spatters of blood and gore covered the cabinets and ran down the wall by the time she finished. Little lumps congealed on the floor and twitched. His left hand curled in on itself, a crab flailing for purchase on the yellow tiles. As the fuel that had fed the cells, the blood and meat of human DNA faded, the parts slowed.

And the ravenous urge was back, full force. Mary panted with the pain. Her temples throbbed and her eyelashes stuck together. Her scalp itched.

Bingo barked, sharp yips, followed by his version of a menacing growl, though she knew his tail would be wagging. Hunger raced through her, insistent and persisting. Mary put her head in her hands.

During the struggle with Donald, her thumb, the one she had bitten by accident, had started bleeding again. The smell of it ripened in her nose, sent signals throughout her system. Fresh meat.

Oh god, she thought. The choices I have left. Mary could kill others, kill her pets, or...

She stuck her thumb in her mouth and began to chew.

JUDGMENT

by Stephanie Kincaid

Vivian had been right; the Tarot reader was a big hit. Charlotte hadn't been sure that one woman could provide enough entertainment to keep a roomful of twelve-year-old girls busy for an evening. She'd discussed backup plans with her daughter, but Vivian adamantly insisted that all she wanted for her birthday party was a fortune-teller. Charlotte had rented a stack of movies just in case, and so far nobody had even looked through the pile.

Charlotte's analytical mind had nothing but bemused scorn – carefully concealed, of course, in deference to Vivian's enthusiasm – for the very idea of "reading the future." To the girls, however, the promise of seeing the unseen meant one precious thing: a way to access otherwise hidden knowledge about boys.

There were variations on the theme, of course. "Does Chris like me?" "Will Justin ask me out?" "Will Nathan kiss Vivian this month?" The last elicited universal squeals of disgust, and Vivian expressed profound relief when it was revealed that certain obstacles stood between her and the hypothetical kiss. Charlotte wondered what was wrong with Nathan. She felt sorry for the poor kid. She also wondered what kind of questions the girls had started asking once she left the room.

After the matter of the kiss was resolved, Vivian quickly decided that the girls might be more comfortable opening up to the Tarot reader without Charlotte listening in. "It's not that we don't want you there, Mom," she said earnestly. Charlotte wondered if she were expected to actually believe that or simply act as though she did. "It's just that we have to be able to bare our souls. We want an accurate reading, after all."

Charlotte bit back her smirk. "You'd just better not be talking about baring your souls – or anything else – to any boys, young lady."

Vivian rolled her eyes. "Mo-o-om!" She stretched the word into three syllables, each one emphasizing just how ridiculous she found Charlotte's statement. "There aren't any boys I even like."

"That's a relief," Charlotte responded, immediately wondering what Vivian would consider baring if she did find a like-worthy boy.

Vivian rejoined her friends, and Charlotte plated two slices of pizza to take upstairs to Dave's office. Overwhelmed by all the estrogen, Dave had retreated to the office shortly after the party began, and Charlotte didn't think he'd emerged since.

Dave eagerly accepted the pizza, clearly relieved that he wouldn't have to leave his hidey-hole to look for food.

"How's it going down there?"

"They love her. But apparently the most pressing issue among those bundles of hormones is boys."

"Yeah. What'd you expect? What else did you think about when you were that age?"

"Getting ahead on SAT prep," Charlotte answered with neither a pause nor a trace of irony.

"Well, that's why you're my little freak."

"At that age, I would rather have dissected a boy than kiss him."

"And aren't we glad that changed?"

The thunder of bare young feet pounding up the stairs interrupted their banter. Dave looked faintly horrified as seven grinning heads popped into the doorway.

"Mrs. North! Mrs. North! Come down and let her do your

66

cards!"

"Yeah, come on Mom."

"I already have a boy," Charlotte protested, gesturing toward the rapidly blanching Dave. "I certainly don't need another one."

"You can ask her about your big work project. The one that makes you get home so late all the time."

Vivian's words hit a nerve. Charlotte felt guilty every day about the project that forced her to spend so much time away from her husband and their only child. Even though she felt a bit ridiculous doing it, having her cards read was a small thing to do to make her daughter happy on her birthday. Charlotte agreed, and the girls bounded back down the stairs, hollering to the other partygoers, "Mrs. North's gonna do it!"

"Guess they finally ran out of boy questions," Charlotte observed.

"Not going to make them call you Dr. North?" Dave teased. Charlotte glanced over her shoulder to make sure that none of the girls remained in view, and then quickly flashed her husband the finger. She grinned wickedly as she backed out the door, hands at face height, ready to defend against well-aimed pepperoni.

"I would like to know the outcome of my 'big work project'," Charlotte declared obediently. The girls clustered around her as she sat across the card table from the reader, cutting the cards as she was instructed. The fortune-teller had an earth-mother vibe to her. Her green peasant skirt and blouse flattered her abundant curves, and her auburn hair hung nearly to her knees. Lanky, angular Charlotte felt a quick spark of relief over the fact that Dave was hiding upstairs. As soon as she admitted it to herself, she felt silly. What did she have to be threatened by?

"Death," the woman announced.

"Excuse me?"

The reader tapped an unmanicured finger on the table,

drawing Charlotte's attention to the upturned card. It depicted an armored skeleton riding implacably along on a white horse, mowing down humankind. Beneath the hooves of a horse lay a man whose crown had clearly toppled from his head.

"As long as he gets the king, too," Charlotte quipped. In actuality, she was thinking that this card had more to do with her research than the reader could possibly know.

"Now this card does not necessarily refer to a physical death," the woman began. Several of the girls let out dramatic sighs of relief. "It refers, rather, to change. And the change can be positive. In the case of your work project, for example, you might turn an unexpected corner or have a development that you had not foreseen. Perhaps a sudden triumph that necessitates the 'death' of a previous way of doing things in favor of a better way?"

"Perhaps," Charlotte said enigmatically. The reader was clearly waiting for her to offer more, but she remained silent. After a few moments, the reader flipped another card.

"Judgment," she declared. On this card, an angel leaned down from an unseen heaven, trumpeting the dead from their graves. In the forefront, a man, woman, and child rose from their coffins, cyanotic arms raised in rapture.

"Here we have the Last Judgment, when the graves open and the dead are reborn." The reader gave Charlotte a look of approval. "This card indicates revival and new life. Perhaps your project will take on new vitality? Does this mean anything to you?"

Charlotte's scientific skepticism did not quiet her human heart. Revival? New life? It was a coincidence, of course, but this spoke to everything toward which she was working.

The reader nodded. "I can see that this is significant for you." Clearly Charlotte's poker face needed some work. "It's perfectly all right if you prefer not to say. We'll continue."

The next card was labeled "The Tower." Lightning ripped through the two-dimensional sky, striking the titular structure and setting it aflame. Two human forms plummeted from the tower to an ominous fate.

The reader's eyes flicked over the girls' faces, then back to Charlotte. After a pause that lasted a little too long, she took a steadying breath and spoke brightly. "Admittedly, this card is not one I like to see too often. It looks kind of scary, doesn't it? But, you know, change can be scary, even when it is all for the good."

She swept the cards back into the larger pile and began shuffling. Charlotte took this as a cue that her reading was over. The fact that the reader had never offered a meaning for the last card did not escape her.

Once the fortune-teller had departed and the girls had demolished Vivian's birthday cake, they set up camp in the game room, where Charlotte was certain no sleep would be had that night. After making sure that everyone had adequate floor space and pillows – not that she anticipated their being used as anything but cushy projectiles – she opened her laptop and started an Internet search for "the Tower card in Tarot." As she suspected, the results were less than encouraging. She repeatedly encountered such phrases as "sudden downfall" and "catastrophic change." It was a good thing Charlotte was such a rational woman. A more superstitious individual might have taken this as a bad sign.

A more superstitious individual might have lived longer. The morning after the slumber party, Charlotte's pager went off. She flailed into consciousness, chased there by an angry bee only to find that the furious buzzing went on even in the real world, the code for an emergency at the lab flashing on the miniscule screen. It was just a little after four; as she dressed swiftly, she could still hear muffled giggling through the wall. She shook Dave and said a quick goodbye, regretting even as she bolted for the garage the panic he'd feel having to fend for himself in a houseful of preteen females in a few hours.

Charlotte and her partner arrived at the lab within seconds

of each other. The security team should have been waiting for them. They weren't. The doctors debated what to do for only a few moments. There was only one door to the windowless facility, and it was closed and locked. Only the doctors and the security crew had keycards and alarm codes. If someone had broken into the lab, the door would not have rearmed.

Dr. Finch swiped his card and opened the door. Charlotte followed him down the hall. They both had the same thought: They had to make sure the subjects were safe. It occurred to neither one that they might not be safe from their subjects.

As they approached Room E, where the subjects were kept, dizzy fear swept warmly through Charlotte. The light was on and the door was ajar. So much for new vitality! If the subjects were damaged – or worse, missing – the project would be set back by months.

The scene inside Room E was not reassuring. It was as though a tornado had torn the room apart. Everything breakable seemed at first glance to have been smashed. Tables and cabinets were overturned. Every surface had been spattered with blood. This super-intelligent pair, these geniuses in their field realized, as though with one great shared brain, that they had more to fear than a research setback.

Calling the police was out of the question. While Charlotte believed their cause was noble, she was well aware that not all of their methods were technically legal. They had no way of contacting the enigmatic but apparently very wealthy organization that had sought out the pair and was funding the project with nearly unimaginable generosity. Their benefactors contacted the doctors when the need arose; the communication did not go both ways. They were on their own.

In the stunned silence, they both heard the noise. A faint scrabbling sound barely reached them from across the hall. The doctors looked at each other. Where was the security team? The bespectacled Dr. Finch with his potbelly and comb-over did not exactly present a threatening figure, and the slight

Charlotte was no more imposing. Their work was more important, though, than their personal safety. Their research held implications for the health and longevity of humanity as a whole. In wordless agreement, they left Room E, following the muffled sounds to the office across the hall.

They were met by more chaos and more blood. The desk and chairs were shattered. Papers lay scattered everywhere, and the heavy-duty file cabinets that had lined the far wall had toppled like dominoes on steroids into a great metal heap. A wet snuffling came from the far corner. Charlotte stepped uncertainly forward.

"I've got your back," Dr. Finch said in a low voice. Charlotte wondered what defense the pudgy little man planned to offer if someone snuck up on them, but this didn't seem like the time to ask.

Charlotte picked her way over the debris, her shoes peeling sickeningly up with every sticky step over the dark stains on the floor. As she got closer to the file cabinets, her stomach heaved, and she choked back bile that still tasted faintly of soured chocolate.

A man had been pinned underneath one of the weighty cabinets, trapped by one crushed, bloody arm. He did not seem particularly upset about his condition, though his attempt to free himself was admittedly extreme. He had rolled up on one side to face the damaged limb and was contentedly engaged in chewing his way through it.

At the sound of Charlotte's gag, the man stopped chewing and looked up at her, his face a dripping mess. Strands of muscle and splinters of bone stuck to his chin. She could see now that it was Ralph, one of the men on the security team. Before she could speak to him, he started snapping at her, hungry jaws closing and opening like an attack dog. She jumped back, tripped over an upturned lamp and came down hard on one hip.

Either Ralph had finally gnawed away enough tissue or the

promise of prey gave him renewed vigor, and he rolled toward the fallen doctor, leaving his arm behind with an awful ripping sound. Before Charlotte could scramble to her feet, he had his teeth in her leg, tearing away a large chunk of calf. She screamed and kicked Ralph in the face. This fazed him not at all, and he was leaning in for another bite when Charlotte felt someone grab her from behind.

She struggled until she heard Dr. Finch bark in her ear, "North! Get ahold of yourself. We have to get out of here. Now."

Charlotte steadied herself enough to allow Dr. Finch to pull her to her feet. She limped back through the office, leaning heavily on her partner. Ralph was clearly having some cognitive difficulty, and this coupled with the fact that he was down a limb gave him some trouble righting himself. Not one to pass up a free meal – at least not anymore – he crawled after his fleeing snack. Still, he wasn't going to be winning a marathon anytime soon, and the doctors felt a temporary relief at outdistancing the ravenous freak.

The irksome thing about temporary relief is that it doesn't last very long. The commotion had attracted the rest of the errant security team as well as the missing subjects, and they were massed in the hall, stumbling closer and closer to Room E and the office that Ralph had made his own.

"What the hell is this? This isn't a goddamn zombie movie!" Dr. Finch yelled unhelpfully.

The subjects were easily distinguished from the security crew. For one thing, they were all naked, as they had been when they'd been brought into the lab. For another, they moved more slowly and clumsily. The security team, only freshly dead, had not undergone as much deterioration, although they looked to be in universally bad shape. Several of the men seemed to have dislocated joints; some were missing large pieces of flesh; some had bones protruding from their skin. All of them were bloody. And all of them were hungry.

Charlotte thought of the judgment card, the bluish corpses rising from their graves. How did it go? Death came first, then the risen dead, then the tower – the great catastrophe. She started to laugh; it was all dizzyingly funny.

"What's wrong with you?" snapped Dr. Finch, his attempt to drag Charlotte down the hall toward the single escape route hindered by her fit of giggles.

There was something wrong, wasn't there? Charlotte's head was so fuzzy; she couldn't think what it was. Was the pain making her delirious? She mentally scanned her body. Oddly, despite her bruised hip and the ragged wound in her leg, she felt little pain, merely dull aches that reached her as though through a fog. She could hardly stand; she could swear she felt her muscles liquefying.

Dr. Finch's drive for self-preservation was stronger than his sense of obligation to help Charlotte. It was clear that she was becoming dead weight, and the slobbering mob was close enough to smell. He let go of Charlotte and bolted for the door.

Unsupported, Charlotte found herself sliding to the floor with an odd melting sensation. She pulled herself after Dr. Finch, feeling no resentment or anger. She could barely see the blurry doctor fumbling for his key card as the creatures, which appeared to have lost interest in Charlotte, reached him. It did not occur to her to wonder why they left her alone. Dr. Finch lunged out the door, but the zombies were already on him, pulling him back, tearing off bits of well-marbled meat.

Somehow it came to Charlotte that she had to hold on to consciousness long enough to get the door closed. Through the mud that her brain was becoming flashed a vivid picture of Vivian and Dave. This hungry death that the doctors had created in their quest to prolong life had to be contained. She dragged herself forward, every limb impossibly heavy, passing the feasting beasts, the door only seeming to get farther away.

And suddenly getting to the door no longer mattered. The fog lifted, and all that mattered was the hunger.

HATFIELD THE USURPER

by Matthew Louis

Carl Hatfield ignored the sweat that seeped from beneath his overgrown, oily hair and ran down his forehead and neck. He blinked and wiped his brow with almost timed regularity but never allowed himself to push thumb and forefinger against his eyeballs. From long experience he knew the sweat would carry desert grit and he didn't care to grind the matter into his eyes and render himself blind for the next several minutes.

He was seated on a large, red, plastic cooler, in a tent that was enclosed on three sides and offered only nominal protection from the heat. Numerous crewmembers had left in a panic, some looting the set for supplies on their way out, and someone had even broken into Hatfield's Jeep Eagle and taken his Glock. As he thought of this he once again spat a curse.

But those who remained were taking refuge in their RVs or the air-conditioned common tent, so Hatfield had come here, to this outdoor pit stop, to be alone with thoughts that he found alternately disturbing and exhilarating.

He was dressed as the outlaw Josey Wales. This morning they were due to film the scene in which Josey rescues Laura Lee from the gang of wandering rogues. James Cameron didn't merely want to recreate the original, of course, so the scene had been re-chorcographed so Josey would leap twenty feet down a

75

rocky wall, land on his feet in the middle of the fray, and kill the rogues at point blank range. The leaping was Hatfield's job.

But Cameron hadn't appeared yet, nor was it likely that he – or anyone – would be interested in filming celluloid fantasies for years to come.

Elbows on knees, scowling down at his Blackberry, Hatfield studied the gadget's screen and felt the corner of his mouth twitch. Hannah still hadn't returned any of his various messages. Her texts had ceased and she no longer answered when he called. Hatfield pulled the sleeve of his blue cotton work shirt, styled to look hand-sewn in 1860, across his forehead and thought, *She's dead.* And then, *Life as I knew it is dead.*

A thrill went through him, like a muscle tremor generated in the pit of his stomach and tickling its way down to his testicles. His eyes unfocused and a notion, a daydream of spitting guns, splitting flesh and erupting blood, attempted to impose itself on his consciousness.

He shook his head, bringing himself out of it, and sweat droplets sprinkled on his wrists. Christ, Hannah would be waiting for him, knowing that if anyone could save her, he could. They were only three hours or so from LA, less if he pushed it, and he would probably drive at least ninety since he couldn't imagine sheriffs or cops bothering with him at this point. He knew he ought to be on the road already if he ever cared about the woman at all. Maybe Hannah was alive, holed up in her apartment, waiting for him, but–

"Carl? Is it okay if I call you Carl?"

Hatfield looked up, squinted a moment, then realized Alex Avery himself had entered the tent. Behind the actor the blue Mojave sky was beaten almost colorless by the 11 a.m. sun. Avery was also dressed as Josey Wales, wearing a few weeks of beard growth that matched Hatfield's, except Avery's face had only the lightest sheen of sweat since he had been in his massive air conditioned RV with Brianna Holmes.

"Yessir," Hatfield said. "Call me whatever you like."

"Thanks." Avery gestured toward the soldier's Blackberry. "You know what's happened. Martial law. They don't have anything except chopper footage out of LA anymore."

Hatfield nodded. "It's hard to believe. Two days ago they were saying it wouldn't break out of Mexico and now LA is history."

"You got anyone there?"

"Girlfriend. She's the one I mentioned. The actress, remember? You were going to see about a part for her."

Avery snapped his fingers and pointed. "That's right!"

"But I think she's dead."

The star was alarmed by the word. "No! Things are shutting down, lines of communication. We can't get through to our kids either, but we know everything's fine – at least for now. That's why I wanted to talk to you, actually."

Hatfield studied the terminally boyish face half-hidden behind the blond-brown stubble. It was more like looking at a tabloid cover than a flesh and blood human being. The adorable, slightly upturned nose, the glint of bright perfect teeth, the dreamy blue eyes, were as familiar to Hatfield as his own broken-nosed and scarred countenance. At a startlingly youthful forty-two years old, Alex Avery had twice been *People Magazine*'s "Sexiest Man Alive This Year." With his marriage to the equally iconic Brianna Holmes, and the media's obsession with the couple producing—or adopting from third world countries—a brood that now totaled eight children, Avery was grander Hollywood royalty than Paul Newman or John Wayne had ever been. The joke around the set was that Hatfield was Avery's evil twin. If one didn't see their faces, the two men were the same height, had the same lean, strong build and the same coloring.

"Okay," Hatfield said. "Talk."

Avery sighed and rubbed his hands over his buttocks, which were clad in blue wool Civil War trousers. "You know about my kids." He grunted. "I mean, who doesn't, right? Well, like I said, Brianna and I haven't been able to make contact – with anyone. For about seven hours. I asked around and Jimmy told me to talk to you, because of your background."

Hatfield nodded. Moving in Hollywood circles he was accustomed to being a bit of a novelty. A real life soldier of fortune. After Somalia he had done a lot of private – illegal – stuff through the '90s, working for various millionaires around Los Angeles. He'd reenlisted in the Marines after 9/11 and done two tours in Iraq, but decided not to go back because of Hannah, the dancer and aspiring actress he'd met in a bar on Sunset Boulevard one afternoon. It was Hannah who had him reconnecting with his associates who were tied in with the film industry, and he'd lined up this stunt double gig for her benefit. Funny how things worked out.

"You probably know what's coming," Avery continued. "I want to go get my kids. There's a Humvee on the set and I've already made arrangements to use it. I'll give you whatever you want."

"I don't mean to be rude, Mr. Avery, but–"

"Alex. Call me Alex, Please."

"Okay, well, Alex. I don't mean to be rude, but do you know exactly what's happening out there in civilization?"

"Virus," Avery said. "Rioting and looting. I know, it's scary as hell. There are rumors about other things, but come on."

"Listen." Hatfield brandished his Blackberry. "This is more than a bunch of rumors and you know it. People are fucking eating people, Alex. People are getting up after they been shot a dozen times. You want to go tearing into the middle of that?"

Avery nodded, held Hatfield's gaze. "I do."

The soldier looked the actor up and down and scoffed. The pants and old-fashioned work shirt were artfully torn and soiled by wardrobe technicians. "Alex?" Hatfield sighed. "Listen, you're not a hero. You're not Josey Wales. You're not even Clint Eastwood. This is the end of the world we're looking at. People aren't talking about rebuilding society, they're talking about places to run and hide. This disease, or whatever it is, it's not slowing down, it's picking up momentum. The people who get it, they become monsters – undead. You understand that?"

"Well, my kids–"

Hatfield raised a hand. "The way I see it is, I got something worth a lot more than money. I can survive. Whatever happens, wherever I am, I can survive. Way things look from here, I can do whatever the fuck I want from now on."

"I see." Avery nodded. He began backing away. "Sorry to bother–"

"Hold on," Hatfield said. The guilty, delicious feeling had returned, a drug of infinite possibilities, and one particular possibility had his breath coming short. "Do you want to see your kids again? 'Cause you're absolutely right, you know. I'm your only chance. With the population density in LA, every damned street's gonna be choked with these undead. Everyone that gets infected infects ten, twenty, fifty more. There's no way my Hannah's alive, but you, you got a compound, and I know you got some guys who know how to shoot on your security team, right?"

Avery nodded.

"So you're right. They're probably still fine, at least for another day or two, I'd say. Long as your guys figure out they gotta shoot for the head–" Hatfield held up his Blackberry again, indicating where he'd gotten this information. "And long as they got plenty of ammo, they can probably hold 'em off. Do they? Have plenty of ammo I mean?"

"I… don't know," Avery said. "They weren't hired for this sort of thing."

"Who's your head of security?"

"Craig Hagman."

79

Hatfield grunted. "I know him. Not the sharpest knife..." He looked up. "Your decision, Alex. I can get you in and out of there by midnight. If the kids are there to be gotten, we'll get 'em. I don't care about money, but there's one thing I want." He palmed the sweat off his forehead, lifted his chin and peered into Avery's eyes. "Your wife."

"What?"

"Your wife." Hatfield's heart was thudding. This must be how a queer feels, he thought, when he first goes public.

"You're not serious," the actor said, pushing thumb and forefinger into his eyes as the sweat suddenly became too much.

"I am serious. I just mean, let's say, one hour with her in that RV. That's how I'll accept payment. That's my price. Take it or leave it." Hatfield kept still, but he watched every movement of the actor's body. This was the moment of truth, when Avery would attack him or not. But the actor was now digging at his eyes, having rubbed granules of dirt and dust into them. He sniffled, let out a light cough and said, "I can't believe this! I can't fucking believe this!"

Hatfield continued to watch.

"You just wait here!" Avery said, and turned and waded back into the sunshine.

He's actually gonna tell her! Hatfield thought. And what else could she say but yes?

He wiped his forehead again, drew his lungs full, and tried to think around the solid, urgent thumping of his heart. He was on an adrenaline high that equaled anything he'd ever experienced in a combat zone. He couldn't tell if he was losing control or finally taking it. Had he ever been civilized, or was it a part he was forced to play? And he began to smile, thinking he was like a man looking down, holding a winning lottery ticket in work-hardened hands, not quite able to grasp the implications but knowing life was going to be one hell of a ride from now on.

He then thought of Brianna Holmes. The perfect proportions, the couch cushion lips, the nice-sized, healthy breasts. And he swallowed, feeling almost frightened because he wasn't thinking of merely ravaging her body. He was seeing her as a woman on the cover of a forgotten novel from his youth; a prized, luscious female in a barbarian world, crouching under the protective will of a powerful male killer.

* * * * *

It took ten minutes. Hatfield had gotten up off the cooler long enough to extract a Michelob Ultra from the box's slushy, arctic innards. The soldier thought this incredibly light, one-caloric beverage might actually sober a man up, but it was ice cold and tasted more or less like beer and that was quite a comfort just now. He imagined in the very near future beer would be hard to come by.

Hearing movement beyond the tent's wall, he looked up, and a moment later Avery reappeared. The men's gazes locked and the actor nodded. "We're going to do it," he said, ducking into the tent. "But we have a condition: It only happens after we get the kids. All of them."

"Hmmm ..." Hatfield rubbed his chin bristles. "Let me just give you a scenario, Alex. Let's say I get you in there and all them kids are, you know, dead. Or, let's say there's only two of them still alive. Why should I bother with them two? There's no longer anything in it for me."

Avery looked stunned, but after a moment his face slackened and he exhaled. "Okay, this then: You get as many of our children as you can back here safe, and we – Brianna, I mean – will keep our side of the bargain."

Hatfield was oddly impressed with this adjustment. He could sense the actor already hardening, acclimating, bowing to the law of the jungle. He'd seen it happen to many, many young soldiers – the ones who had the real guts – and he thought, maybe this guy's made of better stuff than I thought ... either that or he's planning to kill me on the way back here.

"Where's your Hummer?" Hatfield said as he stood and hooked the bottle into sand outside the tent. "Let's get this thing underway. First off, these," he slapped the Civil War style bowie knife in the scabbard on his belt – Alex Avery had an identical weapon, "ain't gonna help. We'll stop at Barstow. I know a gun shop there."

Avery looked ill but said, "Okay."

* * * * *

Hatfield drove the yellow Humvee at an unwavering 95 miles per hour, headed west on the I-40. His heartbeat was cantering and every minute or two he had to dry his palms on his thighs despite the vehicle's potent AC. He was acutely aware of the actor in the passenger's seat. He wondered if the man was sneaking glances at him, but did not allow himself to do other than glare straight ahead at the strip of asphalt that rolled away to the horizon, bisecting the dead desert landscape.

Notions that could be interpreted as insane – that, just yesterday, Hatfield himself would have deemed insane – were assailing him. Like electricity arcing between two points, the soldier's mind was connecting his present situation with the books he used to devour as an adolescent: *Conan – The Conquerer, The Buccaneer, The Usurper.* He could almost smell the waft off the pages of a newly opened paperback, almost see the typeface racked up in wonderful rows and clumped in intoxicating paragraphs, describing the million conquests and adventures of a warlord who lived by cunning and brute force in a world without laws. It was these books that had first compelled him to join the Marines; the only way open to a modern day warrior, he used to say. This last memory made him think, strangely, of a circle closing.

He stole a glance at Avery. The actor was lost in his own

thoughts, staring straight ahead, and by the time he became aware of Hatfield's interest the soldier had looked away. I'm sorry, pal, Hatfield thought. But you're already dead.

Outside, man's works had begun overlaying the desolate terrain, buildings, streets and landscaped tracts spreading over the sand with ever increasing frequency.

Avery straightened in the passenger's seat as they pressed into the outer reaches of the town proper. Hatfield lifted his head, narrowed his eyes and felt the hairs rise on the back of his neck. He had been through Barstow dozens of times and it certainly never looked cheerful, but he had never seen it quite like this.

The scene they persevered into was as lifeless as a photograph except for the heat shimmers on the broad, vacant, main street. For a moment Hatfield was sure the town had been vacated down to the last soul, but then, far ahead, he made out a few figures shuffling on the sidewalks. They were alive, evidently, but moving with no more purpose or enthusiasm than curtains stirred by a breeze. Not a single car was in motion, although by the time they entered the heart of the hot dusty town they had seen two separate pairs of cars that had been abandoned after being crunched together in low-speed collisions.

"They're coming," Hatfield said.

Avery just blinked out the window. The Humvee was cruising now, easing along the sun-battered asphalt at 30, and the figures were materializing all around them. They were men and women, regular citizens in regular clothes, except many were dirty-looking, like dolls dragged around by a careless child, and some had untreated wounds. They all seemed drawn to the moving vehicle, dragging themselves into the street behind the Humvee, beside it – and in front of it.

"Look out!" Avery said.

"Hang on!" Hatfield snarled.

In the middle of the street was a blond man, tall, maybe

thirty, and he came at the advancing car in a foot-scraping hustle, as if he was eager to meet it. He wore a short-sleeved, collared shirt and a black tie and there was a metallic nametag pinned on the left side of his chest. He looked like a Radio Shack employee. Hatfield pressed harder on the gas. The hood of the Humvee was at collarbone level and the man lifted his arms as if to seize the vehicle just before the metal thumped into him and he dropped out of sight. They felt him rolling and breaking beneath the Humvee's undercarriage, and Hatfield watched in the rearview as the figure tumbled on the scorching asphalt in the vehicle's wake. The soldier applied the brakes, still watching in the rearview, and said, "I'll be god-damned!"

Both men turned and through the back window they saw the blond man stirring and then lifting his head – which was now torn and misshapen. His lower half seemed useless, and when he pushed himself up his left arm gave way like a candy cane broken inside its wrapper. So he used his right arm, clawed at the asphalt, and began inching toward them.

"That's why you've got to shoot them in the head," Hatfield said. And then he gasped as he turned back around. Since the Humvee had stopped the residents of Barstow had gravitated to within feet of the vehicle. Hatfield fingered the button on the armrest, clicking the locking mechanism although he knew the doors were already locked. The people drew nearer. Up close their faces were indeed those of corpses, their eyes stuck open, glazed and unseeing, and their clothes dusty and rumpled.

"Drive," Avery said, shifting in his seat as the hand of what had been a young Hispanic thug bumped the window. The undead man's brown face was soon mashed flat on the glass, his tongue leaving streaks. Avery leaned away until he almost touched Hatfield.

"I seen worse in Iraq," Hatfield said, pushing the gas and swerving so he knocked an older woman over with the driver's side fender. He felt her ground beneath the front and then the back tire and they sped forward, a parade of one, drawing the undead onto the sidewalks, around cars and into the street.

"There it is," the soldier said, pointing to a yellow sign with square black letters that read, MAKE MY DAY SPORTING GOODS. "You ready, Alex?"

The actor looked green under his Josey Wales stubble but after a moment he said, "Yeah."

"Good. Here's how we'll work it." Hatfield had fallen into a familiar groove, eager to hurl himself into an episode of deadly adventure. His knuckles were white on the steering wheel. "These motherfuckers got one thing they can do: overwhelm us. 'Sides that, we got every advantage. They couldn't use a weapon if they had one. They can't even throw a punch. Now hang on tight. I'm getting my door as close as I can to the front door of that shop and I'm going in. You climb out my side, close the door behind you and follow me into the store, I click the lock on the Hummer, we lock the store from the inside, and then we go shopping."

The engine's RPMs wound up to a scream and the Humvee jumped the curb, bouncing the men as if their joints were unfastened, and then they barreled up to the front of the store, rocking hard as Hatfield stomped down on the brakes. His door was open before they had stopped sliding and he was outside the vehicle, jerking on the doorknob at the front of the store – which was almost too hot to touch in the afternoon blaze. He could hear Avery climbing out behind him, as instructed. He wished he had a gun to blast through the lock. The windows had wrought iron bars bolted in front of them and the door was covered by a heavy iron screen that had a hole cut out for the doorknob and deadbolt.

"Look!" said Avery.

Hatfield's gaze darted to where the actor was pointing and the soldier said, "Holy Jesus!"

It was a crowd. They were like protesters, like angry marchers, only they marched in broad daylight, moving sluggishly, relentlessly, and in absolute silence.

"Fuck! This way too!"

From the opposite direction on Main Street, more came. Regular people robbed of words or thoughts, held upright as if by the strings of invisible puppeteers, being made to sidle up the super-heated asphalt toward the living breathing men.

Hatfield knew they could get back in the Humvee if there was no other choice, and he resolved to wait until the last possible second. He hammered the iron screen that covered the door and looked in the window. Was that–? Yes! He saw movement. A figure approaching in the store's murky interior, and it was armed. An older man's face, pink and white-bearded, was soon close to the glass and Hatfield pressed his face to the opposite side, saliva flying from his lips as he barked, "Let me in! I'm a living man! Let me in or I'm dead!"

The locks were worked and the door came open. Hatfield began to enter and said, "Close the car door, Alex!" and as soon the door was closed he clicked the remote lock on the key chain. He then shoved the old man and kicked the iron-screened door shut in Alex Avery's face, heaving a shoulder against it and twisting the deadbolt.

He felt the barrel of an automatic rifle – an AK-107 he believed from the moment's glance he'd gotten at it – press against his neck.

"What the fuck're you doin', mister?"

Hatfield breathed. "He's one of them. He's infected. It just happened two minutes ago so there aren't any signs yet. I had to do it."

"You motherfucker!" Alex Avery screamed, his voice cracking, the door rattling under his fist.

Hatfield felt the gun barrel lift away from his neck. The old man took two steps to the window. Hatfield stepped over to look also, his heart thundering. Like a life sized image on a television screen, Avery was running around the Humvee, pulling the door handles, then glancing up and down Main

Street.

"I've seen that guy before!" the old man said in a hushed tone. "He looks exactly like, like ..."

"Alex Avery?"

"No, Josey Wales!"

"I'm gonna fuckin' kill you for this!" Avery said, jarring the door with a kick. Then they saw him turn as the first of them arrived, a gray haired man whose glasses were glinting sunlight where his eyes would have shown. Avery yanked his Civil War Bowie knife into the open and shoved it toward the man's face in a way that would have warded off a regular attacker. The knife's point cracked through the left lens of the man's glasses and dug into the eye beneath, but the man didn't seem to regard it as even a minor irritation.

Avery drew back and a black woman clutched his shoulders, bared her teeth and lowered her face toward his neck. The actor squirmed away with admirable agility but now the crowd was intensifying. Beside Hatfield, the old man worked his hands on his AK and cursed under his breath at the spectacle, watching Alex Avery, time and again, slip from the clutches of the undead. Finally the actor had scrambled atop the Humvee, trying to menace the creatures with his Bowie knife as they piled all around the vehicle like rabid fans. They were fifteen, twenty deep, with the creatures in the back clawing at those ahead of them, and the creatures in the front being lifted by the tide of the crowd until they could reach Avery's ankles.

He went down silently, gritting his teeth, kicking and slashing with his knife until he disappeared beneath them. Hatfield and the old man looked away.

"Jesus fucking Christ!" the old man breathed. He was extremely short, but large-headed, which gave him a leprechaun quality. He didn't look at Hatfield when he spoke. "I thought I seen everything. Josey fuckin' Wales eaten by fuckin' zombies!" He turned and began walking toward the back of his dim, cluttered store, saying over his shoulder, "Come on, mister. Hurry up. I got food rations, and if we stay downstairs maybe they won't smell us."

"Alright," Hatfield said, stepping behind the man, pulling his own Civil War replica Bowie knife. He scuffed forward, grabbed a handful of thin white hair, yanked the head back and drew the knife hard across the soft old throat. He had done the same to much tougher specimens.

He eased the elderly frame to the floor as it twitched, tensed and finally slackened, being sure to pull the AK away before letting go of the body. His eyes were adjusting and he could see dozens of firearms and swords on wall racks behind the counter, and more in glass display cases. The store smelled of stale cigarette smoke, gun oil, and now the coppery stink of the old man's blood. Outside the window, under the downpour of desert sun, masses of undead were still clumping around Avery's body.

Hatfield hustled to where a staircase dropped down to some private storeroom. His pulse was jumping. There was no telling what an old gun nut like this might keep – the AK was already more than Hatfield had hoped for. The soldier's mind leapt ahead. It would be easy. He only had to wait until the coast was clear and then click the Humvee unlocked and load up everything that he needed, and then his new life would begin. He would be a warlord, ruling by force and raw nerve, crushing whoever dared challenge him. And when he got out of here, tomorrow or late tonight, he would drive east, back to the Josey Wales set, and get his woman.

RUMINATIONS FROM TRI-OMEGA HOUSE

by David Dunwoody

I had to lock myself in my room. Well, I don't know that I had to – maybe I'm just not much of a thinker, or a doer either. The frat is pretty much where I always end up when things go south (assuming it didn't all start there) – be it a test, a date or an apocalypse.

This is the latter. I think I'm the only Tri-Omega who made it back here; or rather, again, the only one who ended up here. See, its Thanksgiving break and everyone is at home with their families and girlfriends and whatnot. Me? Well, my plans went south – so here I am, in my room.

At least it wasn't my fault this time.

The entire Miskatonic campus and most of the surrounding township was pretty much deserted this morning. There was a light dusting of snow and the sky was this odd gray color, unbroken by the sun; just a smear of clouds from horizon to

89

horizon that completed the feeling of a dead world. I felt like the last man on earth as I shuffled across the quad with a McDonald's bag in my gloveless hands. Does anyone remember that movie, The Last Man on Earth? It's based on a book by Richard Matheson. The first one had Vincent Price, and then they remade it, once with Chuck Heston and once with Will Smith. I'd give my left nut to have any of those guys here with me now.

Anyway, back to crossing the quad. The burger in the bag was keeping me warmer than my ratty old coat, so I slipped it under the coat and shoved my hands in my pockets to keep it from spilling out.

I had decided to leave campus this morning, despite the fact that my parents weren't going to be home and no one else had extended an invitation. I just had to get out of this ghost town. I had to, and I didn't, but that's me getting ahead of myself.

So I got in the car and started her up. She coughed a few times then started that uneasy purr that reminded me I hadn't changed the oil in almost a year. "Sorry," I told her, patting the dashboard. I opened the glove box and sure enough, gloves fell out. I pulled them on, only to take them off again so I could get at my fries.

The "plague," as they called it, had gone global on September 2nd. Now it was the end of November yet I still felt strangely remote – detached from the awful thing spreading out from the southern states – sluggish in its progress towards us here in New England, which had already hopped the pond to Britain before all the planes were grounded. I've never felt like much of an "elitist" but I guess that's my only excuse for going along with the local mentality that, despite all that had already happened, life must stubbornly go on. The arbitrary values and priorities of Man would surely outlast some bug. The greatest precaution taken by most MSU students was a facemask, but there wasn't even evidence that the plague was airborne. Few had fled the campus even as the outbreak reportedly drew closer. No; most just went on like usual and then drove home for Thanksgiving.

Meanwhile, in the real world – every day, every news correspondent used the word "Panic!" at least once a minute, and every hour another country reported that the outbreak had reached them despite their best efforts – but here it was quiet and calm, always, a world apart from world's end.

I fumbled with the radio tuner. All of the stations were either looping a Top 40 playlist or had given themselves over completely to the talking heads, those who thought their spinning wheels could save the world, men muttering over a microphone, righteous anger expressed in flying flecks of spittle. The federal emergency frequency that was set up was irrelevant to my region, so I didn't bother. Settled on a self-made preacher belting out his screed:

"This is it, people! You want a revelation – look outside your window! Look down your street! God has something to tell you and He's writing it on the streets in blood, praise His name, God damn it these walking dead are the bringers of the message. See it in their faces, their eyes! Do you see? Have you looked at a motherfuckin' zombie? I'm comin' straight from the survival scroll to tell you to look into their empty eyes and realize that there is nothing left on this earth for us! The planet is as corroded and hollow as the shambling husks that took the streets of New Orleans yesterday! We must vacate this place – vacate our homes, our bodies –"

I had to change the station. I didn't want to hear another on-air suicide from the Bible Belt. They'd almost become cliché.

As cliché as the zombie that leapt onto the hood of my car and started pawing at the windshield. If my bud Casey were here he would have laughed as the zombie, coat billowing, face frozen, knocked on the glass.

I don't know why I turned on the wipers. It was an

instinctive move. You would've done it.

Wiper fluid ejaculated into his sallow face, frosting his glasses, and he stared hard at me, alone, just the two of us in the parking lot. He, hunched over the windshield, and me, clutching my Big Mac to my chest.

It was Professor Rand.

I aced that test, dammit, and there he was, clawing at the windshield of my Geo while that smug T.A. of his was fucking off somewhere (or being digested). I knew I'd aced that test and now I'd never get the score because Rand with his broken bloody grin and brown loafers was jumping up and down on my car. Undead.

I popped the clutch, dropped her into reverse and made a big semicircle through the thin layer of snow on that parking lot, tossing the prof face-first into the asphalt at thirty-five miles per hour.

Equal parts elated and horrified, I sped across the lot with the intent of leaving Miskatonic and never coming back. I gunned it, leaned into the wheel and gritted my teeth. I ran upside a curb, blowing both tires on the passenger side.

I spun through some grass, tearing it up pretty good, and came to rest in the middle of the quad. It was quiet for a few minutes.

"Maaaaaaaa..." A distant moan drew my attention to the limping shadow in the empty parking lot. The prof. I stepped on the gas. The car lurched forward a little, fell back, and died.

I got out and, with a good football field's length between me and the prof, I started running. The snow was that thin, slick kind that just loves to send you stumbling and reeling like you're Jerry Lewis, like you're running on paste. I slipped and banged my knee pretty good, and all the while Rand just kept staggering after me, unhindered. He was closing the distance quickly. With every glance back I saw him in greater, more horrible detail, more so than when he'd been slavering over my filthy windshield. One of the elbows of his tweed jacket hung open and ragged and was dripping as he ran. Someone had caught him by the arm and taken a bite. Still bleeding... it hadn't taken long for him to turn.

I made it back to Tri-Omega House, on a craggy hill overlooking some overgrown beach property that we'd wanted to clear out for a kegger last year but Sheriff Combs was an asshole about it. Used my key to get in, slammed the door behind me, threw both bolts and ran upstairs. The burger was cold when I got to it.

Huh. I hadn't paid much attention to the phone after learning it was dead. But I just noticed there's a message on my machine.

"Hey Larry, its Crystal. I know you're bummed that plans fell through, but maybe this'll make you feel better. Tonight, around nine, I'm coming up to your room with a bucket of chicken and a bottle of brandy. I know it's cheesy, but it's the closest thing to a Thanksgiving either of us is gonna get. Your roommate's gone for the break, right? See ya."

Crystal. Oh God, Crystal. Please come.

No!

Don't come!

Not because Professor Rand is still out there, along with anyone else who didn't blow out of town in time. No, I know you're smart, Crystal, and that you'll be able to avoid them. But you're still going to come for me, I know that too, because you're a sweet girl. And, well.

He bit me. Before I got into the house and locked the door, while my half-frozen hands fumbled about, he grabbed me and he bit me.

My hands have thawed, and I can write, but a new numbness is creeping through me. I've become acutely aware of the way that every part of me is alive, a machine whose every component is constantly working so that I can get up early every morning and play old-school DOOM II and skip Sociology. I've suddenly become aware of all these different

93

components and systems because I can now feel them shutting down, in some mad sequence, as the virus takes over.

My parents. They cancelled the usual get-together because of the weather from the north, not the apocalypse from the south. Soon it will reach them. They're not going to make it. They'll leave the house, try to make it somewhere like everyone else, and get stuck out in the open.

I love you, Mom. I love you, Dad. I'm sorry about the weather.

The prof's teeth took a sheet of skin off the back of my right hand. I've bandaged it, though the bleeding isn't much. I just don't want to look at it.

I've paid so little attention to the CDC reports. How long will it take? When will I no longer be me?

I have a sister in Michigan – liberal earth mother, confined by palsy to a chair. Her friends – real friends, she has – will try to safeguard her. She'll fight them off, calling herself a "liability" and shutting herself up all by her lonesome to await... what, I don't know.

I thought Brad (roommate) had a gun but I can't find it. Maybe he took it when he left, just in case. I hope it serves him well. I don't know if I could really shoot myself anyway. What if I fucked it up? In all the zombie movies, every headshot is lethal, but it doesn't really happen like that in real life. Sometimes people eat two shotgun shells and live to tell about it. What if I put a gun in my mouth and only succeeded in disfiguring myself?

Pounding downstairs. Sounds like two sets of fists. The prof has made a friend.

There's bleach and shit downstairs but I don't think I could bring myself to use it. I've heard it's not a pleasant way to go. And, again, it might not work.

I don't have the guts to run outside and take my chances among the undead. Besides, who knows, they might not even want to kill me. I might be one of their own already.

Pulse is dropping. I can barely find it in my neck. I don't want to become one of them.

Hand doesn't hurt anymore.

I just pushed a pin into my thumb. It doesn't hurt at all. Weird. Maybe it wouldn't hurt to hang myself with a belt in the closet. No pain, maybe, but there would still be the instinctive panic of having my airway cut off. I can't do that.

Sorry. I was away. They came in. They got into the house. My hands, the papers are smeared with blood now. Can't read the last paragraph. I had been thinking about hanging in the closet, and I remembered Brad's letter opener that looks like a sword. I was rummaging around for it when I heard the door downstairs break down. I froze. Two sets of lumbering footsteps thumped around in the foyer. There were no moans, no grunts, just shuffling. Then it stopped for a while. I may have been standing here, hunched over with the letter opener in hand, for a good ten minutes. Then they clambered up the stairs.

They hit the door with their hands and heads. I threw my weight against the other side, forgetting all about the bite and the infection, thinking only now of being eaten alive. Thoughts of suicide gave way to the need for self-preservation. I guess it was the same need driving them to hurl themselves at the other side until the hinges started to come loose. I slammed the letter opener through the wood, at eye level, and heard one of them – Rand, maybe – slumping against the door. I think it was Rand. I heard the crunch when the blade went through his glasses.

The other one continued to beat at the door for a while, but I think he's lost interest now. I hear movement downstairs again. He won't leave the house. And she – she's on her way – I can't remember her name.

Maybe the Army will come? Or Sheriff Combs? Maybe they will come with a cure. Turning on the radio. Most stations are dead air, Mr. Survival Scroll included. I hear that they're closing everything down, that you need to avoid local area hospitals and shelters at this time, that major roads are deadlocked, that everything is coming apart and we're all cast off into the wilderness. The National Guard is moving into the Miskatonic Valley. To evacuate.

I'm going to die here. But I won't be dead long.

Breathing is still labored, from the struggle at the door I guess. But it's like I have to make myself do it. Odd.

Now I'm not breathing at all.

It's like an energy. I can feel the virus giving it to me, the energy suffusing my meat and bones. I'm beginning to understand.

Getting hard to write now. Hard to connect with external world – that make sense? Feels like fog out there. Crystal? Her name is Crystal. I just opened the door and pulled Rand down. Left the door opened for her. The one downstairs isn't bothering to come up. He knows.

The Last Man on Earth is really depressing. Vincent Price spends all day alone and all night hiding from the monsters. I always felt bad for him, and in a way it was like the monsters had it better than him. It's like it might not be so bad.

Why is the door open?

I am being driven from my own mind, I think.

Hungry now. It all makes sense now.

I want you to come now, Crystal.

I will wait.

ZOMBIES ON A PLANE

by Bev Vincent

The guy wearing the Phish t-shirt tells Myles he can fly anything, and if he's lying they're all dead. It's that simple. The guy – Barry, who looks like he's under thirty – says he trained to be a pilot "over there," where it all started, but he's skimpy with the details and it sounds like an idle boast, the kind of line someone would trot out in a bar late at night to impress women. If women were still hanging out in bars, that is.

"A lot of people said the war was a bad idea. I supported it at first," Barry says with a shrug. "Never figured it would turn out like this." An understatement if Myles ever heard one.

Myles became the group's leader by default. The nineteen people aboard the dilapidated bus are following him because they think he knows what he's doing. Myles wishes that his plan didn't rely on the unproven skills of a guy who looks like he's never worked a day in his life.

"We'll go someplace remote," he told the people who gathered around him, apparently attracted by his aura of confidence, something he'd cultivated during thirty years in sales and middle management. "A place where we'll be safe until all this is over." They followed him onto the bus like rats after the pied piper. No one asked what they'd do if "this" was

97

never over.

Heading for the airport seems like their best option. The city's overrun, much of it is on fire, and people are being killed in the streets. Those that aren't consumed by their attackers get up again a few seconds later to join the ravenous army of the undead.

Myles met up with this small group at an inner city school gym, a place with strong doors with sturdy locks. Once Barry volunteered that he could get them airborne, Myles presented his plan, sketchy as it was. Under his direction, they raided the cafeteria for food and the work shed for weapons. Barry also said he could start the bus parked in the loading dock even if they couldn't find the keys. Myles didn't ask him if he'd learned this trick "over there," too, but he proved up to the task. Maybe there was hope for him after all.

The fuel gauge on the old school bus registered an eighth of a tank. The last working gas station in the county ran dry six days ago, and the promised supply tankers never showed up. Probably never would. They have enough gas to reach the airport, but if Barry can't figure out how to get one of the planes going, they're screwed.

The bus is a piece of crap, but it runs, so long as they take it easy. Every time Alfie pushes it past thirty miles an hour, the engine light comes on. They can't afford to break down. They haven't seen many of those abominations now that they're out of the city, but no place is safe. Those devils can pop up anywhere, and Myles's group has only knives and axes for weapons. Like gasoline, bullets are a precious and rare commodity.

Thirty miles per hour is fast enough, though. If there's a plane and enough fuel to get them wherever they decide to go, it can wait a few minutes longer while they lumber along the highway. When he was in field sales, before being forced into a desk job, Myles hated the long trek to the airport, but today he's happy to put some distance between himself and the city.

There's no other traffic on the road as far as the eye can see, in either direction. They pass stalled out vehicles on the side of the road, but when they slow to see if there are any occupants in need of help, the bus wheezes, hiccups, and threatens to stall. Alfie eases it back up to thirty, the only speed at which it seems content to run. Myles thinks he sees a head pop up behind the steering wheel of one car after they pass, but he can't be sure, and it could just as easily be one of them instead of a real person.

He pushes the fleeting glimpse from his mind. It might have been a trick of the light, after all, and even if it wasn't, they can't save everyone – he's not even sure they can save themselves. Never give up, though, that's his mantra. His most rewarding sales were the ones where the other person intended to buy from a competitor and Myles won him over with persistence and passion.

Myles has no idea what will happen once the zombies kill everyone. Will they wander the planet in a futile quest for food until they fall to pieces and writhe on the ground like a child's toy with failing batteries? Six billion zombies searching for the few remaining survivors of the human race.

Even if his group escapes, they won't live forever. They'll all die eventually, and when they do, the virus – or whatever it is – will bring them back as one of those creatures. All they can do is forestall the inevitable and hope that somewhere people are working on a solution. Mankind has survived for thousands of years – this scourge won't eradicate us, Myles thinks. Someone will find a way to cure this plague. They always do. This belief is what drives him. Otherwise he might as well set himself on fire and be done with it.

When they reach the airport, Myles tells everyone to hold on tight and orders Alfie to crash the bus through the chain-link fence that separates the parking lot from the runways. The bus lurches and pulls to one side as the fence wraps itself around the bumper and the windshield like chain mail, but they make it through and onto the tarmac.

There are several Airbuses and Boeings parked at the terminal, but Barry opts for a commuter jet, big enough to hold them all but small enough that they'll be able to land it wherever they want, even on a remote airstrip designed for private aircraft. It's an Embraer with a range of at least 2000 nautical miles, according to Barry. Maybe a little more if they top off the tanks, since they'll be flying light. Enough to get them just about anywhere.

But that's the catch – where should they go? Barry releases the jet's door, which drops down to reveal a set of stairs. He ducks inside and emerges a few minutes later with a set of navigational maps. Myles spreads them out on a bus seat while Barry and Gilbert hotwire a fuel truck and pull it up next to the Embraer's wing.

Alfie leans over the seat back. "How about Alaska?"

"We can't get that far. We could make Labrador or northern Ontario."

"Too cold," Terri says, hugging herself. Myles isn't surprised. She's complained about just about everything since she joined their group.

"Snow slows them down," Phil says.

Even if that's true, they have to go someplace where they'll be able to survive, perhaps even grow crops. Also a place where they can stay in touch with the rest of the world, so they'll know when the situation improves. Myles doesn't share his thought process with the others, though. He doesn't want them to realize that he's as uncertain as they are.

"Look," Emily yells. She's the youngest of their group, a teenager who has barely said a word since they left the city, concentrating instead on trying to reach someone – anyone – on her iPhone, clicking the keys with her thumbs.

Myles looks in the direction of her outstretched arm. Several zombies emerge from the airport terminal, shambling across the tarmac toward them, guided by some primitive instinct.

Barry and Gilbert are stowing the hose on the fuel truck, so they must be finished. Myles grabs the wad of maps and dashes out onto the airstrip. "We have to go," he yells. "Now."

The two men look up and see the zombies headed their way. Gilbert gets behind the wheel of the truck and drives it clear of the wing.

"Onto the plane," Myles yells, and the others push past him without any further encouragement, backpacks full of food and supplies slung over their shoulders, weapons clutched in their hands. The zombies may be slow, but they're relentless, and they've already covered almost half the distance between the terminal and the bus. Another few minutes and they'll be on them, ripping and tearing and shredding humanity's last, best hope for survival.

Myles is the last one on board the jet, huffing and panting and trying to ignore the pain shooting down his left arm. Two men – Myles thinks their names are Matt and Chet – pull the door closed while Barry heads into the cockpit. Gilbert volunteers to be the copilot, even though he's never flown a plane before. This is it, the moment of truth. If Barry can't get this thing started and off the ground, they're through, trapped like sardines in a tin can.

Myles leans back in his seat and tries to catch his breath. When he closes his eyes and concentrates, the pain in his chest subsides. He has only three pills left in the little plastic case in his front pocket, and the odds of finding a refill range between slim and none, so he isn't about to waste one now. This will pass. This will pass. Another mantra.

He looks out the window. The zombies have reached the bus and are sniffing around the open door. A moment later they lurch toward the jet again. They know we're in here, Myles thinks. He pulls back from the small oval, not wanting to fall under their penetrating gaze.

The others are pressed up against the windows, watching

the slow but steady procession. The cabin door is closed, so they're safe for now. But what if the creatures take a bite out of their tires before they start taxiing? Or if they're smart enough to find a way in – through the luggage compartment, perhaps?

The thought no sooner enters his mind than he hears a thump coming from the underside of the aircraft. It reminds him of the sound of handlers opening or closing the cargo bay doors.

"We have to get going," he yells, hoping their putative pilot can hear him. He prays that Barry isn't sitting in the cockpit staring at the dizzying array of readouts, dials and switches wondering which one is the ignition key.

Another thump, this one strong enough to cause the fuselage to sway.

"I can't see them any more," Alfie says. "They're under the plane."

"How many?" Terri asks, her voice barely more than a whisper.

"Eight, maybe ten," Alfie says. "More on the way."

Myles looks out the porthole window again. A second group of zombies is crossing the tarmac, at least forty or fifty strong.

"What's taking him so long?" Myles mutters. He inhales deeply, assesses the tightness in his chest and decides that moving won't kill him. Besides, if they don't get in the air soon, a heart attack will be the least of his worries.

He lunges from his seat and heads toward the cockpit. Through the door he sees Barry flipping switches as Gilbert reads instructions from a sheet of paper on a clipboard.

"Can you fly this thing or not?" Myles demands, dreading the answer.

"Of course," Barry says. Gilbert looks up from the checklist and shrugs.

More thumps come from beneath Myles's feet. "Now would be good. Reinforcements are on the way – and not for us."

Barry nods, waves Gilbert off, and throws a few switches. "To hell with the checklist," he says. "I've got this." The small jet trembles as one engine roars to life and then the other. Myles can feel the power building, the potential energy that will get them off the ground and headed... where? In the panic and confusion, he still hasn't picked a destination. The others are expecting him to decide for them.

"Just get us out of here," he tells Barry.

Barry pushes a lever and the jet begins to roll forward. "Hope one of those things doesn't get sucked into the engine," he mutters.

The thumping beneath the plane is non-stop now. There's nothing they can do about it, so Myles refuses to worry. If any of them manage to get into the luggage compartment, they'll deal with that once they're in the air. They still have their axes and knives.

As the jet picks up speed, the thumping peters out, and then stops. Myles tries to look behind the plane, but the view out the small window is limited. All he can see is the second group of zombies standing on the tarmac, staring at them like a group of well-wishers.

He takes a deep breath. "Everyone strapped in?" he asks. "We're about to take off." He hopes that's true, that they aren't about to hurtle off the end of the runway into the trees beyond. If that happens, the best-case scenario would be for the plane to burst into flames and consume them. That would put an end to their misery, at least.

The others take their seats and fasten their belts. Myles wonders if they should be worrying about weight distribution, but Barry didn't mention anything about that and so far he seems to know what he's doing. He picks up the navigational charts. He has to make a decision soon.

The jet jerks to the left and pauses. They've reached the head of the runway. The engines roar and the jet lunges forward, accelerating rapidly. Trees whip past the side windows. Myles leans back, waiting for the nose to rotate upward and, a few seconds later, it does just that. Gravity presses him into his seat as the small jet leaps into the air, buffeted by the invisible pressure of air beneath their wings. All the problems of the world fall away below them. If they could remain airborne forever, they'd be fine.

The jet levels off a few minutes later. Out of habit, Myles's eyes are on the seatbelt sign, but Barry probably isn't worried about the niceties of commercial air travel. He undoes his seatbelt and returns his attention to the charts. He might as well close his eyes and point at a random spot. He doesn't have any information to aid his decision. Are there places where the plague hasn't yet spread? An island, perhaps? Maybe Barry can pick up something on the radio.

The need to choose a destination before they burn up too much valuable fuel paralyzes him. Why do they expect me to make all the decisions? All I want to do is go to sleep, he thinks. I'm so tired.

Weight pushes against his chest again, the same sensation he felt during takeoff. But he shouldn't be feeling gravity from acceleration now – they're at cruising altitude, high enough to minimize the friction of the air around them and maximize their range. He tries to inhale, but his chest is constricted. Suddenly he can't catch his breath at all – the heaviness is so great that his lungs refuse to expand.

The others are staring out the windows, like zombies. There's nothing to see, just the clouds and the occasional glimpse of the earth below. They're probably wondering what lies ahead, he thinks. What we'll find when we touch down.

Myles no longer cares. He knows what lies ahead, and there's nothing he can do about it. Shooting pain immobilizes him. He can't reach the plastic case in his pants pocket, or make a sound to attract anyone's attention. His breath comes in short bursts. The pressure in his chest builds, like a wall of water at a dam ready to burst.

He hopes the others will be prepared when he comes after them. He wonders whether zombies feel pain. It can't be worse than this. Can it?

IN DUBIOUS BATTLE

CATEGORY FIVE

by Richard Jeter

"When the rescue workers arrived, I shot at them. In fact, I think I killed one. Single bullet, straight to the head. Works the same for everybody. Poor lady. Obits made her seem nice enough."

He stares impassively into the camera across from him in their corner booth at Lucky's. His eyes, sunken and hollow beneath his Saints cap, dart reflexively around the room any time a noise exceeds even a dull thud. He is not alone. Every patron's head is on a swivel. Every nerve tense, three months later. No one can provide any guarantee it won't be the same three years, or three decades from now. The mud on the floor, the glass in the streets, the scars of the flood will fade. Others will not heal so quickly.

The place had once been a neighborhood dive bar. Before black mold and bloodshed had warranted re-paneling the whole interior, the smell of cheap gumbo had been soaked into the wood, so deeply ingrained that Buck and Lucille could close up shop and go on vacation for a week, come back, and it'd still smell like they were cooking. It was a good, homey smell; the kind that kept drawing people in even if the beer tasted like they were renting it and the karaoke was so bad you couldn't think. This had been a place you came when you didn't want to think. Now it was where people came to do nothing but.

It was a memorial née bar, no longer accepting applications for regulars. You had either been here, or you hadn't. Newcomers were not escorted out, but the sullen stares and pockets of silence that formed around them made the point clear all the same. They would never belong, and the palpable envy of everyone who did would never let them feel comfortable.

"I know how it played out on TV. They blamed the violence on the poor folk, 'cause people'd believe that. But we were all doing the same thing. It wasn't just the ward, it wasn't the Dome – it was everyone. Don't let anyone tell you otherwise. There's a reason they let the Guard have a few days 'fore they'd even let a civilian near this city."

A squirrelly, scrawny sort of fellow in his mid-twenties sits next to the camera's operator. In between chirping encouragement at his subject in a Yankee accent as misplaced as his polo shirt, he scribbles notes on an oversized legal pad that only emphasizes his lack of stature.

His interviewee, a mountain of a man by comparison, thumps his glass down a little too forcefully, sloshing some amber liquid over the side. His drinking is forceful, aggressive, as he attempts to build up the nerve to broach the subject at hand. The pounding of his glass would likely have continued had the bartender not called over and asked him to stop. The old timers were getting jumpy with all the thumping.

The filmmaker presses on, oblivious to this mental toll.

"Right, which is why I appreciate your candor, Mr. Kelly."

"James. Please. I think if I'm gonna tell you this story, Robert, we might as well be on a first name basis. Doesn't get much more personal without screwin' me in the bathroom." A grin splits his pepper-gray, stubbled face.

Robert simply flips back a few pages on his pad and makes another note concerning PTSD defensive humor. "Fair enough, James. And is that why you've agreed to speak with us? To set the record straight about the corporate media's spin on this whole debacle?"

Kelly shrugged, her shoulders a tectonic motion in time lapse. "I don't know about all that now. Got no lofty goals, don't follow the news, figure people got a right to the truth but just don't want it. Not my place to force 'em.

"Now MY truth is, I got cancer. Pancreatic. Survived the damn apocalypse to get diagnosed with cancer. Ain't nothin' they can do about it neither, so now I get to tell ya what all these other folks you see here want to, but can't. 'Cause whoever says it's gonna get called crazy. I figure there's no harm in bein' crazy for another four months or so."

The camera zooms in tight, trying to capture any stray emotions that might flicker across the dying man's face, for the human-interest angle. Off frame, Robert nods in what his limited people skills hope is a sympathetic fashion.

There was a time when James Kelly would not have taken this kind of condescending treatment from some northern film student that didn't know a thing about the real world. Events and illness had granted perspective. If some of his bar buddies wanted to take it up with him outside afterwards for poking his nose where it didn't belong, that was fine. James just wanted to talk this out, once, while he had the chance.

"The first thing you need ta understand, son, is that down here, we're used ta storms, and a lot of folk feel like–"

* * * * *

"Evacuatin' is for cowards, 'cause a true swamp rat hides and rides!"

A deafening chorus of cheers filled the dim, hazy air inside Lucky's as James Kelly finished his toast and jumped down off the bar to return to his wife's side. Every inch of table and counter space was being utilized by the raucous crowd. A record-setting hurricane deserved a record-setting hurricane party. Suspended in every corner and again behind the bar itself were TVs locked into all the available weather coverage they could get, radar pictures smothered in violent shades of red and pink providing an ominous, circulating backdrop to otherwise carefree proceedings.

The one local station that chose to continue broadcasting live was beginning to have power issues, as the winds outside edged past the tropical storm threshold and into category 1 hurricane territory. All the other stations failed Mr. Kelly's swamp rat test, having left feeds of their radar data on screen for video, but only pleading, looped recordings from the sheriff's department begging people to evacuate for audio.

It had technically been a mandatory evacuation, with Jasmine bearing down on them as a category 5 monster, but standing one's ground was a point of pride on the coast. Kelly, New Orleans police department badge hanging from his belt to remind patrons he was all that passed for authority at the moment, was a very proud individual indeed. If people weren't going to leave anyway, he might as well bring them somewhere he could keep an eye on them. His wife had joked that it'd be hard to slap some cuffs on a hurricane. Personally, he was more worried about the sort of opportunism a storm could bring.

They'd chosen Lucky's because it was familiar, far enough off the channel on the north end of the French Quarter to avoid the worst of the storm surge, faced away from the prevailing direction of the hurricane's winds, and would be nowhere near the absolute madhouse the Superdome was. Preliminary reports had some 20,000 souls who would not or could not leave the city heading for its relative safety. That many people was just fine for a Saints' game. An extended en masse camping trip posed larger logistical issues.

Here, in the bar, the only logistical concern was whether or not they'd be rationing alcohol before the all clear was given.

* * * * *

Jasmine made landfall at 11:34 PM, bulldozing her way over Point-aux-Chenes on her way into the city. The surge pushed ahead of her great eye wall roiled its way up every river, channel, and tributary it could find. When their banks could no longer hold them, it consumed the land as well.

Several hours into their bender now, the crowd at Lucky's cheered at the declaration that she was on land. Several threw back shots, part of impromptu hurricane drinking games created for the occasion. Sustained category 2 and 3 winds had beaten every TV's channel save two into blue, absent signal screens.

The locals were running on generator power, and reporting concerns about the structural integrity of their studio. The man from the national weather station was still standing outside somewhere downtown, as he did every hurricane, but even as they watched a particularly strong gust sent him sailing to the ground. More cheers, more shots.

When he returned to the frame, he looked significantly more rattled than when he'd left few involuntarily moments before. James Kelly was one of the few people to notice the change in demeanor, but couldn't hear for the crowd what the man was saying frantically as he and his crew began packing up gear, cameraman backpedaling the whole way. At some point Lucky's jukebox had been cranked up, John Fogerty asking the world at large if they'd ever seen the rain.

"Dammit, James, yer... yer not even lissnin' to me anymore, are you?" The accusation was hurled by a surly, gnarled looking older gentleman, reeking of gin that had soaked all the way into his sweat and hunched over with the hardships of a life that had driven him that far into the glass.

"Gus, I'm listenin' to ya just fine. I gotta keep an eye on this lot too, ya know."

"Yea? Well whadda jus' say then, mm?"

A ripple passed through the room, a subtle change in the energy of the crowd. Kelly's mind was keyed on it like a wolf to the scent of prey, tempered in the service of nearly two decades of trying to keep the peace at Mardi Gras night parades. He began scanning, analyzing, looking for signs of trouble, all while attempting to assuage the lonely regular.

"You were gripin' about these weather jockeys always overreacting to storms and driving people out of their perfectly good homes."

"Thassright! T'ain' never s'bad as they says s'gonna be, people runnin' 'round the innerstates fer no good reason, makin'–"

"Ugh, did someone just puke on my shoes?!" The question was yelled from the direction of the bar's front, doors and windows all boarded up, taped up, sealed up, but still rattling in their frames under ever worsening conditions.

There was another ripple, this time definitively from that same region, as people began attempting to back away from the entrance into space that wasn't there. A mass of humanity, a wall of flesh pressed against flesh at increasing pressures, expanded outward from the door. Water was beginning to rush in underneath it.

"The levees are breaking!" someone yelled from the back, a voice beneath the TV who had heard the reasoning for the national weather network's hasty retreat. The floodwaters weren't just rising. They were attacking, laying siege to a city naturally disadvantaged by its station below sea level.

"We figured there would be some flooding!" Kelly lied, though he'd acquired some supplies for this contingency just the same. "Let's get the sandbags out of the back and start shoring this place up!"

Participating in or observing the sandbag brigade's attempts to secure the bar replaced the drinking games. Mute stares at the test pattern where the local station had once been replaced musings about whether the male and female anchors were sleeping together. And not long after, the howling wind replaced the soothing sounds from the jukebox, the last vestiges of the power grid giving way.

Standing there in the dark, marveling at the inhuman

noises a storm like this could make, the crowd at Lucky's maintained a relative calm. They had faith in James Kelly, and this wasn't their first rodeo. Most hurricane parties eventually reached a point like this, an equilibrium achieved between the festivities of the run-up and the realities of the storm wreaking havoc on basic amenities.

No one panicked. Not until the windows gave way.

The flood waters, driven on by their unrelenting mistress, had risen enough to actually reach the level of the building's dingy glass eyelets, the pressure finishing the job the indirect wind could not. The bar began taking on water like a wounded ship, and no amount of sandbags was going to change that fact.

* * * * *

The counter and table space once utilized for every shape of bottle and glass imaginable was still being occupied. Only now, it was entirely by the former imbibers of the drinks they contained, the vessels themselves floating and bobbing along in the wind and storm driven currents circulating through the bar itself. What wasn't taken up by people was filled with candles and lanterns.

James had seen to it that the women and the older patrons had been given priority once the waters had become waist high on his six-foot-five frame. They had been lifted up on to tables, chairs, the bar; they had been laid down across wine shelves and helped on to pool tables. Whoever was left clung to what they could and tried not to think about what might be sharing the water with them.

By the light of his glo-watch, he could tell that had been nearly an hour ago. The unnatural tide continued to rise, the walls of Lucky's now providing respite from the wind, but little else. At this rate, they would be floating out to sit on the roof before sunrise.

He was brought of his situational reverie by gasping, sharp

and loud enough to be heard over the gale outside. Everyone was pointing, gawking. Following their stares, James saw a body, face down, being drawn inexorably inside the bar through the drainage current provided by the remnants of a window. Based on the details of the outfit he could make out in the dim firelight, it was a city utility worker.

"Boy's dead as a doornail, and serves him right for bein' out in this mess," remarked Gus, considerably more sober but every bit as bitter. The comment brought back another unfortunate piece of knowledge from Kelly's police experience.

"No, body takes longer than that to surface once it's dead. Sinks first, lungs fill with water, don't come back up until the rot sets in. Someone snag him! Poor bastard may just be unconscious, took some debris to the head or somethin'."

One of the college aged kids who hadn't qualified for a perch, LSU hoodie saturated to the neck, slogged over to the form and lifted its upper body out of the water, a hand under each armpit. As he did, the utility worker half-lunged, half-kicked forward. Teeth met exposed throat and pulled away hard, tendons once straining with the effort of the lift now exposed to the open air. The young man barely had time to gurgle before the jaws clamped down once more, severing windpipe and jugular, cutting any further protest short.

There was a moment of stunned surreality, minds refusing to process what they were seeing, refusing to react accordingly. There was only the wind, and the horrible chewing noise. Then bedlam broke loose, some people rushing forward to try and restrain the worker, some trying to will themselves through the back wall, others standing in place and screaming.

James pulled his gun from where it was habitually tucked into the back of his pants whenever he was off duty. It was a bit waterlogged, but loaded with cartridge ammo he hoped had not yet been rendered inert by the conditions. The panicked motion in the room had sent most of the candles careening off

116

into the water, significantly diminishing the quality of light and his chance of getting a clean shot. By way of mixed blessings, a kerosene lantern was booted over and inadvertently stepped on, releasing its contents and setting the bar ablaze, along with the unfortunate soul who had broken it.

While the immolated bar fly dove into the water and another group set about putting out the flames before they could reach any alcohol, James used the momentary boost in light level to draw a bead on their new cannibal friend. He had been pulled off his initial victim, but was chewing on the arm of one of the first men to reach and restrain him. It was now unclear who was holding on to whom. Another kid James recognized as the first victim's friend was near the body, sobbing with what Kelly first interpreted as grief, until he noticed he was missing two fingers on his right hand.

Sighting down his .45 and yelling for everyone to move, James took the first available shots he could once the angle took the innocent out of the way. Five rounds in a three-inch grouping, straight to the chest. The worker didn't give way. He didn't even bleed. Instead, he kept lunging after the man whose arm he had been gnawing on before he'd wrenched away at Kelly's warning, splashing off; grunting in pain each time his open wound was exposed to the flood waters.

"Aim for the head!"

James hazarded a sidelong glance to see who was speaking. In the dimming light, bar fire very nearly extinguished, he saw a girl in drab gothic gear standing on a table, mascara streaming down her face, Misfits shirt clinging to her, torn fishnets that were probably that way when she got here. In a situation as morbid as this, she seemed as good a person as any to take advice from. His next round impacted cleanly with the workers skull, right above the left ear.

Its outstretched arm, clawed grasp reaching out for its wounded quarry, stiffened. An unearthly groan passed unmoving lips, an evil mimicry of the maelstrom outside, and then it was still. All that remained were the cries of the injured, the sobs of the traumatized, the diminishing crackling of the bar's varnish as it boiled up from the residual heat, and the ever-present, maddening wind.

"How'd you know what to do with that guy?" he asked the goth girl, keeping his weapon trained on the corpse.

"He was eating people and wading through gunfire. In the movies that's just what you have to do."

"This sure as shit ain't the movies, but thank ya just the same. Since you're the expert 'n all, any idea what might be causin' it?"

Goth girl shrugged. "Sometimes its radiation, sometimes its chemicals, but you want my opinion? Dude, we are in a flooded city full of voodoo shops full of freaky weird powders and crap, and all our cemeteries are above ground. I am totally not surprised by this."

The response, the cavalier attitude toward it all, amused James. Probably just another day at the office for her type. He chuckled, a manic sort of laugh at the absurdity of it all, downshifting from trained public protector to husband and human being. Locating his wife among those huddled at the back wall he began the sluggish push through the currents toward her, passing as he did the burly patron with the chunk missing from his arm. Using the hand attached to the still intact limb, he clamped on to Kelly as he went past.

"The water really... really burns..."

"I reckon it would, god knows what it's got in it, even if our spooky friend over there ain't right. We'll get you cleaned up and... and would ya loosen up on the arm there, buddy?"

The hand's grip was now white knuckled and only getting tighter. The whole body it was attached to began shaking violently.

"Burrrrnsss... Burrrrrrr... Rrrrrrr..."

Acting on some reptilian-brained instinct alone, James planted one submerged foot on the man's stomach and pushed backward, breaking contact just as teeth snapped down where his shoulder had been moments before. Another round popped off, barrel flash pronounced in the newly descended darkness. Another unearthly moan. Another uneasy silence.

"Get some candles back up, we need ta be able to see what the hell's going on here!" A memory, nagging and persistent, pushed its way past a score of other frantic thoughts. His eyes darted around the room, but night had reclaimed the corners and all but the back few tables. "Where's the kid with the missing fingers?!"

A feminine scream and a thud was all the answer he needed. An arm shot out of the water, two digits missing but still more than capable of clamping around her ankle and pulling her off her precarious perch. Her head cracked the corner of table as she fell, sending her into a dazed half-consciousness from which she would never recover. The rest of her attacker emerged to catch her and began feeding before gravity was even done with its work.

Before James could reload, having expended far too many shots into the torso of the first creature, Old Gus, who for all his faults maintained that pretty girls deserved respect and protection because he didn't have much else left to stare at these days, was off his table and splashing toward her assailant with remarkable speed for a man his age. He managed to get a couple good whacks in with his cane, straight to the head, but didn't have the strength to truly mean business.

James was beginning to fear for the old man's life when he saw the silhouette of someone else come in from the edge of the firelight to assist. Relieved, he diverted his attention to getting his spare clip out of his pocket. The replenished ammo clicked into place in time as a wizened old voice screamed and was silenced. Eyes and gun both locking in to where Gus had been, Kelly realized his mistake. Missing fingers was still on the goth girl, and now LSU hoodie was eating Gus. Each bite he took from the old man slid down into the cavity where his throat had once been before tumbling ineffectually back out and into the slurry of water and gore below.

Swearing with each successive shot, he put down both new revenants before ordering everyone in the bar to look away. Now knowing what was apparently inevitable with these attacks, he splashed over, offered up a small prayer, and put a pre-emptive bullet in each of their victims' foreheads. He thought Gus might have still been alive, but tried to tell himself it was a trick of the light.

There was blood everywhere. He could smell it, metallic and cloying as it mixed and swirled with eddies of the bar, carrying out in a trail to the tempest-stricken world beyond the windows. Gut-wrenching dry heaves dictated he climb onto something, anything, to get out of there, while Discovery channel specials about predation and the scent of blood in the water came flooding to mind almost as rapidly as the storm surge. Its level was rising again, noticeably, an inch or two every few minutes. Another levee, this time nearby, must have given way.

"What if this is happening everywhere?!" his wife shrieked, mirroring his own thoughts.

"We gotta get to high ground!" he replied over the eerie moan of the wind as it picked up outside. Or what he hoped was the wind, at any rate. "I ain't saying I think we got more of those things to worry about. I'm just sayin' this water's gonna be over our heads soon. Let's worry 'bout what we can actually do somethin' about, aight?"

There were wary nods from the assembled crowd. James glanced from the ruddy mixture now lapping at his ankles to the distance between his outstretched arm and the ceiling. Some quick estimation affirmed his idea.

"We're goin' to the roof! Taller men lead! In a few more moments, you should be able to reach it from the surface of the water!"

Agonizing seconds, stretching out for a small eternity, saw

the deluge reach shins, then knees. What little light they had left came from candles and flashlights held in hand, no surfaces remained to set them on. When the surge had almost covered the tops of the windows, James led the first wave of men out into the storm. One hundred mile per hour winds whipped at them, tore at even soaked clothing, and swept one volunteer loose of his hold on the bar's window frame. James tried to reach him as he went sailing past in the monstrous current, but could not compromise his own grip.

Then there were arms, a forest of them about thirty yards downstream, surfacing and clutching at their detached friend. A few badly chewed upon faces broke the surface for a moment, illuminated by the strobe-effect lightning searing the sky. If he had a chance to scream, the wind had carried it off into the uncaring night.

Buck, the bar's co-owner, leaned and yelled straight into his ear to be heard over the hellish cacophony. "They're everywhere! We gotta get everyone now!" He pushed himself back into the window and began barking orders, audible but not intelligible from outside. James and the three remaining volunteers hurriedly hauled themselves onto the roof, flattening down against the wind and preparing to bring others topside.

Buck returned a moment later, and patrons began to surface, one or two at a time, arms reaching up over the edge of the roof in a desperate grab for life. James and company waited for bursts of lightning to find them. They yanked, tugged, strained and struggled, as those they rescued crawled to the other side of the peak to seek some shelter from the winds. James frantically hoped that each new face breaking the water would be his wife's, but he knew better. She would be ushering everyone else out, too kind for her own good.

Lightning forked through the sky, and Buck reached out to grab the next available hand. Light was not consistent enough to make out details. Buck was not strong enough to keep the mottled, inhumanly strong zombie's arm from pulling him over

121

the ledge and into a feeding frenzy. More arms and gnashing teeth joined the struggle. James unloaded his gun in the vicinity of the splashing, saving his last bullet. Just in case. Then–

* * * * *

"There weren't no more arms after that. Least not livin' ones. Everything come up after they got Buck was twisted, gray, missin' bits. Blood drew 'em straight to the bar, is all I reckon. We got twenty of us out. Death certificates on everyone else'll list 'em as drownin' victims. Even my own Amanda.

"They forgot all about us on the roof, after we stopped playin' over the edges. Guess they couldn't smell us, and certainly couldn't hear us. We hunkered down on that damn roof for three days, goin' mad from exposure, from the noises below, from the memories. I was layin' there, thinkin' of puttin' my last round ta good use on my own self, when that Red Cross woman stuck her head up over the edge of the roof without callin' up. Pure reflex."

His eyes glaze over a moment, staring into the middle distance between Robert and his cameraman, both visibly shaken.

"Obits made her seem nice enough."

SURVIVORS

by Joe McKinney

The ramp dropped open and Canavan's squad un-assed from the LAAV to take up their positions amid the rubble. They'd been fighting for weeks, street by street, building by building, trying to retake San Antonio from the zombie hordes that had overrun it, and now the city lay in smoking ruin all around them. Everywhere he looked Canavan saw dead bodies, and most of them were still moving.

They were facing south down Broadway, right into the heart of downtown. Echo Sector. Their mission was simple. The lieutenant had located some survivors but now he was surrounded and taking shelter in a fire station off Bonham Street. Canavan and his squad were to extract the lieutenant and the survivors, and fall back.

Quick and easy.

A pair of helicopters passed overhead, flying so low Canavan could feel the thropping of their blades echoing inside his helmet.

One of the pilots spoke to him over his headset. "Squad Two, you got bogies ahead and to your left. Clear behind and to the east."

"Roger that," Canavan answered.

He turned and motioned to PFC Bill Travis to position his M249 machine gun forward. Noise from the fighting was bringing more and more zombies into the area, which is what they wanted. It would ease up some of the pressure on the lieutenant and at the same time put the infected into the meat grinder they'd set up with the LAAVs.

Clouds of smoke and powdered concrete floated across the street ahead of them, blanketing everything in a depthless, churning gray fog. In the haze, Canavan saw zombies staggering toward them. He scanned the rest of his squad. Their eyes were bloodshot and hollow, exhausted, but they knew their jobs. They'd been through this plenty of times before. They were steady, and Canavan was proud of them.

Above them, one of the helicopters banked hard and came in low, the downwash from its props momentarily pushing the screen of dust from the street.

It was enough for Canavan to see how deep the shit really was.

Thousands of zombies choked the street. They poured through the gaps made by the abandoned cars and crumbling buildings, and their moaning was audible even over the rumble of the LAAVs and the ear-splitting shriek of rockets overhead.

The gunners in the LAAVs opened up and Canavan gave Travis the signal to do the same. Before the fighting had really gotten bad, back when clearing the infected from the overrun cities was still a matter of bullpen strategy, some of the pundits on TV had said it wouldn't work to unleash bombs and machine guns against the zombies – that only carefully directed sniper fire would work. That was the only effective way to ensure the headshots that would stop the zombies, they had said.

Well, whoever said that had clearly never fought on the ground with a seasoned urban combat group, Canavan thought.

White lines appeared in the creases at the corners of his mouth as he smiled.

They were kicking ass.

For nearly two minutes the LAAVs churned up the advancing hordes with a steady stream of fire. Swollen, rotten bodies were perforated by large caliber shells and oozed their gore upon the ground like wet oatmeal bursting from a plastic bag. The roar of gunfire echoed off the sides of the buildings. The sky was laced with the smoky trails of rockets. Canavan took it all in, his eyes moving from side to side as he scanned for gaps in the fire pattern.

But there were no gaps. They were thinning them out in huge swaths. The operation was going smoothly, and he was already planning their route through the rubble when the LAAV to their left went silent.

Canavan turned back, but all he could see of the LAAV in the dense screen of dust was a dim, dark outline.

A moment later, the LAAV one block east of them fell silent too.

Above them, the helicopters banked again and sprinted over the rooftops to the east. Canavan waited, maintaining radio discipline.

Then one of the pilots came on. "Squad Two, you got a whole bunch of bogies to the east. Ya'll need to hump it out there. Head for Delta Sector."

"What about the LAAVs?" Canavan asked

A pause.

"Negative," the pilot finally said. "Your fire support's been compromised. Ya'll need to hustle yourselves back to Delta Sector."

"Roger that," Canavan answered. He could almost picture an out of work rodeo bull rider up there in that helicopter. "Travis, take right. We got hostiles on the way."

All at once the radio erupted with the sounds of men shouting in panic. Canavan recognized the voice of Carlton Weir, the gunner from their LAAV, screaming about zombies entering the gunner's hatch of his LAAV. They heard three pistol shots and a whole crowd moaning as one and then Weir screaming with sounds that didn't seem like they could come from a man before somebody got smart and cut the feed to Weir's headset.

Images of a flooded street in Houston a year before

crowded his mind, a young girl being pulled under a sheet of brown water by the living dead, and he had to labor against the confines of his MOLLE gear to breathe.

He raised his right hand to deliver orders to his men and realized his fingers were shaking. Canavan closed his fist and his eyes and forced himself to focus. When he had mastered the fear and trembling in his extremities he ordered his squad to move out, putting Travis' heavy gun in the lead. He guided them back the direction towards Delta Sector, keeping them tight. To the north the street was awash in smoke and dust. The air was an ink wash of gray shot through with black roiling clouds of oily soot so dense that in places it seemed to have no depth at all and left him with a terrifying sense of vertigo.

And then, through the swirling dust, he saw a flash of red.

It stopped him in his tracks.

It was a woman. Her red dress was vividly bright against the haze, and he rose subconsciously from his crouch to watch her.

She wasn't a zombie. He could see that plainly enough, even from fifty meters out. She was looking to the east, towards the silenced LAAVs, her body tensed and uncertain, as though she couldn't figure out which direction to run. Canavan called to her, but she didn't look his way.

A screen of dust passed between them, and when it cleared, the woman was gone.

Canavan stood confused.

"Corporal!"

Canavan spun around. Travis was pointing into the haze, at a figure coming their way. Canavan squinted into the swirling dust and saw their lieutenant. He had his right arm bent in front of his chest, his palm showing, waving his arm around in a large horizontal circle.

The signal to assemble.

Travis and the others moved forward obediently, but Canavan stood his ground. Something was wrong. The order made no sense. Not when they needed to un-ass the area as fast as possible.

Only then did he see the blank, dead look in the lieutenant's eyes, the blood staining the hips of his trousers.

He yelled for Travis to halt, but the words didn't come in time. The lieutenant fell on the machine gunner and both men went down, the gun sprawling off to one side, the gunner's arms flailing awkwardly at the air as the lieutenant tore into him with his fingers and his teeth.

Stunned, it took Canavan a long moment to look away.

When he did, he saw dark forms staggering closer through the haze. He turned, looking for a way out, and realized he was surrounded.

His team was gone.

He raised his rifle and fired into the crowd, burning through three magazines as he hunted for a way out.

But there were too many of them.

He screamed into his radio for air support, reloaded, and went on firing.

He was still firing when he heard the whistle of artillery above him. He dropped to his belly, covered his ears and opened his mouth to equalize the pressure. But the explosions were too close, and the blast bounced him violently off the pavement.

For a moment, he was too stunned to think. He was bleeding from his nose and his mouth and he couldn't breathe.

He had just staggered to his feet, driven by a desperate, instinctive urge to get the hell out of there, when the second wave of artillery rolled in. A concussion blast knocked him off his feet, but he was unconscious before his back hit the ground.

* * * * *

When he came to, Canavan was on fire.

He could smell his hair burning beneath his helmet, and

127

even beneath forty pounds of gear and ammo, his skin felt like it had been splashed with hot grease.

Canavan tore at his clothes frantically, pulling off his helmet, protective mask, body armor, and even his tunic. Right down to his t-shirt. He rose to his feet, swatting at his body as though he were covered in bees, his head reeling.

The air was full of dancing sparks that slanted across his field of vision like snowflakes in a light breeze. He thought his optic nerves had been damaged by the concussion blast. His inner ear, too. He couldn't walk straight. The ground felt like it was rolling beneath his feet and there was a throbbing pain in his head that made his eyeballs shake.

He staggered drunkenly and dropped to one knee.

He heard moaning and looked up. A zombie was limping towards him, carrying the stench of burned flesh and decaying meat with it. Most of its clothes had melted into its skin, leaving it encased in a slick, black slime. Only then did Canavan understand that the sparks he saw were actually burning bits of airborne dust. This zombie had no doubt been at the edge of the blast area, for Canavan could see dust mote lances of light passing through the holes in his chest.

Canavan reached down to his right thigh and pulled his pistol from its holster.

The front sight was swimming in the air in front of his eyes. Canavan fired and missed four times. He teetered backwards and took aim again, and with his next shot managed to hit the zombie in the left shoulder, blasting off a piece of charred flesh and spinning the zombie around.

But the zombie didn't drop.

The thing moaned and raised the stumps of its arms as though it were seeking absolution and came at him again.

Canavan stepped back. He raised the pistol and fired through the entire magazine before landing a lucky head shot and dropping the wrecked corpse to the ground. It lay there in a heap, and Canavan, moving backwards uncertainly, could only gape at it.

Some vital connection between Canavan's mind and muscles and bone had short-circuited. Walking was a painful, doubtful process. He felt like he was moving through water, and in his confusion his mind tumbled back across the last year to the flooded streets of Houston in the wild days following Hurricane Mardell, the city whelmed beneath the oil-streaked waters of the Gulf of Mexico. Once again the air was unnaturally green and cool and wet, like it was made of damp cloth. He was up to his hips in water the color of melted caramel. It stank like raw sewage and shone with an unnatural chemical luster. The living dead were in the water with them, survivors waving their arms over their heads frantically as they screamed for help from the helicopters racing overhead.

For two days he and his twelve year old daughter Sarah had wandered the wreckage in a numb stupor, chased ever onward in a blind frenzy of helplessness by the living dead and the looters and the flood waters. Shots rang out constantly. The bodies of deer and dogs and human beings festooned the limbs of fallen trees. And worst of all, they were unable to tell the difference between those bloated, lifeless corpses bobbing in the water and the infected zombies that could seem part of the trash, but were in fact only waiting for someone to come too close. All the hospitals had become necropolises, and they learned quickly to avoid those. The flooded houses, too – for the moans coming from the attics were not all made by the living, and they could never be sure when a submerged section of a roof had been punched through by the limbs of a live oak or a snapped telephone pole, allowing the zombies an easy place to hide.

On the morning of the third day they saw a bass boat appear from behind the leafy top of an upturned pecan tree. A National Guardsman with a rifle was waving them on.

Turning to Sarah, Canavan stuck out his hand. She was holding a pink backpack by the straps, splashing frantically as

129

she struggled to keep up. "Come on," he shouted at her. "They're right there."

The girl was exhausted, and every word out of her mouth took the form of a plaintive whining that at first had touched the atavistic protectiveness all fathers possess for their daughters but now met only with an impatient hardness and more shouting.

"Daddy, help me."

"Come on, move!"

A zombie sprang out from beneath the canopy of an immature live oak right next to Canavan, and in a moment of pure base fear Canavan leapt onto the roof of a nearby car. He spun around, only to see his daughter bent forward at the waist, her hands reaching for him, her eyes flashing with fear as the dead man strapped his arms across her middle and pulled her down.

She sank beneath the debris-strewn water yelling, "Daddy! Dad-dy!" and he reached for her, but she was already gone.

"No!" he shouted. "No."

He scanned the water, unable to believe what had just happened, when more of the living dead emerged from the water.

Another wave of burning ash hit his skin and he swatted at his face.

The memory of Houston vanished and he was back in the dusty ruins of downtown San Antonio, disoriented at first because the memory had seemed so vivid and so very horrible. A small crowd of zombies, about a dozen or so, were closing on him. There were more behind them, picking their way through the rubble of a collapsed building.

With his mind still numb with guilt and loss for Sarah, he raised his pistol and tried to fire.

Nothing happened.

Confused, he looked at the weapon. It took him a moment

to figure out it was empty.

He had two more magazines on his thigh next to his holster and muscle memory took over as he ejected the spent magazine, slapped a fresh one into the receiver, and released the slide.

Canavan fired through his second magazine and reloaded the third.

Moaning behind him.

He turned and saw another badly burned zombie coming toward him, trailing a shredded leg. Canavan pointed the gun at the zombie's head and fired until it fell. Then he dropped his hands to his side and staggered off into the swirling clouds of ash and dust, the moans of the dead trailing away behind him.

* * * * *

He walked on until he heard the sounds of a woman sobbing.

It was coming from a white stone building with all the windows on the first six stories blasted out. The lobby on the ground floor was littered with plaster and garbage, lath visible through the walls. There was an acrid, dusty taste of acrosolized concrete and ash in the air that collected in Canavan's mouth, leaving his tongue dry, like it was wearing a sock.

Looking in through one of the openings he saw the woman in the red dress, the vivid splash of color he had seen earlier muted now with a fine powdering of dust. She was sitting on the floor, her legs spread out in front of her like a little child, her hands on the floor between them. Her hands were wet with blood.

He stepped inside the lobby and the crumbled plaster and broken glass on the floor crunched beneath his boots.

The woman in red spun around and screamed. Her sudden movements scattered photographs across the floor. Canavan watched the pictures skid toward his boots, then turned his attention on the woman. Her chest was heaving, her eyes wild. She held her mangled hands out in front of her, as though to push him away, the gore dripping from them a stark contrast to the bloodless pallor of her face.

"Don't hurt me," she whimpered. "Please."

She thinks I'm one of them, he realized. Without his gear, and with the blood leaking from his nose and mouth and the punch drunk stagger in his walk, he must have looked just like a zombie.

"I won't hurt you," he said.

A long pause.

Three of the fingers on her right hand had been bitten off. She let the stump drop to her side and made a low huffing noise that came from the somewhere deep in her throat.

Canavan reached down and picked up one of the photographs. It showed the woman in front of him, younger, smiling, nestled in the arms of an overweight, dark haired man in a Hawaiian shirt and sunglasses. They were on a small boat, a heavily wooded shoreline in the distance behind them.

He held the photograph out to her. "Your husband?"

"My brother, Paul."

He nodded. When she didn't take the photograph from him he dropped it in front of her. "What's your name?"

"Jessica Shepard."

"I'm James Canavan."

There was a beat. The muscles at the corners of her mouth twitched, as though she might smile. "Are you a James or a Jim?" she said.

"Either. Jim to my friends."

"Well, Jim, pull up a chair. The place is kind of dead tonight."

He couldn't really laugh, but he liked the easy way she used his name, the gallows humor, the way it gave him a glimpse of her personality.

She was staring up at him, her eyes yellow and bloodshot and almost lifeless, rimmed with red. Her face was lost in shadow and her hair clung to her damp forehead and cheeks like wet thread. When she breathed she made a labored, painful sound, as though she had fluid pooling in her lungs.

"Can you get me out of here, Jim?"

He shook his head. "You've been infected."

She closed her eyes and let her chin sink to her chest. She was silent for so long he thought she hadn't intended to answer. But when she lifted her head again there were tears cutting rivulets down the dust on her cheeks and a knot was working itself up and down furiously at the base of her throat.

The look in her eyes made him turn away.

"I'm sorry," he said.

"You're sorry? You fucking bastard. You God damned fucking pig-headed bastard." She wiped a forearm across her eyes, her bleeding, fingerless hand trembling. "I'm dying," she said. "I don't want to die. I don't want to be one of those things."

The air seemed to go out of her lungs.

Then, so faintly he barely heard her, she said, "I've been one of them for too long as it is."

Canavan had no idea what to say, and it shamed him. She was pleading for some sign of human compassion, and it was just her lousy luck to meet with a man who could no more give it to her than he could cure the riot raging in her bloodstream.

"Will you do it?" she asked.

"Will I...?"

"Please. I don't want to be one of those things."

He followed her gaze to his right hand and was dumbfounded to see his pistol still there, the slide locked back in the empty position.

"I don't," he said, and trailed off. "It's empty. I'm sorry."

"Stop saying that." Her voice was muted in resignation. "Stop saying you're sorry. It only makes it worse."

133

He nodded.

A helicopter passed overhead, its blades a padded staccato rhythm. Soon they would start hearing more gunfire, he realized. He'd need to be ready to signal the rescue squads before they gunned him down like one of the dead.

She started to cough, and to Canavan it sounded like her insides were being shredded by knives. The coughing went on for a long time, and when it subsided and she could once again lift her head to look at him, the deep valley between her breasts was flecked with black, clotted blood.

"Can't you do it? Please, Jim. I don't want to be one of them. I can't..."

Canavan forced himself to swallow, as though there was an almond was stuck in his throat. His chest hurt when he breathed. The shame of his own impotence in the face of this woman's pathos at first left him speechless; but gradually, his feelings of sympathy gave way to a vague, unfocused anger. He resented her for making him remember how lost and helpless he could feel.

He turned to leave.

"Wait!" she said. "Please, don't go. Please. God it hurts so bad."

He knew it did, and he wasn't without pity. During their training, Canavan and his fellow Marines had been given the skinny on the necrosis filovirus and how it worked its way through the body, how it waged war in the bloodstream and gradually took complete control of the host body, leaving only a staggering train wreck of a virus bomb.

This woman was pretty far along. Infection had probably happened as much as an hour ago. Her temperature was spiking, leaving her face flushed in sweat. Already the blood in her veins was coagulating. A blueberry stain of cyanosis was forming around her mouth as her cells starved for want of oxygen. Her eyes were milking over. The coughing and the fluid in her lungs had affected her ability to speak, her voice taking on a whiskey-edged roughness that was becoming less and less human with each passing moment.

He wanted very much to leave her.

She began to cough again, the hacking shaking her like a rag doll in a dog's mouth. She seemed unable to control her movements. A sudden sour odor of defecation reached him, and he knew she voided her bowels. She didn't have long to go. Complete depersonalization would no doubt happen within the next ten minutes, probably less.

"Please, I need you to do this," she said, barely able to lift her head now. "One bullet. Don't you even have one bullet? That's all it would take. Please, I hurt so bad. I can feel it inside me."

He shifted uneasily and the glass crunching beneath his boots sounded very loud in the sepulchral stillness of that ruined lobby.

She watched his feet. She lifted her milky eyes and webs of wrinkles spread from the corners of her mouth. Within the few minutes he'd been with her she seemed to age horribly, as though she was a peach left on the sidewalk and puckering in the sun.

And then her face cracked with rage as she screamed at him.

"Why won't you fucking help me? You bastard. All I want is a bullet."

Canavan had to force himself not to look away. The look on her face, the baffled anger and desperation, brought images of his daughter into his head. Once again he saw her slipping under the waves. Heard her screaming, "Daddy! Dad-dy!"

He realized he was crying and swiped the tears away angrily. But the dying woman didn't notice. She had started to cough again. When it subsided, she seemed detached and blunted, as though her mind had been scrambled and left her little more than a babbling idiot.

But he would not have told her about the depth of his self-loathing and shame, even if she had been capable of comprehending it. Perhaps she had her own issues, her own regrets, and perhaps she too had failed someone who had depended on her for their very life; but there were some things that cut so deeply into a man's conscience that they could not be mentioned to anyone.

"One bullet," she said.

"I'm sorry."

She groaned once and his gaze fastened on her. Her breathing slowed, her mouth working like a fish that has been left on the shore by a wave. She tried to speak and couldn't. He watched her struggle through two final breaths. There was a phlegmy rattle in her throat and her shoulders sagged, as though at rest after carrying a great weight.

Stillness descended on the lobby.

And then, slowly, laboriously, she climbed to her feet. Her head drooped to one side, her mouth hanging open. A fine patina of dust coated her lips. She reached for him, but he did not move until she began to moan; and when that happened he slid the collapsible baton from its holster at the small of his back and snapped it open.

She never acknowledged the danger. He sidestepped the woman and slapped her in the back of the head with the baton, knocking her forward onto her face. But he was still dizzy from the concussion bombing and was uncertain on his feet, and the force of his swing also knocked him onto his hands and knees.

She was still moaning, still trying to get up. He climbed to his feet, raised the baton high into the air with both hands, and brought it down again and again on the dead woman's head, grunting and sobbing with each savage blow.

In the stillness that followed, he heard something small and metallic drop to the ground.

He looked into the puddle of broken glass below him and saw a single, perfectly clean bullet glittering amongst the dusty rubble. At first he didn't know what to make of it, but gradually it came to him, the loose round he'd accidentally ejected while clearing a malfunction in his pistol during the fighting the evening before. He'd put in his trouser pocket. It must have fallen out as he was beating on her with the baton. He'd forgotten it was there.

That one bullet.

He stared at it for a long time. He could have helped her if he'd only had his wits about him. It was like Sarah all over again.

The thought curled around his heart like a cold, wet vapor.

He heard the echo of automatic rifle fire in the near distance, like people clapping in the next room.

"Marines, stand and identify."

"In here," Canavan shouted.

Another Marine appeared in the doorway, his rifle at low ready. "Identify," he said. "Are you wounded?"

It was a question Canavan didn't quite know how to answer.

* * * * *

Fourteen months later, Canavan made his way up the front walk of a one story white wooden house in a Nashville suburb and rang the doorbell. It had been raining all that evening and the air was thick with the damp scent of mown grass and vibrating with the sound of frogs. He had researched a lot of dead leads, but now his hunt was at an end. This was the house.

Paul Shepard was the spitting image of the smiling fat man Canavan had seen in Jessica's photograph, though he had begun to gray at the temples and the bright smile had been replaced by nests of wrinkles around his eyes. He invited Canavan into the entryway but no further, and the two men stood in a web of soft white light and shadow cast by three glass chandeliers in the hallway that led to the rest of the house.

"My twelve year old has the flu," he said in a whisper. "She just got to sleep about twenty minutes ago."

Canavan nodded, though images of Sarah rose in his mind like corks that won't stay submerged.

Then Canavan told him about San Antonio, and about his sister Jessica's final minutes. Shepard listened to it all without interrupting, the expression on his face never wavering.

A woman poked her head around the far corner of the hallway and said, "Paul?"

"It's okay. This is Mr. Canavan. He was with Jessica when she died."

The woman looked at Canavan without expression. "I have Cokes and Dr. Pepper in the icebox," she said. She waited a beat. "Scotch, if you'd like something stronger?"

"No, thank you, ma'am."

She nodded and slipped back into the quiet darkness at the back of the house.

Shepard said, "You've come a long ways, Mr. Canavan. Are you sure I can't offer you something?"

"I'm fine, really. I ought to be going."

But before Canavan could leave, Shepard put a hand on his arm. "A moment, Mr. Canavan."

"Yes?"

"Fourteen months is a long time to spend looking for somebody."

"Your sister wasn't completely lucid there at the end," Canavan said. "She never told me anything about you. Besides your name, I mean. It took a while to find you."

"I don't mean that. I want to know why you didn't stop looking. You didn't have to come tell me this. We all figured my sister was dead. Deep down we knew it. You must have realized that too."

"I guess I figured I owed it to... I don't know. To her."

Canavan's eyes slid off of Shepard's face. "Maybe to myself."

Shepard's brown eyes seemed to soften, and the knots of veins that stitched his temples seemed to slacken.

"Mr. Canavan, when my sister left for San Antonio she did so to escape our mother. The woman was dying of cancer of the small intestine. Have you ever known anyone with that particular condition? She was in terrible pain. There at the end she was living with Jessica because we couldn't afford a hospice nurse and sometimes when I'd visit I'd see Jessica sitting on the curb in front of her house, crying her eyes out. You could hear our mother moaning all the way out in the driveway. I've sometimes asked myself if Jessica didn't go down to San Antonio knowing what she'd find there. I think maybe she found what she was looking for."

Canavan just stared at him.

"Did you know, Mr. Canavan, that the Japanese have a word for the people who survived Hiroshima and Nagasaki? Those people with the thousand yard stares. Those people who cannot hold down a steady job or stand in a crowd without wanting to cower into a ball or even carry on a conversation that goes beyond a few inane pleasantries. They called them Hibakusha. It means sufferers. Our word for it is survivors. But I think their word seems much more fitting, don't you?"

Canavan said, "Are you trying to tell me something, Mr. Shepard?"

"I think I just did, sir. I think all survivors carry hell around with them like a turtle does his shell."

Canavan thought about those words several hours later, as he washed his face in the sink of a gas station bathroom south of Nashville.

He went into a stall and closed and locked the door and sat on the toilet with the bullet that had dropped from his pocket back in San Antonio in his hand. He turned it round and round in his fingers, feeling the oily smoothness that was as slick as bacon grease against his skin. Out the grimy window to his left he could see the wind gusting across the station's roof shingles, feathering the rain off the corner flashing. His mind was crowded with images of the living and the dead and those in between. The screams of the innocents wouldn't stop.

He looked down into his lap and studied the single bullet and the pistol that rested there.

Hibakusha, he thought. *It means sufferers.*

Then he loaded the weapon.

PIERRE & REMY

HATCH A PLAN

by Michelle McCrary

After the zombies came, me and my friend Remy used to like to sit on the front porch and talk about what we was gonna do when them zombies finally made their way down here.

You see, we live down in good old Louisiana. The home of LSU football and the best gumbo you ever done wrapped your lips around. It wasn't none too long ago that the dead just stopped wanting to stay dead, you know what I mean? Well, me and Remy stayed in the swamps, a long ways away from the big city of Lafayette, so it took a little while for them zombies to get to us. We figured we was lucky; we had us some time to prepare.

Last we talked on the porch, I was sucking the foam off a Pabst I had just popped open when Remy said about the dumbest thing I ever done heard.

"Pierre," he said, "how about we catch us a gator! That'll keep them zombies away!"

"Now listen Remy," I done told him, "How you 'spect to catch a gator?" I then took a big ol' swallow of my beer and let out probably the best burp I ever had in my whole life.

"And if you was a lucky enough sonfabitch to catch one, how you think a gator is gonna keep a zombie away?"

Remy looked at me with those glazed over eyes that meant

141

he was a'thinking. I always wondered if I could see smoke coming out his ears when he did that.

"Well, the way I figure it, you old coon-ass," Remy started, "them zombies can't eat no gator – they's skin too tough. Plus that newsman said that them zombies don't eat animals and even if they did, animals ain't turning!"

I let out a guffaw at this and proceeded to tell my very stupid friend that he ain't driving with a full tank of gas, if you know what I mean.

"Man Remy, you really on something. What you been smoking? We ain't ever gonna catch no gator, and it's damn near impossible to get one to fightin' zombies for us!"

Poor old Remy got that glazed over look again. I listened to the frogs croak and the crickets sing while I stared at Remy, and I swear that I saw a puff of smoke come out his ear that time. He sat there in a daze and I kept sucking on my beer until he snapped out of it.

"Maybe you are right, Pierre."

"Ain't no maybe to it, dumbass, I am right."

We sat there in silence for a spell and that's when I formulated my plan. Remy's idea gave *me* an idea. It was much better than his. After I slipped into my purple and gold jersey, we headed to Baton Rouge. It's about a two-hour drive from the swamp to where we was going on campus.

* * * * *

Everybody and their mama here in the pelican state is big fans of LSU football. Even us folks who never stepped foot on campus for a lick of learning got purple and gold running through our veins. It's in our blood, you know what I mean? Now don't it stand to reason that there would be a real tiger mascot at the Louisiana State University campus? Ol' Mike been living large in that million dollar cage they got him in and we was gonna bust him out!

142

Remy thought having a gator was a good idea, but I thought maybe we can train ol' Mike to fight by our side instead of some dumb ol' gator that ain't got a lick of sense. What else is he but a 'fightin' tiger' like they all say? The way I figured it, ain't nobody fed poor ol' Mike in quite some time. We was gonna stop and pick up some meat for him; maybe bring him to our side of things mighty quick, I reckoned. I mean, he really ain't nothing but a super-sized house cat, ain't he?

We grabbed our shotguns and jumped in my Ford. It was slow going to the capitol, what with the roads being congested with cars and zombies. It took some steady nerves on my part when those bloody hands started slapping on the windows of my F-150. Good thing I got that Big Tex Grille Guard some years ago when I was hunting a lot. It mowed over them zombies like a knife through my grandmere's cornbread. We made a pit stop at Tramonte's butcher shop on Jefferson. I had to put down a couple of them undead suckers that had been holed up inside. It was worth it – I left with a huge slab of aged beef that would have Mike the Tiger licking his chops for weeks.

It took some time, but we finally made it to the campus. There weren't as many professor zombies running around as I thought there would be. No college type zombies either. You could almost say the place was empty. I bet all them jocks and frat boys ran home to their mamas right after they crapped their pants. No so tough after all, huh?

We went the wrong way up the road that leads right in front of Mike's Plexiglas cage. I shut off the truck and jumped out with Remy right on my heels. We pounded the pavement mighty quick and got right up to the cage. I looked around and around, going from side to side. I couldn't see nothing until Remy finally hollered and pointed him out. There he was cowering in the bushes, Mike the Tiger, and he was a sad sack.

I had figured right; that old pussycat looked like he ain't

eaten nuttin' for weeks. I knew we was gonna have to fatten him up a little before we could use him for what we needed him for. It was gonna take a little figuring on how we was gonna get inside. A steel mesh covered the top of the entire fifteen-thousand square feet cage. Ain't no way we was getting over that. Soon I got to thinking, like I always do. We had to jump back in the truck and head to Home Depot over on Coursey. Traffic wasn't so bad, if you don't count the zombies I mowed over on my way there and back. We smashed in the sliding glass doors and stepped inside, taking out what few employees had settled in for a spell, not knowing they was gonna be dead when they woke up.

I grabbed the best pair of heavy-duty wire cutters I could find, along with some thick ropes and strong chains, and one big cast-iron hook. We was in and out of there in less than twenty minutes and on our way back to Mike's cage.

Now you see, the plan was to hook a big chain onto the mesh and wrap that other end to my truck and pull that thing down. Then me and Remy was gonna climb on over with the ropes we brought. First thing we was gonna do was lower that fine cut down to ol' Mike and let him have his fill, just so he wouldn't go after us next. That was our not-so-well thought out genius plan. What could go wrong, you ask? Well, let me finish and you'll find out real quick like.

We did manage to pull that mesh down – not all the way, see, but enough to get the job done. We plopped that slab down onto the ground and watched Mike saunter up to it slowly then dig in like it was rubbed with catnip. Man, we was really feeling good then and thinking we was the smartest couple of rednecks that ever laid a boot on LSU grounds.

Now, we watched Mike eating for a little while and then he took a little swim in his pond. We was mighty proud that we was taking care of such an important animal. Remy climbed down the rope and I slapped him on the back; he might have been dumb as nutria rat but he was a mighty good friend, indeed.

"What we gonna do next, Pierre?" he asked me.

"Well," I said, "I 'spect we can sit a spell in the Ford and have a beer, to celebrate that we made it this far and still got our skins. Ol' Mike is satisfied for now and we can fool with him more tomorrow."

'Bout that time, the sun was setting low on the horizon and we needed to buckle down for the night. I didn't feel like shacking up in no smart kid's rooms, so we just stretched out in the cab of my truck. Remy grabbed a couple cold ones out my ice chest in the back seat and tossed one to me. We knocked our cans together and hollered our toasts to Mike and the plans we had for him. It wasn't long before we had sucked down a six-pack and passed out cold.

* * * * *

I woke up the next morning to the sounds of them awful things a'moaning and slapping my windows again. That black goo, like old blood, was starting to block the view on my poor F-150.

"Remy!" I yelled, startled, "get your old ass up!" Remy stirred and said something in his sleep about his ex-wife's big ass then he sat straight up, eyes wide and blood-shot.

"Aw she-yut! When they ever gonna go away?" Remy hollered. We both reached into the back seat for our shotguns only to realize they weren't back there. We looked at each other and said the one word our mamas would have slapped the taste out our mouths for. We had left them damn things in the bed of the truck when we were bringing down the mesh. Man, we didn't feel so smart anymore, let me tell you!

"What we gonna do, Pierre? What we gonna do?" Remy started getting all frantic and stammering, which made it harder for me to think right good enough.

"Just shaddup your mouth so I can figure this out!" I

145

yelled at my jackass of a friend.

I knew there weren't no way we was making it to those shotguns. When I looked out and counted, there was about eight of them zombies on my truck and more on the way. They was moaning and jostling us around so much I thought I might waste the beer I had drunk right onto the floor of my truck. I swallowed hard and shook my head to clear the cobwebs out.

"Okay Remy. Here's what we gonna do."

* * * * *

I could tell you what happened next but you gonna figure it out in just a minute. I'm sitting here staring at my best friend and he's got big problems. We tried to get out the truck and get our shotguns, but Remy didn't quite make it as far as I did. I grabbed my gun and took off up the stairs of a building across from the cage. Remy is standing on top of that big ol' tiger statue and about twelve zombies have him surrounded. Slinking up behind him and the hungry crowd is ol' Mike. That rascally tiger must have climbed out that hole we made in the fence while we was sawing logs in the truck.

As soon as I got myself covered in some bushes, I opened my shotgun and saw that all I have left is one shell. I don't think I have ever had to make a harder decision in my life. Now, I know I can't get to my friend. He is dead one way or the other – I gotta shoot him or he is dinner for a horde of zombies, maybe even a college mascot. I can't shoot all them zombies, so it's either Remy or Mike. You'd think it'd be easy to put my friend out of his misery, wouldn't you?

Don't get me wrong now…I love Remy, dumb ass as he is. But what kind of fan would I be if I shot Mike the Tiger? You just tell me that, huh?

LOSING GROUND

RECOVERY

by Boyd E. Harris

We inch our way through the restricting aisles of the Daily Fresh grocery and I do my best to ignore the locals. I squint my eyes, passing through the florescent-lit rows of neatly organized vegetables, when I notice an old man whispering to his wife. They stare at Lacy and I'm stricken with a complexity of emotions.

Ed and Judith have brought us here purposely, to acquaint us with the folks of Quail Hill, our new home, but it's not easy. It's Lacy's first time in public and I worry about her probably more than she does. It's still too early, I think. I want to curse them, to tell them to stop the staring, but my vocal cords are ruined, mangled from the virus that coursed through me months ago.

Judith's warm hand on my back persuades me to twist my misshapen neck her way. I hold back the tears, but she sees through the manufactured smile to the pain hidden behind it. I turn and hobble for the exit and Judith follows.

She sits me down on the ledge outside the entrance and leans sideways to look into my eyes. Tears begin to well. She wipes the drool from my chin and lip.

I see the red lady approaching from the parking lot. She smiles at Judith, but she is not really smiling. She has no choice but to walk past us if she wants to enter the store, so she stops and offers small talk.

Judith brushes my hair out of my face and introduces me.

With a squeaky voice, the lady says, "Hello Pete, you sure

look nice today." I'll never remember her name.

Judith looks to the store entrance, expecting Ed and Lacy. This lady with tall, puffy red hair sneers at me when Judith turns away.

Judith tells her, "Yeah, I think he'll be fully recovered in a few months. See how his eyes have cleared up?"

The lady shifts. "Well, that's just precious. Did the doctor claim that he's safe around people?"

Judith shifts. "He's friendly, can't you see?"

"And what of his mind?"

"We're still not sure. He lost his vocal cords completely, but he reads at about nine-and-a-half years now and he's learning sign language."

The lady knows all about me. They all do, and most disapprove of Lacy and myself not being kept in an institution. Judith says that they will have to get to know us before they understand.

She tells me I've had an amazing recovery. My neck still has very little use, stiffened from several fused vertebra, but I can almost turn it now. She leans down and kisses me on the face. I suspect the lady sees me blushing.

Keeping the forced smile, the lady says, "Well, you must be really proud. What does he eat?"

"We're already beginning to cook his meat. It's still pretty raw, but we char it on both sides just a little and he pretty much finds a way to choke it down."

That's enough for the lady to drop her smile. I know what she pictures and I understand. Her imagination is not far from the truth, though it's under-exaggerated.

Their conversation continues, but I start to feel light-headed. A seizure is coming on, and the awful flashbacks are making their cycle. It's something I've tried so many times to suppress, but Doctor Goldman says it's like a panic attack, and I just have to ride it out. The light switch in my head clicks off, my vision goes black and I plunge into darkness.

Spasms surge up and down the spine and the nervous system cringes from electrical impulses. Lost, unfamiliar with the world. Walking, seemingly to somewhere. Angry swelling in the head and chills in the spine. Enormous throbbing afflicts the extremities, but this body walks, feet directed by something unknown.

Don't understand, don't care. No memory; just sketchy awareness.

Smell is strong. The sweet odor of rotting meat. Everywhere. It hangs in the gut, sourness in the stomach.

Groaning, nearby. Different sources, different pitches. The body harmonizes with the eerie sounds. Hums from inside, escaping jarringly through the bones.

Stumble along the path, legs and back not working right. One foot slides forward, staggers with the other. As a leg swings out, the heels and toes drag together. Can't raise the head; the bones in the neck feel frozen. Stare at the feet. Ragged leather shoes covered in dried blood and dirt. Legs of a cripple, the spine of rigor mortis. A misshapen body

Pass a set of bare feet moving the other way. They are covered in wet blood, though not fresh, and they stagger the same as they pass.

Attention is averted from the path. Impulses run through a decaying nervous system and the left foot begins to slide around, turning the clumsy body with it. Stumble off balance, but find a suitable stance. Don't see well, but something moves.

The caterwauling humanoid on its side in the dirt twitches all over, arms and legs curled in close to its torso. Its unseeing eyes dart around under a heavy, white film. Its legs are badly shredded and large chunks of its neck and chest are missing. The entire body is covered in mud-caked blood. The meat bad, the blood rancid.

Sour stomach gets worse.

Turn back and resume progress, lurching down the trail. A

151

dark tree root catches the foot, tripping the body down and further twisting the neck as the top of the head strikes the dirt. The chin jams against the chest, causing sharp pains to shudder through the spine. The arms and legs don't hesitate. They swing and flail about, working to find a way back up.

Upright and walking again, the body seems to be powered by an everlasting fuel cell.

A sensation surfaces in the nervous system. Hunger is the ailment, the driving force. Need food. Nostrils guide the feet. Detect fresh meat ahead.

Getting closer, picking up speed. The upper body pulls, wanders forward, struggles not to fall.

The scent crosses the nostrils again, and the nose points the way. Raise the head and the chest groans louder. The fused bones in the neck snap, each vertebra cracking in succession like pecans under a heavy foot. Pain explodes in the head and shudders into the limbs. The neck is still buckled, but through eyes stretching upward and across the brows, they can now see ahead. Trees line the path, a glowing sun sets over water and dark structures appear in the foreground.

The food is nearer.

Reach the lake and pass some of the buildings at its shore, but press on. Others surround a building ahead. Many scratching at it with their useless claws. Pounding on it, moaning the aches of hunger.

Arms rise, working the body forward, faster and faster. A door gives way and the others jockey toward it, crawling and fighting across each other. Loud noises pierce the sensitive ears, and several of them fall backwards from the door into the grass, but the rest keep pouring in. As more sharp sounds resonate, something within recognizes gunshots.

Almost there. Hear living screams from the food. The captivating aroma of fresh blood pierces the nasal passages.

Quiver.

More screams through the doorway. Fresh blood vies with

the heavy stench in the humid night air.

Follow the screams, the blood. They pull something freshly bleeding from the cabin. Through a dozen of them, a large human is visible and is kicking, fighting for its life.

They bring another fresh human from the building, and carry it another direction.

The first crowd erupts into turmoil, tearing at the prey. The human screams for its life. Its clothes are shredded and its bare foot is visible, protruding from the crowd.

Move toward the foot.

Bumped from behind. Fall face first.

Another one stumbles over, carrying something in its arms. It's faster than the others and it carries a smaller human. One that screams, but in a much higher pitch.

Recognize the sweet smell of younger, tastier meat. A human child, a girl.

The limbs thump at the ground, once again finding a way back up. The fast one moves alone, carrying the human girl.

Follow

Follow... follow, but... I remember now. I've done this before. I've preyed on humans and I've eaten to abate the pain. It's my instinct and instinct is all I have. I chase the fast one, plotting the pursuit. The girl is still alive, kicking and screaming. The fast one is taking her toward the water. It's slower than me, because of the added weight, so I advance. We trek a distance, it hobbling just ahead, clasping the kicking girl. Along the water's edge, a quarter of the way around the lake, I reach out and tackle them, separating the two.

I hold my legs across the fast one, which is scraping and clawing to get up. My legs hold it down and I squeeze the rest of my body between it and the human girl, shielding her from it. I'm stronger and larger, so this meal is mine. Pecking order rules.

She still screams, crying the dreadful human sounds of terror. She looks at my face as I lower my teeth to her midsection. Thick, reddish liquid oozes onto her skin from my decaying mouth. I stop, though my teeth have scratched her rib cage, peeling skin away and drawing blood, further enticing me to feed.

Why stop? I don't understand.

I feel the fast one fighting to get out from under my knees, to reach the girl.

Unable to look up, I cock my head to the side, my left shoulder turning with it, almost like they are attached. I look into her eyes.

A bright memory flashes across my fatigued brain, the first memory of this questionable life. It's a little human girl, but not this one; another. She's smiling, not screaming in fear. She steps into my arms and hugs me and I feel her warmth. It causes new impulses to sputter through my crackling tank.

I break free of the memory and see this girl, lying under me at my mercy, studying me, imploring me.

Instinct takes over once again and I turn myself down, sensing the aroma of her delicious flesh. I stretch my mouth wide and lean toward her skin.

Her screams stop me a second time. Her fear of me causes unwanted thoughts.

I turn back up, fighting the surging drive to eat my pain away, but she no longer faces me. She directs her agonizing scream toward the fast one, which I realize is no longer struggling under my legs.

I cock myself to the side and see it feeding, tearing at her arm, its teeth ripping away strips of flesh that is gushing torrents of blood. Its cloudy eyes have no pupils, the skin around them yielding yellowish fuzz, a sort of fungus, crusted at the corners. Groaning the sounds of content, it feeds. Thick, reddish mucus seeps from its various facial orifices, hanging from the edges of its furrowed, rotting cheeks and the tip of the tattered nose and chin, as it jerks its head one way and then the other, shredding meat and tendons from the girl's elbow, paying no observance to her screams or my stare.

Then the question; Am I like this vile beast? Is this me?

I look back to the girl's pleading eyes.

The driving instinct is fierce, but it somehow gives way to my will, something I just now begin to understand. I turn to the nasty creature gnawing on her arm and conclude that I'm different. I plunge my elbow into the center of its face, causing its teeth to crumble inward. It rolls over, but relentlessly turns back up. It ignores me, going after its favorite spot on the girl's arm.

I find a rock the size of a large grapefruit, round and shiny. I raise it up and bring it down on the creature's head. The skull cracks. I raise the rock again and force it into the open wound, this time splitting the head apart. Rotten mush where the brain should be spills out, and it seeps into the soft steaming night air. The creature rolls back, its hands and feet thrusting and quaking; its nervous system unaware of its death.

I turn to the girl, who is now barely conscious. My hunger for the fresh meat is still strong, though I resist. I'm gaining control of this deteriorating body.

I need a place to hold up and protect her from the predators. I prop myself up to my feet and lift her. I carry her around the lake, and there I find paved road.

She sleeps as we move down the country road. Her arm still bleeds, what is left of it dangling from her body. I stop momentarily and use part of my torn shirt to cover her wound, but I have no idea how to stop the bleeding. In another life, I might have, but this foggy brain has no clue.

Looking back, I see them coming. They are way behind, but they've found her scent. I turn and move faster, my right foot stepping ahead, dragging the other behind, my head jammed to the left side of my chest by the chin. I lean way back see over the right shoulder.

I hold the girl. Her head is propped in my right hand. Her unconscious body swings with each step as I work us farther and farther down the road. And the pursuers continue to gain ground. A couple hundred feet away, four of them stagger and groan, as they keep to the chase. I sense the inevitable.

Ahead, two humans approach to help. The creatures are gaining fast, maybe a hundred feet away.

I race toward the humans, my legs working harder. I want to call out, but I have no voice, no words. I know they can see us because they are coming. I pull my right leg faster, dragging my left foot farther with each step, sweeping the unconscious girl wider each time.

I look back again and there are now six behind, the front two are only a couple neighborhood yards away. Their arms are out, their groans become more rapid and their bodies shudder with each step.

I turn to my path; help will come before the hunters. The humans are closer, but I notice them approaching in a familiar way. They stagger toward me, moaning like the ones behind!

I stop and set her down. I need a weapon to fight them off, but there is nothing suitable. I charge the first of the two, leading into its midsection with my front shoulder and knocking it to the pavement. It struggles to get up, looking like an overturned beetle kicking for leverage.

I grab the other and take it to the ground with me, rolling with it in the center of the road. The first one finds its way back up and moves toward the girl. From my horizontal position in the center line, I kick out, tripping it up, but not enough to stop it. The others from behind are almost there too. I know now that I can't save her. She's theirs and I can't stop them from their meal. I stand up. The one I just tackled passes me, moaning for its share.

They converge on the girl, with their decaying mouths wide open, reddish slime surging from their faces and their hands reaching for her limbs. Without the use of knees, they stumble to the ground and begin ripping at her.

I stand nearby, beaten and dejected, watching a pile of

feeding beasts smother their victim.

The creatures settle from their feeding frenzy. They stop pulling at her. They prop themselves up, still moaning, but not eating. Nothing more drips from their faces. One by one, they work their way to their feet and disburse. They leave us, the girl is now alone.

I haul myself over to her. She twitches and shakes, jerking her head to and fro, her milky eyes staring into the sky above me. They twitch, focusing on nothing. The blood is now rancid. The meat infected. I fall to her side, feeling another sensation; sadness. I cry.

I pick her up and carry her in the same direction. I work my way down the road, soon losing steam, losing will.

She jerks in my arms, fighting nothing but air. I want her to be human.

Squinting in the dawn sun, which is peaking over the treetops, I can see a tall fence stretching across the road ahead. Bodies lie in the road on this side of the fence. But they are not really bodies. They are piles of rancid mush, their stench rising like steam off hot pavement after a good summer afternoon rain.

I approach the chain link fence with the girl still twitching in my arms. I hear a human voice from above in the trees. The language is familiar, though I don't understand. My brain recognizes the words, but it cannot process them. It's aggressive. It warns. I stop, intimidated by the angry tone. I look up, trying to find its source. It comes from different directions, but above. I want so badly to understand what it says.

I stand still, waiting for what will come next. I hear a gunshot and something strikes the girl. A bright orange, fuzzy bug protrudes from her head. She stops twitching.

I hear another shot and something hits me in the exposed part of my neck. I set the girl down and retrieve a bug, just like the one in her head. Even through my cloudy vision, I can see a shiny stinger on the nose of the insect.

That's always the last thing that happens before I come to. My vision returns fast and I find Judith in front of me holding my cheeks.

"He'll be okay, she says. "He's coming out of it now."

Standing a few feet back from where she was before, the red lady says, "He couldn't relapse, could he?"

"No, of course not," Judith scolds. "Dr. Goldman say's it's his way of purging the chemical imbalance still affecting his brain stem."

"That was scary," the woman says.

You have no idea, Lady. I don't like her. Wish I could scare her for real, but Judith won't have any of it.

The flashback never takes me to when and how my neck was broken. I've thought long and hard about it and figure it happened during a feeding, when one of my victims probably kicked my head as he or she fought to survive.

Likewise I have absolutely no memory of my life before I got the infection. My childhood, adolescence and early adulthood have been effectively stricken from the database in my brain.

I recall very little of my wife and kids before they were eaten. Several images of my wife and each of my two children have returned, but nothing definite. There is one memory I have of the two crying to me from outside our basement door, and my wife pounding nails into it by my command. The memory jumps to the three screaming, being pulled out of the house. I'm locked in the basement, unable to save them. But really there's nothing else that makes definite sense.

"Yeah, it seems scary, but we've grown used to it," Judith says, smiling and still combing my hair with her hand. "He gets these seizures a couple of times a day, especially when he's in stressful situations."

The lady asks, "Are those his new dentures?"

Judith pulls my upper lip out and say's, "They did a

wonderful job, don't you think? Late in his second month, it was obvious the teeth were all going to rot away, so we went ahead and did the whole job then."

"Oh," the lady says, accompanying it with a slow nod.

Judith reminds her, "You know the plague has vanished. The fever's gone. Whatever infected most of the counties in those four states vanished as mysteriously as it appeared."

I get to watch the news with Ed and Judith nightly and I'm interested in all the different theories going around, though I don't much understand them. It looks as though this lady pretty much doesn't care for the subject.

Judith continues, "The strain of the virus in each of the survivors has generated into a harmless form, so they no longer pose a danger. You can touch him if you like."

The lady steps forward. From an unsteady hand, two fingers brush over the side of my head. I want to snap at her hand for a reaction, but I don't, because it would make Judith mad. She steps back, gives an obligatory smile and looks at Judith.

She asks, "And what about the little one?"

Judith glances again at the store entrance and lowers her voice. "Well, you know she started her recovery much later than Pete here. She's got a little way to go, but we're hoping she'll do as well as him."

Ed steps out of the store, followed by Lacy. The red lady quivers at Lacy's sight. She doesn't look directly at the recovering, one-armed girl.

"And here she is," Judith says, with admiration.

Facing Ed, the lady says, "Hi little honey." She won't look at Lacy. She barely looked at me.

Lacy and I smile at each other. Her teeth are just little nubs, barely poking out of her black gums. They have just begun to grow back and her entire body is still swollen and dark purplish-blue. Watching her get better is the sweetest thing I've ever seen. I won't ever forget how close I came to ...

well, it was close.

Ed sits down next to me on the rock wall in front of the store, a bag of groceries in his right arm. Looking at the lady, he says, "I still can't get over how few of them recovered. To think the authorities let us adopt both of these guys is remarkable. I mean these kiddos can be a lot of fun, huh Judith?" He tousles my hair and Judith nods at him.

Judith says, "What's more remarkable is they tell us these two were together when they found them. Both had the defense antibodies in their systems to kill the virus. The authorities think Pete bit her at one point and passed his strain on to her."

Ed adds, "And you know, the Federal Post-Outbreak Adoptions Council made an exception and allowed us to take both, thinkin' it was best to keep them together."

The woman says, "Lucky you. And to think they were just this close to nuking some of those counties that were quarantined." She holds her forefinger close to her thumb. She motions with the back of her fingers in Lacy's general direction, refusing to look that way. "Some still think it would have been the most humane thing to do."

Lacy looks at me and rolls her eyes. She turns her head down and begins coughing heavily. Leaning over, she allows a large, gelled sack of dark, bloody phlegm to spring from her mouth and splatter the sidewalk. Her hair hasn't begun to grow back yet, so her blistery purple head points up at the lady. The pressure from the coughing cracks a couple of the large blisters and clear liquid dribbles off, speckling around the thick oral discharge. The smell of something that resembles a rotting rodent rises from the cement.

I enjoy watching the lady draw back. Her nose curls up and she turns away. She says, "Well, it's getting late. Got dinner to cook." She doesn't look back at any of us, but waves at Judith and Ed and hurries away.

Lacy looks up to see her leaving, turns to me and grins. A greasy reddish wetness glistens on her blackened lips and clear puss oozes across her forehead, down her cracking nose.

I grin back.

Ed hands Judith a clean handkerchief and she leans over to Lacy. She carefully dabs at Lacy's head and nose and then holds her cheeks. "You feeling bad again, sweetie?"

Lacy looks at her, drops her grin and gives her a bashful nod. "Wanna' go home."

Ed and I stand up and we all head for the station wagon in the parking lot. My feet work a lot better now. I gingerly walk around to Lacy's right side and hold her hand. We smile at each other again. Though I'm over fifty and she's only six, we're like brother and sister. Together we will recover.

IN THE MIDDLE OF POPLAR STREET

by Nate Southard

Ginny stood at the upstairs window, looking down at them all and trying not to cry. She had burst into tears twice in the past, and her mother had scolded her for it both times, telling her the thing in the street didn't deserve her sadness. Ginny couldn't help it, though. The people were just so mean it, and the scene unfolding now was just too strange, too awful, to be real.

A man in the coveralls was peeing on the thing in the middle of Poplar Street. The dead man, now staked to the concrete with pieces of rebar through his shoulders and around his throat, writhed as much as the pieces of steel would allow as he tried to escape the stream of urine. Her eyes darted from the groaning creature to the limp piece of flesh in the peeing man's hands, and she didn't know which was more horrible. She tried to look away, but both sights horrified her, left her cold and disgusted even as they pulled at her eyes.

All around, the crowd laughed and cheered. A bearded man gave the one in coveralls a pat on the back. A bunch of teenage girls giggled.

Ginny decided she'd never giggle when she grew older.

She felt so sorry for the dead man. She didn't even know if he... it... had feelings anymore, but she still felt sorry.

At least they weren't using the fire hose.

The people did that sometimes. Their small town only had what Mom called a volunteer fire department, and every once in a while, one of the firemen would bring down a hose from the station. While everybody watched, making little giggles and almost shaking with excitement, the fireman would hook up the hose to a hydrant across the street and blast the thing with water. The creature would go crazy, wrestling against the water and rebar while the people cheered. Usually, the crowd kept spraying the hose for half an hour or more, until people wanted to get back in and kick the trapped dead man again. Of course, the firemen didn't bring out the hose much anymore. The last time, a bunch of skin and stuff had come off of the dead man. One piece had hit a little girl, and everybody freaked out. Ginny hadn't seen the girl since.

She was probably freaked out, too.

Suddenly, the blinds slammed shut an inch away from her nose. She gasped, jumping backwards, and screamed when she found her mother standing right behind her.

"I told you not to watch that."

"I wasn't!"

"Don't lie to me."

Ginny turned around, wrapping her arms around her mom's waist. The woman smelled like cookies, and Ginny breathed the scent in deep. She loved her mom, loved her more than anything in the world, but she didn't see why the woman hated the thing in the street so much.

"I'm sorry, Mom. I didn't mean to lie to you. I just feel so bad."

Ginny looked up to see her mom, her face framed by stringy black hair, shake her head.

"Don't you feel bad for that thing, Ginny. It doesn't

deserve it. You should know that."

"But he "

"Don't you 'but' me, Ginny. And it's not a 'he,' okay? It's not a real person, not anymore. I don't care how miserable that monster out there looks. I want you to remember that it wants to kill you, me, and everybody else in this town. If it ever gets off all that metal, it's going to do just that."

"Then why don't the people just kill it?"

"I wish they would. I hate having it this close."

"So why don't they?"

"You know the rules, Ginny. We have to wait for the county's cleanup crew. We're not allowed to do it ourselves."

"So why are they hurting it?"

Her mom turned away then, looking around the room, examining the walls and doing her best to keep her eyes hidden. When she finally spoke, Ginny thought her voice sounded weird, a little bit softer than usual.

"Ginny, you know how the dead people used to be real people, right?"

"Yeah."

"Well, the real people in this town went through a lot of trouble because of the dead. Remember that thing that happened at the school? Well, that truck driver was probably trying to get away from a bunch of those monsters, and that's why he crashed. A lot of people were killed by the ones who came back not just here, but all over and the real people were very afraid for a very long time. In a lot of ways, they're still scared, and sometimes scared people get mad."

"But there's not really anything to be afraid of anymore, Mom. Most of the dead people are gone."

Ginny's mom smiled. "I know, honey, but people don't stop being scared right away. It takes time."

"But why do they get angry?"

Her mother sighed, and even Ginny could tell she was getting annoyed, struggling to remain patient. "Honey, scared

165

people get angry because they don't like being afraid, and they think it's somebody else's fault that they were so scared in the first place. That's why they do stuff like what they're doing down in the street. It's because they hate that they're so scared, and they want to feel like they've made it all even. I guess... I guess they just need to convince themselves they're in control again."

Ginny breathed in her mom's scent, trying to make sense of what she'd said. Yeah, people were afraid. She had been afraid, too, but the dead people were mostly gone, now. There wasn't any reason to be scared anymore.

Sometimes people just didn't make any sense.

"You understand, honey?"

Ginny looked up at her mom. She smiled and hugged her tight around the waist.

"I do, Mom. I'm sorry."

It was the first time she could ever remember lying.

"So," her mother said, "What do you want for dinner?"

Ginny pretended to think it over.

"Cheeseburgers."

"I don't have any hamburger thawed out. We can have some tomorrow, if you want. Is that okay?"

"Sure. Can we have spaghetti tonight?"

"Yeah."

"Good. Let's have spaghetti."

Mom smiled. "Okay, and I'll set some hamburger in the fridge to thaw."

"Thanks, Mom," Ginny said as she hugged her mother again. "I love you."

"I love you too, honey."

Her mom walked to the door, turning back to give Ginny a sad smile. "Stay away from the window, okay? I don't want you upsetting yourself."

She nodded, gave her mom a thumbs up. As she made the gesture, she realized how stupid it looked, how... silly.

Mom left the room. A second later, Ginny turned to peer through the blinds.

* * * * *

Ginny pretended to sleep, the covers pulled up to her chin and her cheek against the pillow, until the noises from the street disappeared as the crowd dissipated and all she could hear was her mother's soft snoring. She waited a while longer, her eyes roaming the bedroom, and then climbed out of bed. The hardwood floor was cold beneath her feet, but she tried to ignore it. The air outside would be colder, the pavement ice against her soles, but she couldn't risk putting on her shoes or coat. Any unnecessary noise might wake up her mother, and then she'd have some explaining to do.

She crossed the hall and stepped to the window, pulling back the blinds the slightest bit. Poplar Street stood dark and empty, the way she had expected to find it. Squinting through the night's shadows, she could made out the sickening garden of rebar, the twisting figure it pinned to the pavement. The people always left the reanimated alone at night, and they never bothered leaving a guard, either. They knew it was harmless. Without its arms or jaw, it was just a thing. A punching bag or something more pitiful, and most didn't appear to like torturing it without an audience. Ginny shook her head, thinking about the people, and then stepped away from the window.

She made it to the kitchen without creaking any of the floorboards and pulled the refrigerator open as quietly as she could, her hand darting inside to shut off the interior light. Heart thumping behind her ribs, she paused to listen to the house, remaining still until she decided her mother was still asleep. The hamburger sat on the bottom shelf, still wrapped in plastic. Ginny removed it from the fridge and tucked it under her arm, closing the door behind her.

Almost done. The other item she needed was under the sink. She remembered last seeing it on the right hand side, and she hoped Mom hadn't moved it. Searching under the sink would be so loud it might wake the entire neighborhood, not just her mother. Luckily, her fingers closed around the object right away. She breathed a sigh of relief, and her heart calmed the slightest bit. Moving slowly, careful to keep the hinges from squealing, she opened the back door and left the house.

The winter air slashed at her as she rounded the house and stepped onto the cold concrete of Poplar Street. The dead person staked to the street like some kind of weird science project looked up, sensing her approach, and moaned.

"Quiet," Ginny said. "You have to be quiet, or I'll get caught."

The dead man didn't understand. It continued to groan, the sound both ominous and pathetic, as she stepped closer. When she finally stood over the creature, it could only wheeze in excitement, staring up at her and the objects in her hands.

Without a word, she set one of the objects down so she could unwrap the hamburger. The reanimated dead man caught the scent of blood and meat and began to thrash against its metal bounds. She placed the hamburger on the ground and then pushed it forward with her foot until it was within reach of the creature's ruined mouth. It looked up at her, eyes wide and glazed, yet somehow thankful. Then it dove into the meat. It worked with its dead tongue, doing its best to lap up the raw beef, and paused only to groan in pleasure before returning to its meal.

Ginny watched it eat, and she wondered what it might have looked like when it was alive. She could tell it had been a man. Maybe he had been handsome. Or maybe ugly. What about the man's family? Had he been married, had kids, maybe a little girl around her age?

Nobody in town seemed to care. They just used the thing in the street as something to beat on and torture. Did it really

168

make them feel safer? How could it? She doubted it. If people really feared the thing in the street, they wouldn't leave it alone at night.

"Monster," Ginny said, and she leaned forward to spit on the dead man. The glop of saliva struck the back of the thing's head and began to trickle down its ruined scalp. Ginny expected the thing to look up at her or try to shrink away or something. Anything. But the corpse didn't do a thing but work at the hamburger, its moans growing louder as it managed to eat more and more.

She drew in a deep breath and held it. The smell of hamburger mixed with the clean, empty smell of winter, but beneath it all, a rotten smell lingered, and she knew it was the miserable thing staked to the pavement. Disgusting.

Baring her teeth, her face morphing into an angry sneer, she picked up the other object and stepped forward. Slowly, she raised the hammer over her head, her fingers curling tighter and tighter. The reanimated continued to ignore her, not noticing the growl in her throat or even her presence until she swung the hammer as hard as her arms allowed, slamming the metal against the creature's shoulder. A screech split the quiet night as the dead man's head arched away from the pavement, flesh and bone scraping against rebar.

Ginny caught a scream in her throat as terror burst up from her stomach and lungs. She scrambled away from the thing, making a trio of hurried steps across the pavement before her ankles twisted and she landed hard on her bottom. Then she scurried like a crab, forgetting the hammer, until she reached the sidewalk and the grass beyond. Its moans chased her, and soon she began crying, wiping at her eyes as she drew her knees under her chin.

"I'm sorry," she whispered. "I'm sorry, I'm sorry." Sitting in the grass, she found herself scared of her ability to hurt the thing. If she could hurt it, did that mean she could enjoy hurting it? She didn't want to find out.

Shivering, she watched the reanimated and waited. It continued to groan its pain into the street for several long moments, and she watched the houses for any lights flicking on or doors opening. No one appeared to notice, however, and after a few minutes the dead man returned to the package of hamburger. The night filled with slopping sounds and groans of pleasure.

Slowly, Ginny returned to her feet and started across the street. She stopped long enough to retrieve the hammer from where she'd dropped it, and then a few more steps took her to the reanimated.

"I'm sorry," she told it again.

It ignored her, instead concentrating on the last few clumps of raw beef.

"I don't know who you were," she said. "You probably don't deserve this, though."

Ginny raised the hammer over her head once more. She eyed a spot on the back of the dead man's skull.

The wind picked up, and Ginny held her breath.

SEMINAR Z

by J.L. Comeau

Chief Executive Officer Richard Dresden feared that the sheer intensity of silence encircling him might shatter his spine if his fragile construct of brisk composure should falter for an instant. He dragged a hand through his hair to sweep away sweat droplets forming on his brow and struggled to maintain a resolute demeanor. Dresden's facade wavered momentarily when a reedy voice quaked through the com-unit built into the head of the massive black marble conference table where he sat facing his Board of Directors.

"The package has arrived, sir."

Dresden pressed a button on the right arm of his chair. An embossed steel door directly behind the Chairman of the Board swung open to admit a grim-faced young man. Dresden's gaze locked with the Chairman's returned glare while the aide placed a titanium attaché case on the table before Dresden.

"Leave us," Dresden murmured, detecting a sharp metallic odor of panic stirred by the aide's departing wake.

Dresden entered the code that opened the case. Inside, a digital capture disc and a rectangular metal box lay snuggled into protective foam cutouts. He withdrew the disc and placed it into the slotted receiving orifice of his com-unit. Above the gleaming table where eleven other men sat rigid and expressionless, a whirling hologram coalesced into a tumbling three-dimensional stylized representation of the entwined letters E and C. The men turned toward the colorful image with predatory anticipation.

171

"Begin," the Chairman said, pale vulture's eyes pinning Dresden from the opposite end of polished table.

Dresden pressed the Play button. A trickle of icy perspiration slid beneath his starched white collar and down the length of his aching back. He clamped his teeth together to steady his jaw and awaited the imminent collapse of his career. What Dresden foresaw as the beginning of the end unfolded thus:

* * * * * * *

ECOCORP   CAPTURE   DISC

LEVEL 10 CONFIDENTIAL
FOR USE BY CEO, CFO, COO, AND
BOARD MEMBERS ONLY

DISC TO BE DESTROYED AFTER VIEWING

IZ Division Capture Camera 5/Orientation Theater/Mesa Bldg 20952: TMark 0903/DMark 092453: Video Log

[An athletic, razor-jawed young man bounds towards a stage center podium and waits until the background buzz of his audience wanes. Behind him stylized EC logos tumble across a floor-to-ceiling movie theater screen. He clears his throat and taps the podium microphone to bring the assembly to order.]

"Welcome to what we affectionately call Seminar Z, ladies and gentlemen, and congratulations on having been selected as members of our customer service team. I'm your orientation coach, Christopher Faulkner, and I want to welcome each of you to EcoCorp's new Mesa Arizona customer service facility."

[Audience applause.]

"Thank you, thank you. First, I want to make sure that all of you have your magnetic scan badges. These will allow ingress and egress to your workstations. They have been programmed to recognize your individual retinal configurations and will be fully functional when you report for your first day of work tomorrow morning."

[Pause.]

"You have each been chosen to serve in our elite first line battalion in EcoCorp's ongoing war against customer dissatisfaction."

[Applause and whistles from the audience.]

"As you know, you have each passed through a number of top level background checks to insure that you are intellectually and emotionally suited to the demanding task of servicing our highly specialized consumer base. The InfiniZ Division of EcoCorp's public EcoMart procurement chain is dedicated to providing the highest quality reanimated products to our clientele. Most EcoMart shoppers are unaware that the InfiniZ division exists and, while it is not precisely a clandestine operation, our InfiniZ line of products is – how shall I say it? – exclusive."

[Tentative audience laughter.]

"So let's just get the Z-word out of the way, shall we? Zombies. At InfiniZ, we sell zombies, although it is a requirement of your employment that you use the term "reanimate" whenever speaking with our customers. Any Customer Service Specialist who fails to meet this requirement will be severed from employment immediately. Memories of the zombie infestations of the early 30s still unnerve a certain portion of our consumer demographic, therefore we must strive to keep in mind what a terrible time it was when feral zombies shambled across the land slaughtering unwitting victims until the crudely engineered nanotoxin pathogen created during the last Indo-African war was eradicated. Nearly eradicated, that is."

[Faulkner grins.]

"EcoCorp became the owner of the last known existing specimen subsequent to our scientists reengineering it into what we call Z-Tox, a blockbuster profit generator that now provides our select clientele with top-quality reanimates specifically created to meet their unique specifications. Customers may purchase reanimates for any function they wish, utilizing their products for entertainment, labor, companionship or whatever use they can envision."

[Faulkner smiles.]

"And they can envision some very interesting applications for their InfiniZ reanimates."

[Boisterous audience laughter.]

"Often, however, clients wish to reanimate their dearly departed loved ones and sadly, this situation has generated our highest level of customer complaints when the reanimate's behavior does not approximate the personality of the living person. Consumer expectations have always exceeded reality with regard to these products, and this is why we're currently purging RelativityReanimates™ from the InfiniZ lineup. Because of the phase-out, this is an issue you will rarely if ever be called upon to address during the term of your employment with EcoCorp. But, as with any popular and developing product line, problems and consumer complaints are bound to occur. Your initial training has prepared you to respond to nearly every situation you will encounter, however, new issues are sure to emerge from time to time, and that is why your selection has been so rigorous. You must never allow your emotions to overshadow your professional deportment. You must always behave in an empathetic manner, but you may not allow your personal feelings to usurp your loyalty to EcoCorp. Do we all understand that?"

[Vigorous head-nodding response from the audience.]

"Excellent! And now we're going to watch a short film that will demonstrate an InfiniZ Customer Service Specialist handling actual customer complaints. Lights, please."

[Auditorium dims. Onscreen presentation cues. Dynamic EC musical score thunders from speakers and the words ECOCORP FILMS PRESENTS: CUSTOMER SERVICE TRAINING, INFINIZ DIVISION appear on the theater screen.]

[Music fades out. A compactly built young woman wearing a tailored green EC jumpsuit and com cap appears onscreen. She is sitting on a contour chair inside a transparent cubicle before a com screen fitted into a built-in tabletop. A buzzing sound prompts her to tap the earpiece embedded in her com cap.]

"Good afternoon. InfiniZ Customer Service Division. Ms. Trejo speaking. How may I help you?"

[A meaty red face with a bushy black mustache appears on the EcoCorp com screen. The man is shouting.]

"Come and get your fucking zombie!"

175

[Ms. Trejo smiles pleasantly.]

"Good afternoon, sir. I will gladly help you resolve any problem you may be experiencing. Please state your complaint or concern calmly and clearly."

[The man takes a deep breath and leans towards the screen. His mustache quivers with rage.]

"I own and operate a skating rink in Buffalo, New York. I ordered a Zamboni from EcoMart – Zamboni to clear the ice. You sent me a zombie. When we opened the crate it ran amok and has killed several of my customers."

[The man leans aside to reveal a bloody expanse of ice behind him.]

"Your zombie killed two children and three adults before someone had the presence of mind to stab it in the head with the blades of his racing skates. Then we had to stab the dead customers in their heads before they got up and ran wild, too. What the hell is wrong with you people? I ordered a Zamboni, not a fucking zombie!"

"I'm sorry if there has been a mix-up, sir. However, you should know that our reanimates are engineered to be completely non-infectious, making it unnecessary to deactivate the brain of anyone other than that of the reanimate itself."

"Great. Now I know."

[Ms. Trejo consults a flip-down panel beneath her com screen.]

"This is very unusual, sir. May I ask if your reanimate arrived with its facial restraint in place?"

176

*[The man grasps his head with his
hands, fingers digging into his scalp.]*

"Lady, the fucking zombie stumbled out of the box and started biting people. Does that sound like it was restrained?"

[Ms. Trejo smiles dazzlingly.]

"Sir, this is a problem that can best be resolved by our shipping department because it sounds as though a shipping order error may have occurred. Please hold while I transfer your call, and please have your order number ready. Thank you for calling EcoCorp's InfiniZ Division. We are always happy to help you. Have a wonderful day."

*[The mustachioed man opens his mouth to protest an instant
before Ms. Trejo's screen returns to tumbling EC logos.]*

[Jump cut.]

*[A pinched, sallow-faced man wearing a
clerical collar appears on the com screen.]*

"I am calling to report that the reanimate I ordered does not function."

[Ms. Trejo tilts her head.]

"I'm very sorry to hear that, sir. Could you explain the nature of this malfunction?"

"The nature of the malfunction, madam, is that the reanimate arrived dead; ergo, it does... not... function. It was my misguided notion to order a reanimate from your company to illustrate a grave and weighty sermon about Lazarus. Lazarus is a biblical figure whom Christ brought back from death. I tell you this because people of your age group tend to be appallingly ignorant of The Teachings. In any event, when the dramatic moment in my sermon arrived, my altar boys opened the box and, instead of rising up to Lazarus-like reanimated life, the entire congregation witnessed – and I stress the word witnessed – nothing other than a lifeless corpse lying inert and reeking like last week's fish entrée. The churchgoing public expects theater with their liturgy, young lady, and your product missed that particular mark in epic fashion. It was quite an embarrassing anticlimax to what was meant to have been a monumental sermon."

[The cleric arranges his lips into a
parsimonious moue and glares into the com screen.]

[Ms. Trejo smiles sympathetically.]

"I extend to you my sincere apology for any inconvenience you may have experienced, sir. Although all of our reanimates are encased in and embalmed with a revolutionary elastic silicone matrix to insure freshness, on rare occasions a reanimate's brain will putrefy prematurely due to preexisting cranial conditions or the silicate gel encasement matrix develops a leak due to damage sustained during shipping. I will connect you with our warranty division to determine if you are eligible for a replacement or a refund. Hold, please."
"But–"

[Jump cut.]

[Ms. Trejo's com screen glows with the florid faces of three young men who jostle for center screen position above the keyboard of a portable computer from which they are communicating. A pounding cacophony of loud music punctuated by whooping voices induces Ms. Trejo to lower the

178

volume of her com-unit. A sudden slosh of frothy liquid from a green bottle spews onto the customer's screen and the sweaty, red-faced young men guffaw and wheeze with drunken glee.]

[Ms. Trejo smiles politely.]

"How may I help you today, gentlemen?"
"It's this stupid zombie my dad ordered for my graduation party, right? It's a piece of shit."

[The trio of young men explodes with unfettered hilarity, bobbing heads and gasping for breath.]

[Ms. Trejo squints in an effort to hear above the background din.]

"Is there a specific problem I can help you with, sir?"

[The complainant attempts to compose himself]

"See for yourself!"

[The complainant's com screen swivels to expose a ransacked and ruined hotel room. The screen pans toward a king-sized bed surrounded by whooping and cavorting young men in various stages of undress who edge away reluctantly as the computer is carried toward them. A blood-drenched bare mattress becomes visible where a twitching heap of clotted flesh has been tied down with a network of bungee cords.]

[Ms. Trejo examines the carnage with a neutral expression.]

"I see. Your reanimate has sustained major damage. Did you read the manual that came packed with your reanimate, sir?"

[The complainant rotates the computer back towards his face and stares into the camera.]

"What? No! I didn't see any fucking manual."

[Ms. Trejo smiles crisply.]

"Each of our reanimates arrives packaged with a manual that explains and depicts proper and improper usage. From what I can see, your reanimate may have been misused. InfiniZ warranties and bonds are nullified by any instance of negligent maltreatment of our products. May I ask for what specific use this product was purchased?"

[The complainant places his com-unit upon a stationary surface off-camera and leaps into view, jumping onto the gore-laden bed astride the savaged reanimate, which continues to twitch and strain against its tethers.]

"It was a graduation gift from my dad, like I told you. Just look at this thing! It fell apart! I'll bet it was a hundred years old when it died."

[The complainant kicks at the heap of flesh and gore, dislodging a flapping purple organ.]

[Ms. Trejo consults her flip-down panel.]

"Economy models are not selected for age, sir. If the silicate seals are broken on any model – as your reanimate's certainly have been – your InfiniZ warranty is considered invalid. I must ask you again: For what use was this product purchased?"

[An off-camera hand places a bottle in the complainant's fist.

The complainant takes deep draught from the bottle and spits the contents of his mouth upon the jerking remains of his reanimate.]

"Fun and games! Gangbang, yeah!"

[The complainant's companions raise foaming bottles over their heads and roar approval.]

[Ms. Trejo adjusts her earpiece.]

"It seems to me that your InfiniZ product has fulfilled the purpose for which it was purchased, sir. If you are finished using your reanimate, please press the red metal button located on the left side of the facial restraint device. This will fire a projectile into the reanimate's brain and deactivate your product. You may then place the deactivated reanimate into the red plastic biohazard bag included in shipping. Once the deactivating device has been engaged, our Pickup Division will be automatically notified and a local Pickup Specialist will be dispatched to retrieve the biohazard bag and its contents."

[The complainant smirks and looks down at the convulsing mass of flesh and bone between his feet. He addresses someone off-camera.]

"Bring my com over here, bud."

[Ms. Trejo's com screen fills with an image of a molded stainless steel mask that obscures the reanimate's face. A hand tugs the mask back and forth revealing four massive bolts – temples and jaws – attaching the facial restraint to the reanimate's head. A circular red button is positioned below the left temple bolt. The button is covered by a clear plastic cap.]

181

"Please remove the protective plastic cap and–"
"We ain't done with our zombie, yet, are we boys?"

[Affirmative roar.]

"Get me a knife, Willy. Let's take a good look at this zombie before we croak it."

[Ms. Trejo's smile fades.]

"InfiniZ does not recommend that you–"
"Shut up, bitch. Just shut up and watch."

[A hand stabs at the attachment bolts with the blade of a pocket knife amid laughter and encouragement.]

"Get up under the bolt-head!"
"Use some leverage and pry that fucker out of there!"

[Ms. Trejo issues several unheeded warnings as the blade wedges beneath an attachment bolt. The bolt begins to lift. Ms. Trejo warnings are lost in the cacophony of triumphant bellows. The bolt shears bone and cartilage. Amid primal shrieks of jubilation the reanimate's facial restraint is rocked pulled. The reanimate's jawbone cracks asunder as hands wrench the mask aside to reveal the ravaged, decomposing face of an elderly woman. Cloudy, shriveled blue eyes snap back and forth, withered stump of tongue waggles and lashes in a jawless skull.]

"Ha! I told you! Bitch is a thousand years old! Come get some!"

[The image on Ms. Trejo's screen bobbles as the complainant's com-unit is dropped onto the floor several feet from the bed. A

cluster of bare male buttocks jounce toward the mattress upon which the complainant stands straddling the writhing reanimate. The complainant bends over, wrenches the restraining device free of its last intact bolt and holds the mask overhead like a trophy, half a jawbone dangling above his head.]

[Ms. Trejo turns up her audio volume and shouts.]

"Please be careful, sir! The protective plastic cap covering the deactivation button on the facial restraint is no longer in place and–"

[A sharp bang blasts through the din. Sudden silence. The complainant's gleeful expression goes slack. A dark jet of blood pumps from the top of his head as he topples face-forward onto the reanimate.]

"Oh, shit! Brandon! Somebody call an ambulance!"

[Three of complainant's companions drag their inert comrade from the bed while the rest pick up lamps, books, shoes and other objects with which they batter and hammer the reanimate.]

"Crush the brain! Crush the brain!"

[The entire throng choruses the refrain.]

"Crush the brain! Crush the brain! Crush the brain!"

*[The reanimate's head is thrashed
to puree, deactivating the unit.]*

"Now go crush Brandon's brain before he gets up and tries

to eat us!"

*[Ms. Trejo shouts directly into the
mouthpiece of her com set headgear.]*

"There's no need to–"

*[The gore-flecked face of a young man partially fills Ms.
Trejo's screen. Behind him, a naked youth holds a large
Chinese vase above the head of the prone complainant. The
young man speaks as the vase hurtles down.]*

"Thank you very much, ma'am. We'll call you back,
okay?"

*[Ms. Trejo's screen returns to tumbling EcoCorp logos. She
taps a number of keys on her keyboard. She touches her
earpiece, waits for a moment, then speaks.]*

"Legal Department? This is Ms. Trejo in Customer
Service. I am forwarding to you a video capture for immediate
review. I have red-flagged the capture 'Customer Fatality'.
Subject possibly a minor. Please attend to this at once. Thank
you."

*[Ms. Trejo taps her earpiece and leans back in her contour
chair. Her com-unit buzzes and she taps her earpiece to
answer another incoming call.]*

*[The InfiniZ Customer Service Specialist training film ends
with applause and cheers from the audience.]*

*[Customer Service Orientation Coach Christopher Faulkner
bounds back onstage and positions himself behind the podium.
He waits for the applause to dwindle.]*

"I'm happy to report that each of Ms. Trejo's complaints was concluded with a minimum of liability to EcoCorp. Any questions before we begin our review?"

[At the back of the auditorium a young woman wearing a bouncing auburn ponytail stands.]

[Faulkner scans a seating diagram.]

"Question, Miss Arden?"
"Yes. I would like to know what happened to the men who raped and butchered that old woman."

[Faulkner blinks in obvious confusion.]

"I beg your pardon?"
"I asked what happened to the men who raped and butchered the old woman, motherfucker. Do you know? Do you care?"

[Before Faulkner's fingers can locate the emergency button hidden on the underside of his podium, a trio of large men surges forth from the audience and leap onstage. One of the men grabs Faulkner by an arm and twists until it cracks.]

[Faulkner screams and falls to the stage, writhing and moaning.]

[The men unzip their EcoCorp InfiniZ jumpsuits to reveal black tee shirts emblazoned with the letters "HZL." They brandish automatic weapons that had been hidden in the parachute legs. The weapons are EcoCorp carbonized plastic firearms developed to evade security screenings.]

[Muffled shrieks ripple through the paralyzed audience.]

[The ponytailed woman positions herself in front of the stage, holding a gun in one hand and a vial of glowing green material in the other.]

"Good morning, drones. My name is Annie Linden and I have come to release you from this nightmare. You are no doubt familiar with my organization, Humanitarian Zombie Liberation. The production, enslavement and commercial sale of the undead is an abomination! The formerly living old woman whom you witnessed being debauched and torn to pieces in your training film was once someone's child, mother, grandmother. EcoCorp is a tyrannical vulture that feeds on the carcasses of poor people who must sell their dead to feed their living. And you want to work for EcoCorp? Is this the kind of thing you want to do for a few shitty finance credits each month? Well, my friends, it's not going to happen. What's going to happen is that you and I are going to become freedom fighters in a war of liberation that will bring down EcoCorp and their bloody subsidiaries!"

[The doors at the back of the auditorium – jammed shut with folding chairs – rattle and bang.]

[The ponytailed woman glances at her cohorts then faces her cowering audience.]

"The dawn of a new day begins now!"

[The ponytailed woman smashes the vial of green liquid against the floor in front of her. A shimmering cloud of vapor rises and envelops the auditorium. All camera views are obstructed. When the mist begins to clear, everyone in the auditorium is limp and unresponsive. None are breathing.]

[The doors burst open and a dozen EcoCorp security guards in

186

riot gear edge into the room, guns drawn. Cautiously they move forward. One guard speaks into his wrist-mounted com-unit and calls for an EC ambulance. Another guard lifts the arm of a jump suited trainee. He removes one glove and his helmet before checking for a pulse. One of the trainees moves his head.]

"Hey, this one's not dead, he's–"

[The security guard's sentence ends in a scream when the subject whose wrist he is holding pulls the guard forward and bites off his nose. Pandemonium ensues when all of the formerly dead trainees and HZL members arise and begin slaughtering the security guards who, once killed, rise up within moments to assault their living colleagues. The reanimates are uncharacteristically swift and focused. Several disembodied heads are shattered and brains consumed before reanimation can occur. When no living subjects remain, the reanimates sprint through the auditorium doors and the room is left empty with the exception of the brain-eviscerated dead.]

* * * * * * *
END OF ECOCORP CAPTURE DISC
DESTROY! DESTROY! DESTROY!
* * * * * * *

Richard Dresden leaned forward and flicked a lever that atomized the disc. The Chairman, ensconced at the head of the table in his Terrain Rover Life Support Pod, cleared his throat in preparation to speak.

Dresden often wondered how much revenue the 123-year-old Chairman had sucked from Eco-Corp with his ongoing and self-serving life extension projects. The old man hardly needed to worry about Dresden replacing him since it was clear that the Chairman planned to live forever. It didn't matter now anyway, Dresden thought, since he would consider himself lucky to have a job cleaning the Chairman's personal toilet by the meeting's end.

"I must say," the Chairman began, "that the Mesa situation is a predicament of gargantuan proportions. A most unsatisfactory state of affairs considering that the board has been assured repeatedly that this sort of infiltration by the HZL was not even a remote possibility."

Dresden raised his chin and engaged the Chairman's malevolent glower. "Yes, sir. It is an unforgivable breach of security. The Mesa facility is currently under Code 10 lockdown to prevent–"

The Chairman continued. "Are you able to give me one hundred percent assurance that none of the HZL zombies escaped the Mesa facility?"

Dresden looked down at his diamond cufflinks.

"I see," the Chairman murmured. "So, what do you propose?"

Dresden turned to his flanking COO and CFO, both of whom cringed in their designer suits like a pair of flogged mongrels. No help there.

"It is clear that the unidentified HZL material is an airborne contagion," Dresden began, praying his voice wouldn't crack. "We cannot allow it to escape into the atmosphere."

"Are we looking at an end-of-the-world scenario?" the Canadian board member asked with a distinct tremble in his voice.

"I would hesitate to characterize it as such," Dresden said. "We heard that kind of talk back in the 30s, if you'll recall, but we found a way to halt and control the original pathogen.

"But that was a viral nanotoxin derived from rabies, for Christ's sake!" the Central American chair insisted. "That sickness wasn't airborne; it was conveyed through bodily fluids."

"These new reanimates are so fast!" The Chinese chair added. "I've never seen anything like it."

"That is why we can't allow the pathogen to escape any farther than it already has," Dresden said.

"Already has?" the Chairman demanded.

Dresden drew a deep breath. "There are isolated outbreaks currently under containment."

"By what means?"

"Fire."

"You're burning Mesa?" the Australian chair inquired. "You're setting the city on fire?"

"It goes a bit beyond than that," Dresden admitted. "The entire state may have to go." Dresden rose from his seat and faced his colleagues. "In fact, I'm thinking it should go much beyond than that."

The table erupted in cross-talk and exclamations.

"Gentlemen, gentlemen!" the Chairman wheezed. "Come to order. Please."

This is my moment, Dresden thought. Make it or break it. He drew back his shoulders and spoke. "I've been compiling updated reports on wind patterns from our meteorology division, which indicate that prevailing winds will prevent the pathogen from reaching the upper atmosphere and escaping the Americas for the next twelve to fifteen hours."

"We have at least twelve hours to act?" the Chairman asked.

"Hopefully," Dresden replied. "This new pathogen is also spread via bodily fluids, so contagion patterns will soon become exponential and continue to expand even if the airborne pathogen dissipates. Considering the agility and speed of these reanimates, we will most certainly be looking at the end-of-the-world scenario suggested by our esteemed Canadian chair if we do not act immediately."

"And you are suggesting..." the Chairman prompted, leaning forward.

Say it quickly, Dresden told himself. "I'm suggesting a nuclear solution. Neutron bombs."

Again the table erupted in angry pronouncements while the Chairman sat blinking. The table fell silent when the Chairman spoke. "Neutron bombs." He seemed to be turning the words over in his mouth. "Maximizes damage to organics, minimizes damage to structures."

"Correct, sir," Dresden said with a glimmer of hope.

"Are both of you insane?" the Canadian chair exclaimed with upraised palms. "You wish to destroy the center of this country? And how do you propose to persuade the American government to go along with this plan?"

The Chairman waved away the question with a skeletal hand. "The government privatized oversight and control of missile facilities decades ago. Our subsidiaries own those contracts."

"But the news that EcoCorp used a nuclear weapon to destroy an American city – even to control a deadly pathogen – will destroy us," the Russian chair weighed in. "We could never contain that kind of information."

"We could contain it if the information remains within this room," Dresden proposed.

"How would we explain it?" the Chinese chair inquired. "An accident? Surely not. The American government would eventually uncover the truth."

"That would be a problem," the Chairman said, looking directly at Dresden.

"It would be necessary to expand the solution," Dresden said.

"But you would be destroying all of our valuable American facilities. You're looking at a loss of trillions of dollars," the Canadian chair pleaded in desperate tone. "And the radiation; the bombs would render the blast zones uninhabitable for decades, perhaps centuries."

"Most structures would survive. It would be a matter of

rebuilding. Imagine the reconstruction contracts," the Chairman mused.

"And just whom do you suppose would be crazy enough to enter radiation zones for the purpose of rebuilding during our lifetimes?" the Canadian chair insisted.

The men assembled on both sides of the table flanking Dresden and the Chairman looked up and down the table at each other, considering.

"We've been having a great deal of success with experimental remotely controlled reanimates at our Euro facilities, gentlemen," Dresden said. "In fact, the remotes were going to be InfiniZ's next major product rollout." A sense of triumph spread through Dresden's limbs like a life-infusing tonic. "Did someone mention trillions? Gentlemen, our profits would become nearly uncountable."

Within an hour a consensus was reached and the emergency meeting of EcoCorp's international board concluded. Dresden could hear the thundering approach of EC helicopters bound for the roof above the 60th floor. He shook the hands of each solemn board member and ushered them to the bank of elevators that would take them to the landing pad. Soon only Dresden and the Chairman remained. Dresden walked beside the Chairman's life support pod as it rolled toward the elevators.

"I don't suppose I could take my wife with me," Dresden inquired, but it was not a question. "Or my mistress."

"My dear boy," the Chairman said in an approximation of sympathy. "I am sorry. We must each make our sacrifices for the greater good, mustn't we?" The Chairman patted Dresden's arm. "I would like for you to accompany me to the Euro division and become my right-hand man. You'll retain your CEO status and receive an upgraded salary, of course. Would you be interested in such a position?"

Dresden looked down at the man whom he would gladly choke to death with his own hands to ascend to the

Chairmanship and smiled. "I would be honored, Mr. Chairman."

"Good, good," the old man said, nodding. "A helicopter will be waiting for you. I'll see you in Berlin."

When the elevator had whisked the Chairman away, Dresden walked back into the boardroom and picked up the titanium attaché case that had contained the damning capture disc. He snapped open the hinges and looked inside where a rectangular box lay next to the empty foam cutout where the disc had been. He knew what was concealed inside the box: a vial of glowing green material that an EC HazMat team had collected from air filters throughout the Mesa facility. A little extra insurance never hurt.

Dresden closed the attaché case and carried it to a long window at the end of the room. Outside, the Hudson rolled on and on as though the world would never end. Above the Hudson a late afternoon skyline glittered with a thousand iron and steel towers.

A chattering brown sparrow fluttered past the window and Dresden watched it alight on a ledge several floors below. The phrase 'Ich bin ein Berliner' darted though Dresden's mind like a small impatient bird before he turned and strode towards the elevators.

ONLY NIBBLE

by Bob Nailor

I stood at the podium listening to the raging attack on the outside auditorium doors. The first double set of entrances from the school campus had been barricaded, while the three sets of inside doors, which opened to this auditorium, were locked and chained to provide a secondary bank of security. I watched the fidgeting of the students; the nervous and furtive looks being passed between them. These were the sole survivors of the campus who had heard my intercom announcement of an emergency class to teach them how to survive. The stage lights were turned on over the podium and also the first few rows of seats had some low lighting, but not the rear of the auditorium, which still remained in shadowed darkness. I glanced at the row of windows that followed the darkened recesses of the roofline on the right side. Those windows were at least twenty feet off the ground; possibly safe, but also a potential hazard to our current situation.

"I realize time is running short," I said into the microphone. The words blared over the speakers drowning the assault on the outside doors.

There was a sudden loud thump at the doors on the left aisle. They, those who we now huddled in fear of, had obviously made it through the front doors and were inside the lobby and attacking our second barricade and final defenses. A shiver coursed down my back. There was a scream in the distance. The students jumped and stared at the darkened upper recesses. Some students nervously moved about, unsure of

193

where to go, but they never ambled beyond the circle of light.

"Please, please," I shouted while walking away from the podium and microphone. I now stood in the center of the stage. I waved my hands to settle the audience. "Listen to me." I started a motion of two fingers pointing at them then pointing at my eyes. "Your attention up here. Focus, students. Focus. Sit down and listen."

I hoped my voice didn't crack or waver. I was nervous. It was inevitable. I knew those doors wouldn't hold forever and there was no way we could continue to exist inside this room. All I could do was prepare them, this small collection of students, for the inescapable. I tossed my suit jacket to the floor then yanked on my tie and pulled on it. The tie slithered from the edge of my collar where it had been constricting around my neck to flutter to the floor. My fingers quickly undid the top shirt button. I decided I was going to be comfortable.

"Professor Franklin," a student yelled. "What are we to do?"

I scrutinized him: probably a sophomore, from a well-to-do family and very scared. I didn't know him or at least didn't recognize him from any of my classes, but with such a large campus, I couldn't be expected to know every student.

"First, sit down," I said. "There won't be any need to take notes; anything you write down won't matter in an hour." I grabbed a book from the pile I had perilously stacked by the podium. "Just listen and try to remember everything I tell you. This will be a quick lesson on zombies."

"An hour?" somebody asked. "You think they'll get to us that soon?"

The doors rattled loudly and the moaning, which up to now had been very low, increased in volume and again drew all of our attention to the back of the auditorium.

"Attention. Focus. Focus," I said while once again making the fingers-to-eyes motion. "We all know what exists beyond these walls. We know that at some point they will break the locks, chains and everything else we've put up to hold them at bay. I said an hour but it may only be fifteen minutes. I don't know. Let me get this session going." I slammed the book onto the wooden podium desktop and opened it; the microphone blasting the noise of me frantically turning pages.

The wide-eyed, frantic look of a young girl in the front row caught my attention. I was reminded how many times I had to beg the students to move down front so I wouldn't have to yell. Today? They huddled close to the stage, putting as much distance between them and the rattling chains at the back of the auditorium.

"We have to be able to get out of here, professor," another student yelled. "We have to!"

THUNK! Something hit the doors at the center of the auditorium.

"Please listen to me," I said above the hysterical screams. "I know you don't want to hear this but they will soon break those barriers down and then..." I let the sentence die.

"What can we do?"

"Not really too much except to try to remember what I'm going to tell you now," I said, watching the group. "Take a seat and listen."

I studied them for a few moments; there were about thirty-five students and two other professors. They milled absently, glancing at the doors at the back of the auditorium. Suddenly I was reminded by their actions, short of outstretched arms, they weren't too dissimilar from the zombies just beyond; the creatures we loathed and were hiding from. I motioned for the group to grab a seat.

"Why should we listen to you, Professor Franklin?" came a dissenting voice from the back. "Who made you the expert?"

"I didn't say I was an expert," I replied. "I said this was going to be a crash course on the phenomenon of the walking dead that we're experiencing; welcome to Zombies 101. I only said I can give you information – information that will help you when the unavoidable happens."

THUNK! The door and chains rattled.

"I'll make this quick," I said. "Here are some things to remember. One." I held one finger in the air. "Remain calm at all times. Screaming in a high pitch will only bring attention to yourself. Two..." I had two fingers waving in the air. "Try to stay away from heavily populated areas. You shop for food at a grocery store, zombies look for food at malls, big cities and campuses. Three..." I held the fingers high into the air above my head. I looked left, then right. "If that asshole Professor Holliwell hadn't dropped that vial of viral zombosis over at the Astrobiology lab while studying the zombie epidemic, well, we wouldn't be here, barricaded in." I grimaced and lowered my hand. The answers were flip and not what they wanted to hear, that much I knew.

THUNK! This time the right side was being attacked. The zombies had attempted all three access points. We remained safe but I knew it was just a matter of time.

"When are you really going to tell us something?" a student cried. "Because that last part was a bunch of crap. It seems we're trapped inside here with little chance of rescue. Sure Holliwell might have slipped up and dropped the vial so you can point a finger at him for turning everyone into a zombie. But the fact remains, here we are, barricaded and no hope. You called us here... why?"

"Why? I'll tell you why. First thing," I said leaning into the microphone and glancing at my notes. "Zombies are mindless creatures. You may recognize one as a friend, a lover, a family member. Trust me, it's not them. Not any more. They don't know anyone anymore, except as food. Totally mindless."

"Mindless? That's what you say," somebody yelled. "They're trying to get at us. That isn't mindless. They are working together as a team to get in here. So I'm thinking they know us... they just have to."

"No," I replied and moved to the center of the stage. "First, they don't know you; you are nothing but a food source. Plus, they aren't working together. Each one is working separately of its own volition. They're dead. Rigor mortis has set in and yet, by some strange reason, they continue to move. Totally mind dead. Remember, they can't think, therefore they are not working together."

THUNK!

"That's bullshit!" a young man's voice called out. "It sounds like they have something very heavy that they're trying to use as a battering ram. More than one of them is carrying it."

"Again, trust me," I pleaded. "They are working for their own reasons only. They are not, I repeat, NOT working as a team. Three or four of them may be using some form of battering ram but it is more by trial and error than anything else. At any point, one or more of them may drop the ram for their own purpose of attack. Let me show you."

"The moaning," a female voice cried. "Make it stop."

"I can't," I said. "Now hear me out." I walked back to the podium and picked up the remote to the projector and began flashing images onto the screen. "Zombies can't run, they have no motor skills other than the most rudimentary; hence the rigid walk. Like I said before, a form of rigor mortis has set in. This can work to your advantage for only so long. As more and more humans become zombies, you will have less and less safe areas where you can hide. You can run only so long." I looked about the group. "Some of you may run longer than others; of that I am quite sure."

THUNK. Cr...unch. The door still held even though wood had broken.

"Oh my god!" It was Helen Bigsley, the only female professor to make it to the auditorium. I watched Professor Howard Mueller, my associate, console her with a comforting arm about her.

"Our time is getting close," I yelled to gain their attention again and flashed an image of a cut-away human brain on the screen. "We're at a medical school so allow me to use the resources. There is a logical aspect to this zombie phenomenon that we are experiencing. A zombie's rage is due strictly to an uncontrolled amygdala running amuck with the frontal lobe via the non-functioning anterior cingulate cortex, which is illustrated here in Dr. Mueller's research from 1998. This is what the virus causes." I used the electronic pointer to circle the area of my explanation. "With no frontal lobe modulation or dampening, a zombie only has anger; anger which is exacerbated by hunger."

"Right, professor," a male student yelled. "And it's us they want to eat. How can we stop it?"

This was the question I knew was coming and dreaded. How does one stop a creature with only a single desire? Every zombie's one goal was to devour human flesh; not cows, not dogs, not anything else but soft, living, human flesh.

"Professor?"

I glanced to the source; it was Helen Bigsley. "They're going to kill us, aren't they?"

I hesitated; my answer would cause pandemonium and hysteria. I slowly nodded my head in agreement. "Not necessarily kill us but eat us while we still live. We'll die from blood loss, shock or some other bodily trauma. Due to the base cause of our death, zombie consumption and therefore viral contamination, we will re-animate as a zombie." There was silence; utter silence... except for the banging at the auditorium doors and the rattling chains.

THUNK!.. UNK!... UNK! The sound moved from left to right, like a stereophonic headphone sound moving through the mind. Three hits. All three entrances to the auditorium had been assailed in unison. My eyes widened at the thought of the zombies, that dead group beyond this room, becoming organized. It was unthinkable; they were senseless creatures with no thought processes.

"You said zombies couldn't think! Sure looks like you're wrong, professor." The young man folded his arms over chest defiantly, the expression on his face almost a smirk.

"Never mind," I yelled over the grumbling mayhem the assault had caused. "There are still a few things you must know before they get through... and they will get through."

"I'm too young to die," a female student wailed.

"You're too young to die? I'm too young to die. Face it, dear, we're all too young to die," I said from the stage. I slid my finger down my quickly jotted notes. "Ah... yes. Just remember, if you decide to run, never run up."

"What the hell does that mean? Run up?" It was the male student again.

"Exactly what I said," I yelled back. "Never run up the stairs to a higher location unless you have a definite and safe way to get back down. Stairs and ladders to a roof only puts you on a smaller playing field and that means limited square footage to distance yourself between the zombies. The zombies will get up there and they will continue to come and come. They will surround the house, and if you are up there as a viable food source, they will find a way to you. There is no escape."

My eyes caught a movement at the windows and I stared up at them. There was definitely movement. Could it be birds? I was startled when what appeared as a bloody hand was plastered on the window. It disappeared. How had the zombies gotten that high? How long before they broke the glass. It was tempered, reinforced; it could hold for a bit. I frowned. For a bloody hand, there was no imprint. Suddenly the hand was back – and thankfully I realized it wasn't a hand; it was only a bird. I sighed in relief. At least I didn't have to worry about zombies coming in through the windows; at least, not yet.

I caught Professor Mueller's eye. He shook his head in resignation and held Helen closer. He knew the end was near.

THU... CR...UNCH. The chains rattled loudly and I could

hear them jolting the doors to an abrupt stop. The chains held. The zombies had broken the doors open but they were being tightly held, secured by the metal chains. We were still protected but only for a few more minutes.

"Students! Listen!" I screamed. "The enemy has stormed the final embattlement, but we are still safe. Let me finish my explanation."

We all could hear the wood and metal being abused. The moans, groans and grunting increased in volume. We waited.

"As I stated, the living dead are just that, living dead." I flashed another image on the screen. "Zombies have lost all bodily functions; and only the dysfunctional neural system keeps them going. A part of that system connects to the ventromedial hypothalamus and if that it isn't working properly..." I shook my head. "What that means is this: No matter how much a zombie eats, it is never ever satisfied. Those of you in the upper classes know hyperphagia is the result of a improperly functioning ventrodedial hypothalamus."

A young girl in the front frowned at me. "What?" she asked while scratching her forehead.

"Hyperphagia," I said, reaching down and grabbing another book, third one down from the top of the pile. The top two books fell to the floor, the rest of the books swayed, careened, and then crashed into a heap on the stage. I slapped the retrieved book onto the podium and opened it to the marked page. "Yes, here it is. Hyperphagia is the abnormal or binge eating of great quantities of food. It is usually associated with bulimia." I looked up at the students and smiled. "And, of course, this applies to our zombies. They eat and eat, never filling up." I hesitated. "And they don't have bulimia, either."

CRUNCH! The door broke.

Zombies stumbled through the opening. There was screaming and mayhem in the crowd at my feet. The zombies moaned and stiffly moved in our direction. Their arms were outstretched toward us in a feeble attempt to snag a victim.

They groaned loudly.

The students I'd been dealing with huddled at the foot of the stage then started to climb up on stage, to higher ground, with me. There was a lot of screaming and some of the higher voices were the males. Absolute fear.

"We are faced with death," I yelled. "The zombies are attacking and there is nothing more that I can do to save you. Remember, as best you can, what I have told you."

"Oh, their moaning," the young girl wailed. "I wish it would stop. It's driving me insane." She pulled at her hair and shook her head.

"It won't," I said. "Zombies have to moan. It is their curse. They have lost most body functions and therefore only eat and eat, but can't get rid of it. You see I have determined something extremely important – zombies are constipated. They are obviously moaning from the pain."

"So what is your suggestion, professor?" It was the male student who had been giving me the most problems. He now was in front me, his hands twisting my shirt up in his gripping fingers. He might have even been the one with the high-pitched scream I had heard mere seconds earlier; his eyes were wide with terror.

I smiled calmly and narrowed my eyes.

"When you come back as a zombie... only small bites and extreme controlled eating," I replied softly and felt rough hands grab me from behind, pulling me from the student's hold. Teeth sunk into my shoulder. "Remember, students. Only nibble."

INSIDE WHERE
IT'S WARM

by Lee Thomas

Clouds the colors of rotted meat and tumor spit ashen rain and sleet, and through the pelting downpour, colliding with concrete like the stomping boots of a clumsy army, a scream rises and quickly fades, and I turn to the sound from reflex. Peering between white houses that stare at me like the faces of forlorn ghosts, I see nothing in the gloom and continue my trek down the middle of the road. I am chilled but this is a reaction to the weather, not the fleeting protest of a stranger who is soon enough beyond the fingertips of hope.

My jaw clenches against the cold, knuckles ache from clutching the iron bar, my leg throbs as it has for days, and I think it would have been better to wait until morning to manage my errand, because the early evening is as dimly lit as a waning dusk, except the rain provides cover, masking the sounds of me and the heat of me in icy torrent, and I speculate they do not hunt by sight, or else they would always be at one another. Too little was said about the threat before the newscasts died because too little was known. So I can only guess. I walk down the center of the road, trusting my eyes perhaps more than is wise, and counting on my legs, even the damaged one, to get me far beyond danger should it arise.

I left the city to avoid the problems of a great population, and this decision proved sufficiently warranted, but my preparation was <u>not</u> sufficient – all too shortsighted. I accounted for food and drink and warmth, but failed in one important regard, and it is because of this that I expose myself to the wandering threats as I move toward the center of a town no longer thriving – hardly living at all.

She walks across a distant yard, a spirit in a flowing nightdress, and she turns to me and one of her arms raises in a half wave and I think to wave back, but her gait is familiar and in no way inviting, her steps leaden, her knees locked as if bound in braces. She lifts her other arm and moves across the lawn, untended grass a tide of filaments brushing her ankles, and she approaches me like a crippled mother desperately trying to reach a beloved child. I continue along the white line in the street, and she changes course, and soon her bare feet shuffle onto the sidewalk and seem to disappear as if her skin wears an identical shade to the damp concrete.

Her hope is to greet me in the middle of the road. I survey the landscape, the lonely, unlit houses, the overgrown lawns, the track of street at my back covered in a screen of sleet, and I see we are alone this woman and I.

Led by chipped and torn nails, guiding her to me, she appears serene. Once, not long ago, she was beautiful, with delicate features, lips plumped by nature or needle, and silky skin, but her eyes, which had certainly been lovely, were now bleached of color, many shades paler than the emerald they'd once been, and a thin cowl of sopping hair frames her too gaunt face in an unflattering way. Amid the weather she seems a black and white image, projected on a screen agitated with static.

The iron bar bites into her scalp and follows her down. I step back and observe her fingers, once crowned with impeccably painted nails, which are now serrated and stripped of polish in unflattering tracks. She lies motionless, and I check over my shoulder to be sure none of her breed has found opportunity in my distraction, and we are still alone this woman and I, only she is beyond concern.

Then I continue on my way.

At the edge of town I see five more like the woman, but they are enrapt with a banquet, crouching over the body of an obese man wearing red canvas sneakers and blue sweat pants, the latter being devoured in great swatches along with the meat and fat beneath. I have come to understand they are never quite so vulnerable as when they eat. The ritual of feeding mesmerizes them, and if it weren't for fear of summoning more, I could draw my pistol and execute each of them without disturbing the others until the bullets ended their trances, but the food distracts and incapacitates them and this is an opportunity, so I cross to the far sidewalk and make my way onto Main Street.

My thoughts wander and I recall a party I attended. Like Poe's *Masque*, the privileged gathered in a penthouse apartment to toast their good fortunes while small fires dotted the city below. The crowd, drunk and jovial, made me uneasy, as crowds often do, so I spent much of the evening at the window, gazing down at the panic and the pockets of flame licking the distant streets. A man approached me, a handsome mannequin draped in Italian wool and arrogance. He suggested we spend the evening in a spare room, naked and together while the city collapsed, because it was his intent to overdose on pain pills and found the idea of being fucked as he drifted into death appealing. I turned away from this offer and again peered through the glass, downward. Men and women ran and cars collided, but the celebratory gathering heard none of the commotion. Screams couldn't travel so high. The next morning, I left the party and convinced that the outbreak was not an incident so much as a movement, I packed a bag and loaded the car and drove to the North while the police and army kept brittle control of the situation.

I found this town and settled in. The supply of medication

I brought from the city lasted until this morning.

The glass door of the drug store is smashed. I look into the gloom and take the flashlight from my pocket and shine it over the wreckage within. Shelves are toppled and the floor is littered with boxes and packets and pools of shampoo. That this place has been looted is of no surprise. It offered food for the scavenger, supplies for the wounded and sick, and free dreams for the addict. I step inside and pain flares at my shin. I wince and continue into the shop, stepping over a cardboard display that had once held cheap dog toys. The lantern beam reveals one derelict aisle after another, but nothing moves here save me, and I make my way to the back of the store, picking through the wreckage, cautious so that I don't wound my legs a second time.

The Plexiglas shield that once guarded the pharmacist from his patrons wears an enormous black-rimmed hole. A creative junkie burned his way through a barrier he could not smash. On the floor at the foot of the counter, I see the discarded tank of acetylene and note the tremendous streak of blood it lies in. The smear runs like a poorly painted trail along the back aisle and veers right. I pause and listen, though feel no genuine concern.

The afflicted are quiet in their state, but they are clumsy. It would be impossible for one of them to move through the store's debris with any degree of stealth.

I climb onto the counter and work my way through the hole and drop onto the pharmacy's linoleum floor. Then I begin to search. As I expect, the shelves have been picked through, but I'm grateful to see they are not barren. My light falls over each shelf and I examine the labels on the remaining bottles and on a bottom shelf I am grateful to find one labeled: Truvada. The weight of the bottle is a relief. It goes into the backpack brought for this chore and I return to my search, finding labels that read Viramune, Viread, Zerit and Epivir – all names from the dosage chart I keep in my pocket. They too go in the backpack, rattling like muffled maracas as they drop into place.

Though I consider seeking out a pain medication for the ache in my leg, it strikes me as a waste of time. The addicts – those not dragged away by the wandering threat – would have made a priority of the numbing prescriptions, and the safety and the warmth of the house call me.

Back through the charred hole. I hit the floor, and like an echo of my soles' impact, I hear the hiss of a box whooshing across the floor at the front of the shop. I secure the backpack over my shoulders and put the flashlight in my left hand, retrieving the iron from my belt loop with the right. I stand perfectly still, listening for more noise, but hear only the rapping downpour on the street outside.

Satisfied that whatever shares this chamber with me is not moving in my direction, I follow the smear of blood across the back of the store and turn right, and then I pause again because the weather's chill is intensified by uncertainty as I peer down the aisle. The murky air, visible through the shattered front door, shifts strangely; indistinct shapes drift and sway as if caught in an ocean tide, and a new sound, this one clearly caused by a bit of metal clacking on the linoleum in a nearby aisle, sends tremors through my chest.

I move toward it, iron bar raised, flashlight beam illuminating the side of an end cap where condoms are displayed. This seems the only product untouched by foragers.

He steps into the back aisle. Not long ago he was someone's young son, with chestnut hair grown long over his ears and brow. A pea coat too large for his youthful frame drapes from his shoulders. His cheeks are full and his eyes shine like bits of brown glass in the disk of light bathing his face. The bar arcs high over my head, and I begin the downward swing, when I'm struck by the color in his eyes – still vibrant – and the boy cringes, throwing an arm above his head to ward off the blow, and the bar stops just short of crushing his elbow.

I tell him I'm sorry and that he's safe, and he tells me he was with his grandfather and lost the old man in town, and he saw my light, and he'd hoped to find the man here, and the grandfather was wearing blue sweatpants and red sneakers, and had I seen the man.

I had seen the man, but the truth of what I'd witnessed wouldn't comfort the boy. I asked him his name, and he hesitates to share it with me but finally says, David.

A number of lies, meant to quell the boy's unease and keep him quiet so we would not follow too closely in his grandfather's steps, rolls through my mind, and I know David will fight all of them. So I tell him that I spoke to his grandfather, and his brown eyes light up hopefully. Then I tell him that I had promised the old man I would take David to a house where the man waited with others.

The boy wants to believe me, but he is reticent and shuffles back a step. He looks about uncertainly and when he gazes into the aisle on his right, his face goes slack.

I step forward and swing the light in that direction, and it falls on four trudging figures. Not long ago, the man leading these wanderers was an executive, with a stout confident face and a wave of white hair. He wears a blue suit that would have been expensive, reminding me of the arrogant partygoer who'd considered fucking an appropriate preface to suicide. This executive's hand is missing three fingers and his suit sleeve is torn at the shoulder. Flanking him, two women of diametrically opposed attractiveness teeter from side to side as if each step is their last before collapse. The person behind is unidentifiable save for a swatch of jutting red hair.

Then more of these broken wanderers appear at the front of the aisle, and more still until it is clear this boy, David, has led an ample contingent into the shop. I dash to the far aisle and see that it too fills like a chute guiding cattle to the trough. As quickly as possible, I race back to the boy and scoop him up in an arm, causing him to squeal a sharp protest. Pain flares along my shin from ankle to knee as I support his added weight, but I carry him to the burned portal above the pharmacy counter. With a clumsy motion I throw him at the hole, and he drops heavily across the lower frame, but manages to scramble inside without further sound. Then I follow, and my backpack catches on the upper edge of the hole. I twist and fight, terribly conscious of the vulnerability of my body's lower extremities. Finally I manage to work my way through the hole and drop onto the linoleum, coming down hard on my elbow. Adrenaline deadens the pain. Again on my feet, I turn to the compromised shield and the breath slips out of my chest. From where I stand it seems that these dreadful wanderers occupy every inch of floor space. To the left I see the former executive, pushing against the back of a man in an open bathrobe. The man's torso is shredded, decimated by teeth and nails, leaving only a great sheet of scab running from his throat to the chasm in his belly, and from this hollow to his devoured crotch.

David pulls on the sleeve of my jacket to get my attention, except I can't turn away from the spectacle before me. The people beyond the barrier – those in shadow and those in my light's cast – move forward and back in unison as if swaying to music pumped over a frequency only they can hear, and for a heartbeat's time, I envy their unity and wish to feel it, regardless of the perverse rite of passage joining them requires. It is an odd notion, one that surely has roots in my life before this town.

Then David is pleading with me and I turn away, uncertain of what he thinks I can accomplish. We are meat in a butcher's window. The boy insists we have to leave, and a chuckle of disbelief rises in my throat, but I kill it on my tongue. Telling him our situation is hopeless will solve nothing. We might wait, hidden behind the shelves, hoping the wanderers lose interest or forget of our existence, but that is foolish. Already an overweight, black-haired girl with bloodstained braces, wearing a T-shirt that reads "Unclean," attempts to climb onto the counter, her eyes focused on the gap as hotly as the acetylene torch that created it.

David again pulls my sleeve and I follow him, wondering what this boy intends. He leads me to the last row of shelves and points into a gloomy alcove beyond. I lift the light and it falls on a door, and I feel a bolt of embarrassment that I should have thought the store possessed a single entrance and exit.

Before approaching it, I check the partition and see the plump girl with the grisly braces wriggling through the hole, one arm extended in full as if reaching for an invisible handle to grasp for leverage. Her jaws snap at the light's beam, which glints off her dental work creating tiny blades of reflection. Then I swing the flashlight back to the door and find that David has already opened it, and the sound of rain crackles in the pharmacy. I follow him outside, into the cold and angry sleet, and a sharp wing of wind beats over my neck. The back alley of the store is empty, only dumpsters holding month-old trash, slowly decomposing in the metal bins.

The narrow corridor amplifies the angry sounds of storm as downpour claps on concrete, steel, brick, and filth. I ask the boy to stand behind me and lead him to the end of the alley, and he asks why I'm limping, and I tell him I hurt myself.

Are you bit?

He delivers the question with such disgust and fear, I think to ask him what he intends to do about it if I am, but I clamp down on the ire, pinning it to my tongue, and tell him the truth. The limp is the result of a poorly fashioned booby trap set in one of the neighborhood houses I'd been scavenging soon after trading the city for this place. Upon arriving in town, I met a group of men and women and stayed with them briefly. On one of the daily gathering excursions, my foot went through a sabotaged stair step, and though sprains and breaks had been avoided, a jutting nail had torn a considerable gash in my pant leg and the shin beneath.

David insists I show him the wound, and I lift my damp pant leg and show him the bandage. When he insists I peel this back, I release the gathered fabric, allowing the cuff to return to its place at my ankle and tell him we have more important things to worry about and I'm not about to risk infection – another infection – to assuage his curiosity.

The exit from the town, along a different street, one not littered by the boy's grandfather, is uneventful. Night closes fast, and the ice and water continue to pelt, dropping furiously from the tumor-hued cumulus. The cold is inside of me now, affixing to muscle, vein, and bone. The threats we see are distant, on side streets, wandering aimlessly in circles, and if they notice us, it is without interest. I lead the boy to my house but do not take him inside. Instead, I continue along the street to the house on the corner where the others live, and he asks if his grandfather is inside and I lie and assure him that the old man is safely wrapped in a blanket, chatting happily with a fine group of people.

After I knock, a sour-faced man who not long ago had been a promising corporate attorney opens the door and points a sleek, silver pistol at my face. His name is Cameron and he wears a blue cotton dress shirt over black slacks. His blond hair droops shapelessly over his brow. He asks what I want and I introduce him to David and ask if he will get Erica for me. Cameron frowns more deeply, the expression comical in its extremity. He waves us in and checks over our shoulders to make sure I have brought no threat upon the house in the way that David invited it to the drug store.

Inside a battery-powered lantern glows weakly from the staircase. The windows of this house have been covered with plywood sheets and reinforced with studs so that little natural light enters. Pockets of shadow float at the top of the stairs and in the room to my left where I feel people are gathered, though I cannot see them.

211

Where's Granddad?

David's question takes me off guard. I don't want to have to explain the old man's fate to him and wish Erica would appear so she can relieve me of this repugnant obligation. Cameron presents me with bitter eyes and pinched lips, and I repeat my request to see Erica. He looks from me to the boy and back again and then nods. I hold David by the shoulder and tell him that his grandfather is probably napping in one of the bedrooms, and we will wait for Erica to take him. Faces begin to appear in the wells of shadow at David's back. The men and women come forward slowly, holstering their weapons as they approach and all greet us with smiles and ask me how I am feeling, and I tell them I am fine, and I assure them I will be leaving soon, and this casual statement, delivered without a hint of acidity causes them to frown.

I introduce David to the eight men and women, and he tells them he wants to see his grandfather, and questions alight and then vanish from their brows as they understand why I've brought the boy to them.

Mindy offers to get David a blanket.

Chet hurries off to find the boy a cup of tea.

The others comment on the necessity of these tokens of warmth and how much they will soothe the boy, who has yet to understand the extent of his misery.

Erica walks into the foyer of the house. Not long ago she was a caring, full-figured woman with red hair and compassionate eyes. She still is.

I ask Burt to show David into the living room and then lead Erica to the back of the house. In the kitchen, I explain what has happened to David's grandfather, and that I withheld the information from the boy because I didn't want him to panic, and she tells me I've done the right thing, and she will speak to him immediately. I thank her and open the back door, making to leave.

Erica tells me I can stay. She tells me I should stay. I tell her I can't stay and return to the storm.

Crossing the backyards, through hedges and over low fences, my leg aching with each step, I am barely aware of my surroundings, but no threat approaches and I reach the back door to my house without incident. Inside, I light the lantern. This house has been similarly shielded with boards and studs – a final kindness from the survivors down the street, the men and women who cast me out.

I peel off my wet clothes and retrieve a towel from a stack I keep in the hall closet. Once dry I pull on fresh clothes and wrap myself in a duvet. I take a can of ravioli and a bottle of water to the sofa and sit down for my supper, but the tepid meal slips down my throat like a mudslide landing hard and gritty in my stomach. I retrieve the pill bottles from my backpack and swallow one Truvada and one Viramune, and then I return to the sofa and hike my pant leg to examine the cut on my shin.

It still hasn't healed. The red gash appears wet and fresh in the flat glow of the lantern. Blood has long since stopped seeping from the wound, but it does not scab and it does not close. The skin at the wounds lips carries the same cranberry stain it showed the afternoon of its infliction. It appears neither aggravated nor infected, but it has been two weeks since the nail gouged my leg and it continues to resist amelioration, and though I don't know what this means, I know it must mean something.

I curl up on the sofa, wrapped tightly in the duvet. I think about what I told the boy about my injury. Though not a lie, it wasn't the whole of the truth either.

I entered a home with others, intent on looting supplies, and I did crash through a step that had been worn away with a saw or file. All true. But after freeing myself from the rigged staircase, leg searing with the fresh cut, I returned to the front of the house and found Cameron in a corner of the living room. He had lost his gun or had set it down at some point, leaving himself unarmed. He held his empty hands in front of him as three rotting wanderers closed in. Their focus on him made their deaths easy. I crushed one's head with the iron and the other two didn't even turn my direction. The second was similarly subdued, and all should have been well, except Cameron found his courage and retrieved a bronze obelisk from a tabletop and swung at the third. Its head exploded into a fetid spray of bone and tissue and fluid, covering me from face to foot.

I had not been bitten, but that didn't exempt me from infection.

Upon our return, Erica insisted on treating my wounds and noted the debris covering the wound on my leg. After cleaning and binding the gash, she offered me a distracted smile and excused herself.

They held their arraignment while I dozed on a bed upstairs, and when I woke Erica, Cameron and Burt stood in the room, the two men aiming pistols at my head. I was told that I'd remain under guard to see if my system had been compromised, and I did not argue their logic. That night, while I slept, they held their trial and I woke to find I'd been found guilty. A bite could kill and turn a man in less than twelve hours, and though I had already exceeded this window period the uncommon nature of my wound – its failure to clot – was suspect, and with great sadness and apology they asked that I leave for the safety of the others in the house.

It never occurred to me to argue.

In honesty, I had been considering my future with this band of men and women for days before the accident. Already they spoke of repopulation and of building a society devoted to the Bible's word – for certainly this was a Rapture – and who could say which words from this book would soothe them and guide them in the months to come? I would be useless to them in regard to fatherhood, having carried an established infection into this fresh pandemic – to say nothing of my repugnance for the act – and as to their philosophies regarding a future of god-fearing, black-and-white morality… it comforted me little. I also feared that a gathering of their size provided more opportunity for exposure – the safety of numbers outweighed by the necessity for those numbers to eat and move about. Cameron and the other men relied on their guns, each report a siren, calling the rotted vessels to port, and there were the arguments, the affiliations, the jostlings for power, this group already eager to rekindle politics and government – a new society like a fungus growing from the decay of the old.

So I left the house and they helped me secure this place, and they apologized for their decision, which was unnecessary, and I thanked them, and they returned to the house on the corner. I was left alone and found it acceptable.

Chilled now, I pull the duvet closer to my neck and curl into a tighter ball, staring at the plywood sheets intended to keep the world out.

The loneliness is manageable, if only because it was well rehearsed before the outbreak, not that I practiced misanthropy or reveled in the anti-social. If anything I felt unmoved by the cultural touchstones that so greatly occupied the interests of other people. I didn't follow the television programs dissected and analyzed at office gatherings, preferring documentaries and British crime dramas; nor did I read the latest literary phenomenon, because the voices of Monette and White rang truer to my ears; nor did I take joy or offense at anything a pop musician, movie star, or inexplicable celebrity did or said. This disinterest in glittering culture evolved without calculation, never occurring to me that others should include or exclude me based on such fragile and transient bits of interest. I found politics ridiculous, as logic wasn't allowed to bridge the gaps formed by the Right and the Left. Useful discussion was mutilated as it attempted to cross the laser fences separating the two camps. Religions offered similar obstacles and similar intolerance. I found so many things incomprehensible, so many just plain foolish, and it left me outside – out in the cold, as they say – because I could not with any sincerity claim to belong to this group or that.

Similar estrangement marked my intimate life, not only because of the virus that required awkward disclosure but also for my inability to weave another man into my heart and head. It seemed that my partners always required more than I could give them – more attention, more time, more understanding. They would play games to spark a reaction in me, and I never understood the rules of their games, so I always lost, and they always left. I felt like a cog, filed and sanded, with no teeth left to grip the other gears in the machine.

I drift into dreamless sleep, and come morning the pain in my leg bleats me awake as efficiently as an alarm clock. Through a narrow gap in the plywood, I see the empty street outside, still gray though the storm has passed. The pavement and the grass are wet and the bleak scene sends me back to the sofa, where I doze as the morning hours pass. At noon I take my medications and as an afterthought pop four ibuprofen caplets in the hope that the ache below my knee will subside.

Overnight the pain had escalated, and though still tolerable it concerns me. I check the wound and find it has not changed. No swelling, no discharge, no further discoloration. It remains as it was two weeks ago, and certainly this indicates my system has been compromised, but I am alive long after other infected men would have turned to threat, and I consider the pills I take for the first infection and wonder if they have some affect on this new one. The doctor told me it was a control not a cure.

Fatigued, I lie down and rest my eyes, and I think of the boy, David, and hope that he has come to terms with his grandfather's absence. I know that Erica will do all that she can for him, as she did all that she could for me. Meager light – all the plywood allows to enter – comes and goes, and it is again night. Hunger pulls me from the sofa and I eat a can of deviled ham and a packet of crackers and drink a bottle of water. I take my evening dose of pills and more ibuprofen, and then I put the battery-powered lantern on the table behind me and read a poorly translated German mystery found in the home office down the hall. Soon enough, I am sleep.

I'm startled awake in the middle of the night by a tremor in my leg. Fingers of electricity turn to lightning in my veins, shooting from the cut below my knee to the base of my skull, but then I realize my mistake. The wound is the destination – one of many – not the source of this electrical disturbance. Shocks erupt in my head and fan out, coursing across my system in tingles that at first terrify me and then soothe. The pain in my leg vanishes, leaving only a tickle on the skin, and I lay there in the soft glow of the lantern, gazing at the lake of shadow pooling across the ceiling, and I feel certain that something has passed, though I am unable to identify it.

Come morning, a voice in the street summons me to the window, and I press my face to the plywood and gaze through the narrow opening. In the center of the road, Erica calls my name. My hands form claws against the planks, scratching.

Wanderers close in on her from all sides, shuffling eagerly in a tightening circle. I think she should turn around and run, build up enough momentum to break through the encroaching mass, and I wonder where her people are and why she's alone in the middle of the street. I make it to the door and fumble with the locks, momentarily confused by the knobs and bolts and the chain. I need to reach her, need to help.

I throw the door open and step onto the porch, moving as quickly as my legs will allow. The wound no longer hurts, but it feels as if I'm walking through a pool of gelatin. Relativity makes each step an eternity. Erica sees me and screams for me to hurry, and I want to hurry. I want to help. I briefly think of an iron bar and how it should have been in my hand, except the crowd closes on her, and there isn't time, and I'm compelled forward.

I reach the back of the mob and without concern wade into

217

its midst, throwing my shoulders from side to side to clear a path. Ahead of me, I see Erica's face, but a decaying hand clutches her hair, and holds her tight by a fistful of carrot-red strands knotted in its palm. She cries out to me. David has run away, and it's too late to help her, and I have to help David, but I continue forward, striking out blindly to clear my path to her.

Then she is gone, dragged to the ground as numerous bodies crouch and bend, ripping at her clothes and her skin, and I feel I am too late, but I continue to her, and at her side I find room between a man who shakes his head furiously to rip away a piece of her thigh, and another man who chews hungrily on her left breast, and I kneel down and run my fingers over her bare belly, reveling in the velvety sensation of her. My nails hook into her skin and lines of red open like hungry lips.

I lean down and sink my teeth into the meat and my mouth fills with sensation not flavor. The flesh sends waves of warmth over my tongue and down my throat and into my nervous system until the chill is gone, and only then do I realize how very long I've suffered the cold.

And it occurs to me I am no different from those who crowd me and shove and push for their morsel of heat; we are of a single philosophy, united. Not long ago, I was alive and alone, and now, having shed the detritus of the individual, I find camaraderie in the single-minded horde, and I know each mouthful brings me closer to them.

I tear at the small wound and shovel bits of skin and fat and muscle into my mouth and each grinding of my teeth stokes the fire in my veins. Fingers, painted thickly with blood, gratefully dig, snagging on viscera and shredded tissue, and I want to go deeper, to hollow this thing out, and I want to be small, so I can climb within and swaddle like an infant held by a radiant crib of ribs and flesh, never again to feel the cold, existing forever inside, where it's warm.

SURVIVOR TALK

by Mitchel Whitington

Leslie looked up at the clock on the wall. Five minutes 'til 8 PM – almost time. A quick glance at the meters told her that the signal was strong, and since she'd filled the generator only an hour ago, power wouldn't be a problem.

The last minutes ticked away, and she took several long drags from the cigarette. In her previous life that wouldn't have even been a consideration; she ran three miles a day, ate a strict vegan diet, and drank protein shakes for a nutritional boost. She was a techno-geek then, and her job allowed her time to be outside and exercise.

But that was a different world. She took another drink from the glass of bourbon, and hit the cigarette a final time before pushing the power button on the console.

The board before her sprang to life, lights beaming, and needles on gauges finding their mark. Another button pressed, and an audio intro blared with the familiar words that she'd recorded a few months ago: "It's Zombie-Talk radio, going out to all you folks who happen to still be alive, fighting to claw through another day, and simply maintain your sanity…"

She pulled the mic close to her mouth, and softly said, "Good evening, everybody. I'm happy that you're able to tune into tonight's program." With a glance over at the tally marks on the whiteboard, she added, "And it looks like we're into day ninety-seven of this madness." Another drag, and Leslie blew the smoke up toward the ceiling. "Yep, over three months now since the world turned upside down. I wish that I could tell you that we have all kinds of hope, but I have to be honest... you're probably fucked. But let's take a listen to what's on your mind tonight. Who's on line one?" As she spoke, she pushed the button and waited for the caller.

"Oh God, Leslie, am I on? Oh Christ Jesus, oh, help, I'm in real trouble here. My boyfriend and I were trapped in a gas station bathroom, and we thought that we were safe, but all of a sudden we started hearing all this pounding on the door and–"

Leslie was already shaking her head. "Hold it, hold it, calm down and take a breath; just tell us your story."

"But that's what I'm doing – I'm in trouble! Those creatures broke through the door, and pulled my boyfriend out through the hole. They were tearing chunks out of him and clawing at his body, eating him alive and dragging him outside. When I saw that he was gone, I managed to wedge the trashcan in the hole, and I'm leaning against it now to hold it in place. But I can feel them jerking on it, and... oh God, oh no... Leslie, they're through! Help me! Please, you've got to help me, oh..." The voice stopped, and was replaced by the sounds of screaming, snapping, and tearing.

Leslie punched the Line 1 button with emphasis. "Oh, Jesus, people, what are you thinking? Could you do us all a freakin' favor and not call in if you're about to be eaten? Fucking idiot!" She took a long drink of bourbon, relishing the burning sensation in her mouth and throat. Leaning back into the mic, she said, "Okay, look, we all feel bad for you, gas station girl. But this is Zombie-Talk, not zombie victim radio. You fucked up, lady – you broke one of the four basic survival rules; you let yourself get backed into a corner. Folks, if you do something that stupid, don't even bother calling in. There's nothing that anyone can do to help you. You're food – nothing more – and I'm sorry, but none of us want to listen to you die. We've all heard enough of that."

She sat back in the chair for a moment, staring at the lights on the console, and finally leaned forward again. "Now come on you guys, call in with something good. The fact that the phone lines are still up, albeit only a few here and there, tells me that there are at least some folks out in the world trying to keep communication flowing. A lot of you still have cell phone connectivity, and someone has to be keeping that alive as well... who knows how. Obviously, some of us just don't want to get eaten!"

With another drag from the cigarette and a toss of bourbon she added, "Okay, here we go." Leslie pushed the Line 2 button. "You're on the air, caller."

"Thank you, ma'm," a squeaky male voice said, with a thick country accent. "I appreciate your program a whole lot, but I've got to tell you something important. You see, I've got this whole thing figured out."

Leslie smiled. "Okay, I'm listening. What's it all about?"

"Well, it's nothing less than the very judgment of God himself, that's what it is. And I can prove it."

She rolled her eyes, and took another hit from the cigarette. "Mister, I can hardly wait to hear what you've got on your mind."

"Okay, look at this. The whole thing started with this zombie virus, right? It showed up like a plague to kill us. Doesn't that sound at all familiar? The holy Book of Exodus, right? Just like God did with all those different plagues on Egypt, he's cursed us in a new way. He inflicted this virus on us that raises the dead to life."

Leslie sighed, "Well, I'm not sure that I'd blame God for any—"

"Oh, His hand is right there in this! Don't forget that Jesus raised the dead before – in the gospel according to St. John you can read right there how He brought Lazarus back from the dead. This is the same kinda thing."

"Sure, I remember the story from church." Leslie slowly shook her head from side to side. "But in all fairness, caller, Lazarus didn't start feeding on human flesh when he came

221

back. I don't think that it's the same thing at all."

"Oh, it is, it definitely is. But get this – what do you think's gonna happen when the zombies kill all the living people? Well, plain and simple, there won't be anything left for them to eat, and they'll all die again. The human race will have been wiped from the face of God's earth, just like it happened back in the great flood. And that's what this is – God's judgment, just like back in those days of the book of Genesis."

Leslie's finger was poised above the Line 2 button. "Okay caller, thanks, but–"

"Don't you hang up on me! Just remember that the rainbow tells us that God promised never to destroy humanity by a flood again, but he never said nothing about not doing it with zombies…"

A quick punch of the button cut the caller off. With a laugh, Leslie said, "Well, I guess that the loonies have checked in for the evening. Let's get a little more serious for a moment. I want everyone out there to remember the four simple, basic rules for dealing with zombies." She took a deep breath, and prepared for her nightly recitation. "You've heard them before, but we're gonna go over them again. I repeat them every goddamned night, 'cause they're critical if you're going to stay alive. Ready? Okay, rule number one: always look for a helping hand. I think that the terror that most people feel is that they're in this thing alone. There are others out there, though, and you have to seek them out and ask for their help."

Leslie glanced around the small room that was once a broadcast booth for a top-forty station in Little Rock. Now the entire building was empty, and she always felt alone. "Rule number two: You cannot save them, you can only release them. There's nothing in the world that you can do for these creatures except to put them out of the horrible state of being that they're in. Give them a shot to their head, or anything else that will destroy the brain or sever the spinal column from it." She picked up her glass, saw that it was empty, and reached over for the bottle to refill it. As she did, Leslie continued, "Rule number three, and this one is crucial: never get backed into a corner. That's right… if those bastards get you trapped in a blind alley, up on a roof or down in a basement, you're dead. Always have running room, because they'll swarm you like a plague of fucking locusts. And don't forget gas station girl from earlier – the one trapped in the bathroom. If that's where she and her boyfriend took refuge, then they were just asking to become zombie food… hell, they were begging for it. God rest her soul, but they ran into a dead end, and there was nowhere else to go. But there is a final rule that's much more important."

Leslie stood up, stretched, and pulled a new cigarette from the pack. Raising the mic arm up to her standing position, she said flatly, "This is key. It's the most critical thing that I can possibly tell you. If you take nothing else away from my broadcast, hear this. Rule number four: no matter what else you do, no matter what else is going on, you have to save the last bullet for yourself."

She fired the cigarette up and inhaled deeply, then coughed out the smoke. "Sorry 'bout that. As I was saying, it's imperative that you save that last bullet. If there's no way out, if you're going to die anyway, don't let your last memories be of the flesh being torn from your bones. Don't let them eat you while you lie there and helplessly watch – if it comes to that point, then put a gun in your mouth, point it up at forty-five degrees to get the back of your brain and spinal column, and pull the trigger. Go out on your own terms, and not that of those God-forsaken creatures."

Leslie paused, looking over at the bottle of bourbon. It was still half-full, which would get her through the next couple of nights. There were two full cases stored in the station manager's office, which had become her cache of supplies. Daily outings netted her food, water, gasoline, and other necessities like bourbon and cigarettes, but she found that she was having to venture out further and further to get what she needed. Several times a week she encountered the dead, but fortunately it was from the interior of the radio station van, so she'd never felt in danger.

She had fortified the old station so that she didn't have to worry when she was inside, but still, every night she drank herself into oblivion... just to try to forget about the world outside of her walls.

Plopping down into the seat again, she pushed the button for the third line. "Okay, I see that there's another caller. Who's there?"

Static spewed from the monitor speakers, along with garbled words that were indistinguishable.

In the few months that she'd been operating the station, Leslie still didn't know enough about the equipment to clean up the incoming signals. Instead, she just said, "Hello? Can you hear me?"

More static, and finally, "Lesl... Stanley from Tex...gonna try...oost the sig..."

Leslie laughed. "All right, folks, it's apparently our very own Static Stan back again! This guy calls in several times a week, just to give us little bits and pieces of a phone call. But God bless him, he's still alive." She sat up in the chair, and said, "So, what do you have for us today, Stanley?"

Static blared again, followed by, "...onna try a... oost... tand by..." The noise on the line surged, and then suddenly quieted. "Leslie, can you hear me?" The voice was strong.

"Stan? Wow, after all these weeks, you're coming in loud and clear – perfectly, in fact." She laughed, actually thrilled that he'd finally gotten through. "How'd you manage that?"

"One of our guys was able to boost the signal, at least temporarily. We're still figuring out the equipment here," the voice said. "Look, I don't know how much time we actually have, so I need to give you the details quickly. You must come to Texarkana – there is a huge human contingency inside Lone

Star Army Ammunition Plant here. Before the plague, this place was used as a munitions depot to ship supplies to American troops around the world, so it's flush with resources. Texarkana isn't exactly a small town, so we've been able to scavenge all sorts of things. It's a paradise, and since the plant was heavily fortified after the 9/11 attacks, we're relatively safe from the creatures. Please, you and all your listeners, bring your supplies and come to the main north gate of the plant off Interstate 30 just west of Texarkana. We have guards on duty 24/7, so someone will be there to let you in."

There was a twinge inside of her; a longing for hope, and for the companionship of other people. It seemed like a huge leap to just pick up and leave, but Leslie found herself immediately mapping the route between Little Rock and Texarkana in her head. If her memory served, it was only a couple of hours – a straight shot down I-30. Still, it would mean leaving the station. She shook her head to dismiss the thought. "Great information, Stan, and exactly the kind of thing that we need on Zombie-Talk." She took a sip. "So folks, if you are listening to me out there and are looking for refuge, make your way to Lone Star Army Ammunition Plan in Texarkana – if it's as big as Stan says, then it would be a great destination."

The voice blared again. "Remember – it's on the west side of town, and you can't miss it from the interstate 'cause it has its own exit. But Leslie, you've got to come as well. Do your show from here! We have a full power plant, not just generators; you'll be able to reach three states further in every direction."

She paused for more than a moment, just staring at the lights on the board. "Oh, come on, Stan," she finally said; "I mean, everything's set up here, I can reach people." After another pause, she added, "That, and I'm not getting eaten here."

"You'll reach people from here. Even thought it's all new

to us, we're figuring more and more out about the equipment every day. And you won't get eaten here, either. Speaking of such, how long can you keep going on your own? Do it! I…" the voice went into white noise.

Leslie took a deep breath, let it out slowly, and followed with a drag from the cigarette.

Static Stan's voice broke through a final time. "…remember your first rule, girl…"

She sat back in her chair. Always look for a helping hand; that was the first rule. Still, those folks were two full hours away, if not a little more. To be sure, the interstate highways were said to be safer, because they weren't used as much these days, and the dead weren't lurking there as much anymore.

On the other hand, if anything went wrong – the car died, the gas ran out, or any simple mechanical failure occurred – the dead would surely be on her like fucking vermin. The creatures were like ants showing up at a picnic; they always seemed to be attracted to the food.

Leslie scanned her board, and then went back on mic. "Well, I don't see any more callers tonight, so I guess that it's going to be a short show. I hope that doesn't mean that you're losing phone capabilities, because I've been encouraged that communications have been somewhat maintained." Her cigarette had burned almost down to the filter, so she took one last drag, and then smashed it out in the ashtray on the console. "Goodnight, you poor bastards. But…" She sat back in the chair, staring at the board. Finally leaning back up, she continued, "…if you happen to be by your radio tomorrow morning… maybe around nine… who knows. Tune the show in and we'll see what happens." She blew out a cloud of smoke, and said to herself as much as anyone else, "Maybe I'll make that trip."

She wasn't sure why she'd said that, or why she picked nine o'clock. Most nights she drank until she passed out, and then came to sometime in the late morning hours. Going west would provide an escape, though – and if she got to Stan's place and couldn't find it, or there was no one there, she'd still have half-a-day of light to get back to the station. It would be even better if she could figure out how to broadcast along the way.

Perhaps the biggest unknown was how that would work. She assumed that the station van had some kind of broadcast capability, but of course had never used it, even though she routinely took the vehicle – sporting the small dish on top – for her supply raids. With all the disruption of services because of the apocalypse, who knew what was working and what wasn't. Still, she got calls from landlines and cell phones everyday, and although there were tales of widespread outages, some things were still working.

* * * * *

When the buzzing of her alarm went off at seven, Leslie sat bolt upright in bed. It had been a long time since she'd actually planned her day. She considered going straight to the studio for a morning bracer of bourbon, but then thought better of it – if she was really going to make the trip, she'd need all her senses clear.

The previous night began to solidify through the haze of her memory. She's packed the station van, put an extra battery that she'd taken from another vehicle on board for power, and got everything ready to go. At some point the fog absorbed the evening, because she had no idea when she went to bed. Everything was ready to go, though.

The realization hit her – she was leaving.

It took only half an hour for her to shower and wash her hair, something that was becoming more rare. When no one saw you, there wasn't any pressure to clean up. She even shaved her legs and pits, not knowing what the day would bring.

227

Leslie took a walk through the old radio station, looking for anything else that needed to be packed, but also just reminiscing. When it all started, she'd been chased inside by the creatures, and blockaded herself there. In only a short time, she had begun broadcasting her radio show every evening. Although it had been her home for only three months, it seemed like a lifetime.

As the dead eventually lost interest in her refuge in favor of more vulnerable targets, she came to see it as a bastion of safety. With each week she fortified it more, and it was truly an impenetrable fortress. She felt safe; it was her cocoon, a womb protecting her from the evils of the outside world. But she knew that it was time to leave. In the garage, she climbed into the van and clicked the seat belt across her body.

Before starting out, she checked her revolver in its belt holster – a Smith & Wesson Model 642 with five rounds of .38 Special, Hydra-Shock ammunition... enough to stop a zombie cold. She also had two extra five-round speed loaders in the glove box, along with a box of ammo. Not that she was an expert on firearms, but as her mother used to say, necessity is the mother of invention. In her scavenging over the past few months, she'd found a book on shooting at one of those coffee shop bookstores, and then picked out a weapon of choice from a pawnshop – along with an arsenal of back-up goodies that she'd never had to use. She'd trained herself on the 642 and felt comfortable with it. Hopefully she wouldn't need to fire a single shot today, but Leslie knew better than to take chances.

She took a deep breath, braced herself, and then fired the van to life. Taking the gearshift knob in her hand and pressing the brake pedal, she shifted into reverse and pushed the button on the garage door opener. It slowly rolled upward, and she watched the rearview mirror for zombies. Had they been in the drive, she would have backed over them, and then driven away hoping for clear roads.

As it turned out, the driveway and alley were both vacant.

Out of habit she closed the garage door, even though she would probably never see the building again.

The roads were empty – almost as if the horrible times had never come. She drove the deserted streets of Little Rock, heading for I-30. It reminded her of one far-away morning when she'd gotten up early for a 5K run, and the streets around her neighborhood had been vacant. It was creepy then, and even more so now.

After a few blocks she donned the headphones, and then picked up the mic beside the equipment that she'd strapped into the passenger seat. Leslie took a deep breath, and said, "Well, here we go, folks! I'm on the air much earlier today, because as crazy as it might sound, I'm taking Static Stan's advice – I'm going to join the folks over in the Lone Star State! So far, things are pretty calm."

As she drove along, there wasn't a target in sight. She said, "Before we get the show started, let me settle into cruise mode. I'll be on the highway soon, so hang in there with me." In a few minutes, she'd navigated the van through the city streets to the onramp for I-30, and then headed the van west.

The interstate looked like a wasteland; there were cars scattered here and there on the shoulders and median. As Leslie sped westward, she occasionally saw a stumbling, dead form searching for someone to feed on. While it was tempting to stop for a little target practice, she kept going, and instead continued her morning broadcast. "All right, folks, I'm heading for Texarkana. But let me hear from you – who's out there?"

All she heard in the earphones was silence. "Hello? Anyone there?" she finally said. Again, there was no response. Shaking her head, Leslie added, "Okay, so either no one's listening, or I have something hooked up wrong." She took the van's speed from 60 to 90 m.p.h. and set the cruise control.

"You know, maybe this is a good sign – I'm not seeing the crowds of dead that I've heard about from callers in the past. Could it be that this is an indication that the tide is turning?

Perhaps they're dwindling away, and we're finally winning the battle."

There was still silence in her headphones; for some reason people couldn't get through. There was no time to resolve the problem, so Leslie clicked the mic again. "Okay, I can't hear you, but hopefully you can hear me. In preparation for just such an event, I've prepared a little musical interlude." Pulling a CD from her shirt pocket, she slid it into the player that was part of the equipment stack on the passenger seat. A heavy guitar strain blared in the headphones, and she hit the mic again. "Forgive me for my morbid sense of humor, but we'll start out with a tune from Blue Oyster Cult – Don't Fear the Reaper."

* * * * *

Two hours had passed, and Leslie had played through all the tunes on both CDs that she'd burned for the trip, occasionally breaking in to give a mile marker or comment on the deserted cars and trucks scattered along the way, in case anyone could hear the broadcast. As the strains of Van Halen's Jamie's Cryin' blared through the van's speakers and across the airwaves, she was approaching the Texas/Arkansas border. There still hadn't been a single phone call from the listeners. She hit the mic again, "Okay, just thought that I'd check. Anyone out there? Can anybody hear me?" Only a faint hiss played in her headphones. "Crap; something's gotta be hooked up wrong. Well, in case anyone's listening, I'm crossing into Texas – only a few minutes away from seeing if our buddy Static Stan's a man of his word."

Silence still, so she hit the play button again and settled in for the last few miles of the trip. There was no fanfare as she crossed the state line, and in only a few miles, she was out of town and finally saw the exit that read: Lone Star Army Ammunition Plant.

"I'm here," she said aloud after keying the mic. It was surreal. Leslie had no idea whether anyone had heard her along the journey, or even knew where she was. "I've got to tell you, though, assuming that I can hook up with Stan and his crew, don't hesitate to make the trip. I haven't seen the dead out in any force all day – in fact, it's been a bit of a boring ride."

She was feeling deserted; alone. Turning onto the ramp, she looked over at the equipment stacked and strapped into the passenger seat, and quickly followed the connections. Everything seemed to be plugged in correctly. Leslie steered with her left hand, and with her right began checking each wire, making sure that plugs were seated well, wires were clamped securely, and everything was fastened where it should be. It all seemed fine, but obviously something was wrong.

With a shrug, she looked back to the road just as the van hit the creature.

From there, everything happened in slow motion. First, she saw the monster through the windshield. He was massive – three hundred pounds, at least, and shirtless. Rolls of fat cascaded over his torso, his skin a pale gray. The creature's mustache and beard were matted with blood and other matter that she didn't want to even think about, and his lifeless eyes seemed to focus on her in that split second.

The van hit him at full force, and Leslie lost control. It flipped over once, rolled into the ditch, and continued to toss before it finally came to rest on the driver's side at the edge of a gas station parking lot beside the end of the exit ramp. She froze – and then took a quick physical inventory: she moved her arms, then her legs, and finally rolled her head. She took a deep breath, and then let it out. Although there were some twinges of pain, everything seemed to be functional.

Since the van was on its left side, the driver's side window was resting against the concrete. By some miracle it hadn't shattered, and Leslie laid her head against it and laughed. It figured – a safe trip all the way from Little Rock, and she crashed just short of her destination. Looking up, she saw that the straps were still holding the equipment in the passenger's seat, although it was straining against the fabric and Velcro, bobbing as if it might collapse onto her at any moment.

A shadow moved in front of the van, and in an instant she recognized the fat zombie that she'd hit on the off-ramp. He was dragging his left leg, and his right arm seemed to be elongated as if the bone had separated and was stretching the skin down. With his left fist, he began to bang on the windshield and grab for the edges as if it could be pried loose.

Leslie panicked – she was trapped. Grabbing for the seatbelt, she pulled the buckle and collapsed against the driver's side door. Twinges of pain shot through her limbs, but adrenaline took over. She pulled herself up, using the steering wheel to steady herself, and crawled through the space between the two front seats. The rear of the van had become a maze of equipment that had tumbled in the wreck, spewing all of the gear and supplies that she'd packed for the journey. She hurried through, pushing and kicking anything in her path, and in mere seconds had managed to open the back doors and climb through them.

Free of the van, she took several steps, and looked back. Fat man was now staring at her, and immediately started moving in her direction. He seemed a little worse for the accident, with a gash across his midsection slowly oozing intestines with each step. "Get in front of me, will you?" She pulled the 642 from its holster, took aim, and carefully squeezed the trigger. His head exploded, and the bloated body crashed onto the concrete.

Several yards behind him, she saw three other creatures – a man and two women, all in different stages of decay. Leslie shook her head – some of these things had obviously been around a while. With a glance, she saw movement in the woods around the edge of the parking lot; there were a dozen or more of them, lumbering out of the trees.

It was something that she wasn't prepared for. Some were missing limbs, others had open wounds in their torso where organs were sliding out, and their clothing hung in tatters. Many had dried blood on their face and hands – but they all were moving directly toward Leslie.

"Shit!" she said aloud, and looked around. The bridge over the interstate that she would have been driving over had half-a-dozen creatures on it, and in the distance, she could see that they were starting to come as well. The others from the woods were closing in, and the van was unusable. She saw movement in the convenience store of the gas station, and realized that someone must be manning the counter there. Without hesitation she screamed, "Hey! Over here!" and sprinted across the parking lot. Jerking open the door, she heard a little bell tinkle that had been mounted just above the threshold. Leslie quickly said, "Lock the door, mister, 'cause there are…"

Her voice trailed off as the man behind the counter turned to face her. His left eye was gone, and his face withered as if decay had set in weeks ago. The dark skin was flaking away, and she could see the muscles of his jaw flex as his teeth clacked together, already biting in anticipation of her flesh. She quickly raised the revolver, and squeezed off a shot that sent his head tumbling off the body, which collapsed behind the counter.

She stood there, her heart pounding in her chest, and tried to catch her breath. A sound made her spin with the gun raised – and she saw a young girl, maybe eight or nine years old, walk around the end of the aisle on the other side of the store.

"Oh, honey, it's okay!" she said, and lowered the weapon. "Don't be scared."

The child took a few cautious steps toward her, and then smiled. Leslie saw the dark red matter in her teeth, and then noticed the bloodstains on her hands as she raised them. "God, no, please…"

The girl was moving faster now, almost upon her. Leslie

233

lashed out with her foot, sending the child sprawling back down the aisle. "Don't make me," she pleaded, "you're just a baby."

Leslie watched as the girl righted herself, then stood, and then came toward her again. "No, please," she pleaded. The girl covered the ground between them. "No – I won't – I can't..."

The child's arms extended, grabbing at the empty air between them, desperate for contact. Leslie took a step back, sobbing, "Please..."

As the girl lunged, she raised the gun and pulled the trigger. As her body collapsed, head rolling to the side with the neck severed, Leslie fell to her knees and put her face into her hands. "Oh Christ, I'm going to hell. How can this happen? How can something like this happen?"

She heard the bell above the door jingle. "No..." she said, and stood up in time to see an elderly woman staggering inside. She was wearing a pink fluffy robe, hanging obscenely open, and her bloated, naked body on display underneath. A recent attack had obviously left blood that had dried on her chin, down her neck, onto her breasts and stomach.

Another head shot from Leslies revolver sent her lifeless body collapsing against the door, unfortunately propping it open for the ones crowding in behind her. They stepped over the body, staggering inside, focused on their target.

Leslie said, "Back exit!" under her breath, and took off running. Finding a door, she jerked it open and dashed through – to a small, tiled bathroom that smelled horribly of urine. "Oh, no fucking way..."

As she started to back out, she saw that the creatures were descending upon her. Without a thought, she started to push the door closed. It hung on the fingers of a skinny, bald zombie that had grabbed the edge at the last moment. He slowly pried it open, his face coming in, jaw snapping. Leslie put the gun a few inches from his face and pulled the trigger. The force of the shot blew him backwards, allowing him to pull the door closed and lock it. Based on the throng that she'd seen descending on the station, there were many more behind him.

Leslie took a deep breath, letting it out slowly. With a glance around the tiny gas station restroom, she shook her head and said, "Great. So this is how it fucking ends." The pounding on the door started slow, and in moments had suddenly become deafening. With each stroke, the metal of the door appeared to crease inward a little more.

She knew what was on the other side, and the fate that awaited her. Looking over to the mirror, she saw that her clothes were torn from the wreck, and her hair was disheveled. She smiled defiantly. "I may look like shit, but I'm damn sure not going to become one of those monsters."

She shook her head, and asked her reflection, "So how does a person decide to take her own life? Shouldn't there be grandiose ceremony and fanfare?" With a sigh, she looked away from the mirror and put the gun barrel into her mouth, then closed her lips around it to help secure the angle toward the base of her brain. She made a few final adjustments, closed her eyes, and without another thought, squeezed the trigger.

The only sound was a benign "click" that seemed to echo emptily off the walls of the small room. "Oh, shit," Leslie said, pulling the barrel from her mouth. The horror of the situation hit her – she was out of bullets, and the zombies were almost through the door. She felt her pockets, but knew that the two speed loaders were tucked away in the glove compartment of the van in the parking lot.

She looked quickly around the room; there was nothing but a sink, toilet, and trashcan – not a thing that she could use to end her life in a way that would prevent the inevitable. Leslie closed her eyes tightly, and her head dropped. There was no avoiding it... she was going to become a fucking zombie. She thought back to the previous night's show, and said aloud, "Sorry, gas station girl..."

The pounding became heavier, and the sides of the door began to give. Leslie could see a sliver through them at first, and then on either side, rotting fingers pried their way through. Hands were next, and in only a moment, several arms groped into the small room from either side of the door.

As it buckled, shoulders came next, allowing the creatures more reach, and Leslie said aloud, "Here we go."

Fingers brushed her, trying to gain hold, but she pressed herself into the far corner in a futile effort to escape the invaders. "Oh God," she prayed, "please let it be quick."

A creature had wedged his way past the door in an effort to reach her, and he grabbed her forearm. His eyes were milky and lifeless, but his teeth clacked together, trying to reach her flesh.

In a final, futile attempt, Leslie hit the creature with all her might using the gun. It sank into his face, caving in an eye and his nose. He merely snarled at her, though, and kept trying to move through the opening in the doorway.

Still holding onto her forearm with his rotting hand, the creature pushed himself farther into the room. Leslie closed her eyes and screamed, "No, not this… not like this!"

The monster was struggling past the others. His head and a third of its torso was through the bend in the door. It pulled Leslie closer, and she could see the soulless remaining eye as he opened his mouth to bite into her exposed arm.

Leslie squeezed her eyes shut, waiting for the searing pain to begin. There was a loud CRACK! which echoed through the small room, hurting her ears. Oozing liquid and tiny chunks hit her face and torso, and began to slide down her body. A series of popping sounds ensued, and then the door smashed open. She saw that inanimate zombies littered the ground. Opposite the broken doorway were three men, two holding shotguns, the third with a handgun swinging by his side.

"You okay, Leslie?" the man in front asked.

She stared at him wide-eyed, and then nodded slowly.

He smiled. "Great. What the hell were you thinking – did you forget your own rules?" He offered a hand. "Let's go. I'm glad that you decided to make the trip. We've been listening to your broadcast all morning and started wondering what happened to you. By the way, my name's Stanley…"

* * * * *

She glanced at the clock on the console. Five minutes 'til 8 PM, and the signal was strong.

Stanley opened the door, and held up a bottle of bourbon in one hand and a glass in the other. "I believe it's time for a little kick-start shot?"

Looking at the clock, then the power meters, and finally back at Stan, she said, "Know what? I don't think so." Lifting a diet soda can, she shrugged and added, "Now get on the producer's mic and let's get this thing started."

He smiled and disappeared through the door. She saw him emerge in the windowed booth across the room. Leslie nodded, and then hit the broadcast button.

"Good evening – tonight I start a new show in a new location, it's Survivor-Talk radio coming live from Texarkana, going out to all you folks who are still alive, fighting for your lives, and simply trying to maintain your sanity. It's been a tough few months, but if you can hear my voice, then hope is alive. You're going to make it – in a situation that looks impossible, I promise, you can survive. That's what we're all about here; the hope that still exists for humanity today. No matter who you are, or what's going on, we want to hear your story. Let's start out by going to the caller on Line 1…"

THE ZOMBIE WHISPERER

by Steven E. Wedel

Jana Wikel heard Ken enter the room behind her, but she didn't turn around to greet him. She sat mostly still, staring at the citizen's band radio, waiting for a reply while she gently tapped the microphone against her pursed lips. Behind her, Ken shifted his weight from foot to foot. He smelled of sweat and gunpowder.

"You say the zombie is your father?" The voice from the radio was clipped and curt, an upper East Coast accent. Jana wondered why the man was in Mobile, Alabama, with that accent.

"That's what I said," Jana answered, suddenly very aware of her own Deep South drawl.

"Can you afford Dr. Dragoon's services, Miss Wikel?" the man asked. "You've gathered the items we discussed last week?"

"Yes," Jana answered.

"You shouldn't do this," Ken interrupted at last. Jana continued to ignore him.

"Dr. Dragoon can be there tomorrow morning," the radio man said.

"You've got the directions," Jana reminded. "Land your helicopter on the lawn on the south side of the house. They can

239

see you on the north and it excites them."

"You said the area has been cleared," the radio man accused.

"What I said is that we clear the area daily," Jana answered. "That takes a while. New ones come during the night. Every night." *Every fucking night!* "We shoot them during the day. They can't get in. We haven't had one break through in six months."

"Eight," Ken corrected. "Lance let those two in six months ago."

"Whatever," Jana said. She remembered. "Make that eight months," she said into the mic.

"Good," the radio man said. "Our ETA will be 9 a.m."

"See you then," Jana said. "Over and out." She put the microphone down. Behind her, Ken's military boots clomped across the tiled floor. Jana covered her eyes but noted the sounds of Ken pulling a wooden chair up to the table to sit facing her.

"You know this is bullshit," he said.

"I don't," she answered. "And neither do you."

"Oh, I know it's bullshit," he said. "It's level after level of bullshit. We've got a pretty good thing here. Your daddy built a wall around his big house and it keeps those things out, but that wall fucked with your mind, Jana. You're too sheltered. You don't know what it's like out there."

"No." Jana couldn't completely suppress the shudder.

"You're hiding in here."

"We're all hiding in here," Jana said.

"Most of us are hiding because we know what's out there," Ken said. "You're just hiding from the truth."

Jana dropped her hands to the table and faced him at last. Ken hadn't shaved that morning. His chocolate cheeks and sharp chin were rough with short black-and-gray stubble. The short-sleeved denim shirt he wore was already stained with sweat and gore. It was a busy morning. Jana pulled her gaze from a smear of crimson and gray at his shoulder and was caught by his eyes again. They were hard, dark eyes, but there was more there... maybe love, maybe sad resignation.

"I have to do it," Jana whispered. "If he can tell me, I have to know. Wouldn't you do the same?"

The question broke the spell Ken's eyes had been conjuring. He looked away quickly, sighed, and stood up. The 9mm pistol at his side seemed incredibly black and square as he moved, then he was behind her and his giant, hard hands were on her shoulders, rubbing away the tension.

"They don't understand shit, Jana," Ken said. "They're dead. The soul, if such a thing really exists, is gone. They ain't who they were. I've come to terms with it, and you should, too."

"Not yet."

"This guy you're bringing in here," Ken continued. "We don't know anything about him. They come in here with guns and who knows what, find out there's only four of us, and they might just clean us out. If we're lucky, they might shoot us in the head before they leave."

"They won't."

"How do you know that?" Ken asked. He stopped massaging and returned to his chair. "You don't. All you know is that shit you heard on the radio. A fucking CB radio advertisement. You talked to anybody he's helped already?"

"Yes," Jana said, perking up. "Before I ever talked to his people. I talked to a woman down in Savannah and she said Dr. Dragoon helped her."

"How do you know that woman was in Savannah?" Ken asked. "She could have been sitting on Dr. Dragoon's dick for all you really know. The CB radio ain't no better than those Internet chat rooms were. You don't know who you're really talking to."

"I trust her," Jana said.

"You're still living in your daddy's walls," Ken said, but

his voice wasn't harsh.

"I have to try," Jana said. "If you're right, fine. I'll start going to the stands with you guys. I'll shoot zombies with you. I'll help you drag the bodies to the fire. But right now, I can't. Not while I believe there's still some spark of humanity in them."

"All right, baby. All right." Ken stood up, leaned over and they kissed briefly. Jana's nose recoiled at the smell of gunpowder, smoke and human gore on his shirt, but she held the kiss, nipped his tongue when he tried to put it into her mouth, then pulled away, smiling.

"You stink," she said.

"Yeah. Tom and Lamar already hit the shower. That's where I'm heading. Join me?"

Jana thought about it for a moment, then agreed. She held onto his arm as they moved through the mansion's lower floor toward the biggest bathroom.

"Philosopher Tom don't seem to care about us," Ken said, "But it drives Lamar crazy that you're doing me and not him."

"He should find his own woman," Jana joked, then she remembered Lance and the joke wasn't funny any more.

* * * * *

"Everything's ready?" Jana asked. Her eyes were fixed on the buzzing dot approaching the mansion from the south.

"Honey, it's as ready as it can be," Ken answered.

"I know. Sorry," Jana said. They watched the helicopter from one of the twelve freestanding deer stands set up along the 10-foot-high brick wall surrounding the mansion. Below her, on the other side of the thick wall, two dozen zombies in various stages of decay moaned and reached hungrily toward them. Jana tried very hard to ignore their cloudy eyes, rotting flesh and grasping hands. Ken seemed to sense her discomfort.

"This is what they are. No humanity. They're like sharks, except they don't shit. They just eat and make more like them," he said.

"Where's Lamar?" Jana asked. Gaunt and bearded, Tom stood on another platform to her right.

"Listen, Jana, we gotta play this cool," Ken said, his voice deadly earnest. "I got Lamar set up somewhere to keep an eye on these jokers' helicopter. We're gonna make them believe Lamar was killed, so they think we're down to three."

"But that's just–"

"No, Jana. This is the way it is. This is your place and for the most part I let you run it your way. But I've been out there. I grew up in the ghetto and I've seen what people, not just poor people, but everyone, what they've become since all this shit happened. You can't trust nobody, Jana. You play along when I say Lamar was killed last night. If these people are for real – or at least not here to rob and kill us – it won't matter that they never see him. If they try to fuck with us, he's our ace in the hole. And that ain't much. Look at that." He nodded toward the approaching helicopter. "Blackhawk. Bet you thought they'd show up in some old tourist chopper, huh?"

Jana didn't answer. She suddenly felt uneasy about the approaching military helicopter. Ken took her by the arms and made her look him in the eyes.

"It'll probably be fine," he said. "But be ready, just in case."

Jana nodded. "I will. Let's go."

They hurried off the stand and rushed toward the grassy lawn at the end of the swimming pool. The men had spray painted a circle in the grass with a big H in the center. Looking close, Jana noted there were uneven seams in the grass where it appeared to have been carefully dug up and replaced.

"You mined the landing area?" she asked.

"Yep."

"I hope I'm right," Jana said. "I can't stand the thought of living in a world where you have to suspect everybody of the worst."

Ken gave her a sidearm hug. "The world has always been like that. You white bread rich folks just didn't know it." He smiled as he said it, but Jana was irritated at his constant reminders of her former wealthy status.

"I just hope you're wrong," she said, then the ominous black helicopter descended onto the explosive circle and further conversation was drowned out.

As the engine shut down, three men hopped out of the helicopter. Two were massive, muscular black men, heavily armed, wearing sunglasses and black jumpsuits. They seemed even more gigantic when compared to their lean companion, a mustachioed man with an angular face, dark hair and pale skin. The white man wore a charcoal gray suit, minus the tie, and appeared unarmed. He stepped forward, his hand outstretched to Jana.

"Miss Wikel," he yelled in greeting.

Jana nodded and shook the hand as the propeller blades finally quieted, then became still. "Dr. Dragoon?"

"At your service, ma'am." He offered a low bow, then straightened and fanned his face effeminately.

"Would you like to come inside?" Jana asked.

"That would be fantastic," the doctor agreed.

They started forward, the two armed men following their leader. Ken didn't move. "Your other two men coming in?" he asked.

Jana looked from Ken to the helicopter, where an average looking white man sat behind the controls. Another black man, not so muscular but also in a black jumpsuit, loitered near a Gatlin gun mounted at the chopper's open side door.

"No, they'll stay with the helicopter," Dr. Dragoon said.

Jana caught the look Ken gave her and bit her lip. "That's fine," she said. "Let's get out of this heat."

As they were about to enter the front door of the stone

house a rifle shot rang out. Dr. Dragoon's men reached for the automatic rifles strapped on their backs, but a motion from the thin white man stopped them. He looked questioningly at Jana, but it was Ken who spoke.

"That's Tom," he said. "He's clearing visitors on the north wall. Maybe your men could give him a hand?"

"Oh no," Dr. Dragoon said. "Andrew and James are quite necessary to me. They subdue the fleshly prison of the *spiritus* so that communication can take place."

"Uh-huh," Ken said.

"Not a believer, I see," Dr. Dragoon said, smiling. "We'll change that."

Another gunshot rang out and Jana led the group into the house. There was no air conditioning; that would have put too much strain on the generators in the garage. Ceiling fans stirred the humid air above them, the whir of the motors interrupted by the sound of the men's boots on the hardwood floor.

"There's only the three of you now?" Dr. Dragoon asked.

"That's right," Ken said quickly. "Lamar was careless yesterday. We lost him getting your payment."

"I'm very sorry," the doctor said. "He was a close friend?"

"He was alive," Ken said.

Jana led them to a room near the back of the house, beyond the library. She stopped before a heavy, solid wood door. "This is it," she said. "Daddy's in there."

"He's alone?" Dr. Dragoon asked.

Jana nodded, keeping her face blank. "He … he followed me in there and I ran out and closed the door. He's been in there ever since."

"How long did you say?"

"Two months. He died of pneumonia."

"It's a pity most of our doctors were among the first killed when the apocalypse began," Dr. Dragoon said.

"I thought you were a doctor," Ken said.

"Professor," the man answered. "Not a college man? No matter. I have a doctorate degree in anthropology. I was tenured at LSU."

Jana sensed the tension building between the two men. "So, do I just open the door, or what?" she asked.

"Oh, no, dear girl," Dr. Dragoon answered. "Subduing the flesh-cage can be unpleasant and I don't let the enquirer watch that. Too unsettling. My men here will take care of that. I have a chair with restraints we'll bring in. First, though, I'm afraid I have to take care of the crass business of seeing the payment you agreed upon."

"Of course," Ken smirked.

"This way," Jana said. She gave Ken a look she hoped he interpreted as *Shut the fuck up* but he didn't acknowledge her. She led the four men back through the library to a small room her father had used for an office. She waved her hand at items piled on her father's desk. The professor and his assistants eyed the offerings.

Dragoon lifted one of two wine bottles and looked at the label, his face beaming. "You really did have the 2005s Philippe Leclerc Cazetiers," he said. "Do you have more?"

"Hey, this is what you asked for," Ken said.

"You need to shut your mouth," one of Dr. Dragoon's men said. He held Jana's grandfather's World War II Colt .45 in his left hand, his right hand resting on the butt of the cold black Glock in his hip holster. Jana wondered if this man was Andrew or James. Ken gave the man a disgusted look, but didn't speak again.

"It looks like everything is here," Dr. Dragoon said, his eyes fixed on the label of a caviar can, his attitude saying he was pretending not to have noticed the words passed between the other men. "Andrew, James, please take the payment to the helicopter and bring in the equipment. Jana, love, can we use this room for the reading?"

She nodded. "Yes."

"Excellent. Now then, while my men get things arranged and bring in your father, perhaps you would be so kind as to offer me a cool drink?"

Jana led the way to the kitchen and poured the professor a glass of lemonade. She looked at Ken and he nodded, so she poured two more glasses and the three sat down at a table.

"How did you figure out you could do this?" Jana asked.

"It was quite simple," the professor said. "By observing them, you can see immediately that the zombies retain something of what they knew in life. They are still gathering at shopping malls, grocery stores, movie theaters and other places where humans socialized. When they turn, if offered a choice between a loved one and a stranger, the zombie will invariably go for the person they recognize.

"With that in mind, I subdued one of my students who had the unfortunate luck of waking up dead. I strapped her into a chair so that she couldn't eat me, and, well ... probed her mentally."

"Like a psychic?"

"Yes. Exactly. I've always had the gift, though I seldom let anyone know about it before. Now, however," he paused and smiled. "A psychic professor is hardly the strangest thing even amongst the limited menagerie under your own roof at the present time."

"True," Jana agreed.

"How will we know what you say is real?" Ken demanded.

"Oh, you'll know, my good man. You'll see evidence."

The professor told them two stories about past experiences communicating with the dead and was beginning a third when one of his wranglers entered the kitchen and said they were ready for him.

"Thank you, James," he said, then turned to Jana. "If you'll pardon me for a few minutes, I will go into the room and compose myself and establish a connection with your father.

Once that's done, James here will bring you in. Remember, you must only speak to me. I will relay any questions you have to your father. Understand?"

Jana nodded, then watched the thin man leave with his hulking assistant. Ken broke her reverie.

"This is such fucking bullshit," he said. "I don't care if you give him the wine and fish eggs, but do you have to give up guns and ammunition for this? We could use those."

"We still have plenty of weapons," Jana reminded.

"He asked for more wine. I tell you, he's going to turn those thugs – and that fucking Gatlin gun – loose on us. He's not leaving here content with two bottles of that fancy-ass wine."

"Sometimes, Ken, I'm surprised you have enough trust to get naked with me," Jana said. "Is that why you always have to be on top, the dominant position? Because you're afraid I'll turn on you if I'm on top?"

"I'm a realist." He ignored her questions about their lovemaking. "Greed is the strongest impulse in human nature."

"He's right," James said from the doorway. Jana turned to face the wooden-faced black man who still wore his sunglasses in the house. "About the greed part. But we don't plan on killing you, so long as you don't fuck with us. It's bad for business. Dragoon helps the little lady here, she gets on the CB and tells somebody else, and that person calls on us for help. Dead people and zombies don't use the CB, my man."

Jana sensed Ken about to make some retort. She cut him off. "Can we go in now?"

"Yeah, you can go in," the visitor said.

Jana hurried toward her dead father's office. The door was open, and the smell hit her long before she crossed the threshold. James and Ken were behind her, so there was no turning back. Jana breathed through her mouth and forged ahead, but had to stop in the doorway when her eyes found her father strapped into a tall wooden chair.

His flesh had turned an ashy gray color and was hanging on his frame in most places. In others the meat had erupted and was writhing with maggots. The flesh around his eyes and mouth was loose; Jana could see that he'd lost several teeth and that his gums had receded. A heavy, thick leather strap was fastened over his chest, keeping him in the chair. Two smaller straps pinned his biceps to the back of the chair; his hands rested on the chair's arms as if he'd chosen to sit there and relax for a moment. His eyes were cloudy but focused on the angular professor sitting across from him.

"Dr. Dragoon will ask him yes or no questions," James explained, motioning Jana and Ken into the room to a position out of the zombie's sightline. Andrew remained standing next to the chair the professor sat in. "For yes, the zom– your father will raise his right arm. For no, his left."

Daddy should be sitting where Dr. Dragoon is. It's his desk. Jana shook the thought away. It didn't matter.

Dr. Dragoon and his subject stared at one another and it was hard to tell who was hungrier for whom. There was no sound, only the smell of rot and death. Then the professor broke the silence. "I would communicate with the spirit of Alexander Wikel. I know you are trapped in this rotting carcass. While we share this psychic bond I give you the power to partially control your former body. Do you hear and understand me?"

Jana felt her own eyes widen as the thing that used to read her bedtime stories and tuck her in at night suddenly lifted its right arm several inches. "Oh my God," she whispered. Ken had no comment.

"Alexander Wikel, do you know that your daughter is here with us?"

Again, the reanimated corpse raised its right hand.

"Do you remember loving your daughter?"

Jana watched her father answer positively.

"Do you still love your daughter?"

Yes.

"Do you wish to hurt your daughter?"

For the first time, the left hand lifted a few inches into the air. A tear slid down Jana's face.

"Alexander Wikel, we have the power to set your soul free of the rotting cage that holds you here. Do you understand what I mean?"

Yes.

"Is it your desire that we release you from this hell on earth?"

Yes.

"No," Jana whispered.

"Ask him something only he would know," Ken urged softly.

Jana considered it, wondering if it would be a breach of trust to test Dr. Dragoon in such a way.

"They forget a lot of stuff," James said.

"Ask him if he remembers giving me a paint pony for my twelfth birthday," Jana said. *It was a bay. He'll know it was a bay pony.*

"Alexander Wikel," Dr. Dragoon intoned. "Your daughter asks if you recall giving her a pony on her twelfth birthday. Do you remember that?"

No.

"Told you," James said. "It's like Alzheimer's."

"Yes and no questions are so limiting," Jana said, more to herself. Then, louder, "Is there anything he wants to say to me before … before he's … released?"

"Alexander Wikel, is there anything you wish to say to your daughter before we release you?"

Yes.

"Is it an apology for something you did when you were alive?"

No.

"Is it an apology for something you didn't do?"

250

"A lot of them say yes to this one," James said.

No.

"Is it simply that you love her and miss her?"

Yes.

Jana couldn't stop the sob that burst from her throat. She turned and buried her face in Ken's chest and felt his huge, strong, loving hands on her back, caressing and comforting her. "I'm sorry," she cried into his chambray shirt.

"Alexander Wikel, my assistant will now release you. May you find peace," Dr. Dragoon said.

Jana started to raise her head, believing she should bear witness, but Ken's heavy hand kept her face pressed against his chest. There was a shot, then a long moment of thick silence. Ken's hand slipped away and Jana turned to look at her father.

He was truly dead now. There was a small hole in his forehead and a splattering of thick red-and-gray goo on the floor behind the chair. Andrew holstered his pistol.

"Our work here is done," Dr. Dragoon said, rising from his chair. "James and Andrew will take the body out of the chair, but I'm afraid it's up to you to dispose of it."

"Is he... Did he find peace?" Jana asked.

"I think so," the professor answered.

Jana nodded. "Thank you," she said.

"Let's go have another glass of lemonade. Shall we?"

"Okay," Jana agreed. She slipped out of Ken's arms and turned toward the door. That's when she saw Tom standing in the doorway. He had his 30.06 rifle to his shoulder. A hard hand shoved Jana out of the way and as she was falling to the floor she saw Ken drawing his pistol with his other hand.

Tom's rifle fired first, then Ken's pistol. James and Andrew both fell to the floor. Andrew's feet twitched on the carpet. Ken stepped closer, pointed his gun at the other man's head, and said, "Now you shut *your* mouth." His gun exploded and Andrew was still.

Outside, another rifle sounded. Once, then twice.

"That would be Lamar," Ken said.

There was a moment of silence, then Dr. Dragoon asked softly, "Why?"

"You're a sham, you slick fuck," Ken said.

"Ken, what the hell are you doing?" Jana screamed. She got up and charged the big man, her fists clenched, ready to pound the chest she had been crying on only moments ago. He caught her with one strong arm and held her close.

"It's an old trick, baby," Ken said. "This man kept your attention on what he was doing with your dad while his goon manipulated the controls that made the body answer."

"That's not true," Jana argued. "You're just saying–"

"I'll show you," Ken said. He released Jana, but looked to Tom. "Keep your gun on him. Kill him if he moves."

"Gladly," Tom answered. His watery eyes were emotionless. "Preying on the hopeful. Despicable."

Ken went to the chair where Alexander Wikel's dead body sat. He loosened the leather cuffs holding the corpse's right arm to the back of the chair and pulled the arm free. A red-sheathed electrical wire was threaded through a hole in the back of the cuff and fastened to the body's arm. Ken pulled the wire out to reveal that it was attached to a long needle that had been inserted into the arm.

Dr. Dragoon remained silent.

"Now, watch this," Ken said. He moved to the body of Andrew, pushed the corpse over with his boot, then took a small black item from Andrew's hand. "I push this button on the left and ..." He pushed the button and Alexander Wikel's left arm raised several inches off the chair's armrest.

"You ... you're a liar," Jana said, staring at the man in the gray suit. He gave a half-smile and shrugged his shoulders. "And you killed him. You bastard!" Jana reached for the gun strapped to her own waist.

"Wait," Ken said, his voice sharp and commanding. "We can do better than that. Come in here, Lamar."

Jana turned to see Lamar Kennedy enter the room, his own high-powered rife with its assassin scope held loosely in his hands. He wasn't as big as Ken, but his skin was darker, making his eyes and teeth seem to glow in his head.

"The chopper's ours?" Ken asked.

"Yup. Shot the gunner first. His head fuckin' exploded, G. The pilot tried to get the bird started, but I capped him through the side window. We got us a fuckin' Blackhawk, baby!"

"Get some rope and tie this man's hands," Ken said. "I think he wants to play some tennis."

"Lance will enjoy the company," Tom drawled.

"How could you?" Jana asked, coming to stand in front of the professor. "How could you take advantage of people like that?"

"Wake up, sweetie," Dr. Dragoon said. "People have always been willing to pay shamans to tell them what they want to hear. Only the circumstances and technology have changed. You heard what you wanted."

"I wanted the truth."

"I call bullshit, little missy." His voice wasn't more than a hiss now. "You wanted him to say he was sorry for touching you? For not touching you? For ignoring your mother, forgetting your birthday or screwing his secretary? No. You wanted to hear that your daddy has always loved you and that he *wanted* a bullet in the head so you wouldn't feel guilty about shooting him. I gave you all of that. And you, you gave me this." He motioned to his dead associates.

"Fuck you." Jana turned to Ken. "I'll be waiting at the tennis court."

She passed Tom in the library as he took a length of rope to Ken. Jana left the house, returning to the sweltering heat of late morning. She trudged across the yard, ignoring the helicopter, but listening to the regular gurgle of the swimming pool pump. *No electricity for air conditioning, but we keep the pool pump going.* Down a grassy incline on the far end of the pool was the tennis court with its tall fence and red clay floor.

Locked inside the court was Lance Langam. Once almost corpulent, he was now just a corpse. The two female zombies who shared his pen had eaten most of his soft belly and part of his arms before he reanimated. One of the female zombies noticed Jana and moaned excitedly as she shuffled toward the fence.

I can't believe Lance even thought about fucking these things.

Granted, the young zombie in the black leather miniskirt hadn't been as decayed at the time, but still.

"Lead them away from the gate!" It was Ken's voice. Jana looked toward the top of the rise and saw her man – Daddy never would have approved of her loving a black man – as he led Dr. Dragoon toward the tennis court. The professor's hands were tied behind his back and Ken held the other end of the rope. Both Tom and Lamar flanked the professor, their pistols drawn.

Jana strolled leisurely toward the far end of the tennis court. All three zombies had come to the fence to moan and reach for her now and they followed her as she walked. She could hear the professor begging his captors.

"I'll give you anything," Dr. Dragoon promised. "I have unbelievable wealth at my own compound. Alcohol, drugs, books, gasoline. You name your desire and I can grant it."

"We desire that you shut the fuck up, G," Lamar laughed.

Ken dug a set of keys from his pocket and tossed them to Tom, who unlocked the gate of the tennis court. "Let's see you form that psychic connection with these zombies," Ken said. "The man's name is Lance. We don't know his lady friends."

"I'm begging you, sir," Dr. Dragoon said. "Don't do this."

"Push him in there!" Jana screamed.

Ken shoved the man through the open gate and Tom

254

slammed it shut and snapped the heavy padlock. The professor, his hands still tied behind him, continued to plead his case. Jana began the stroll back toward her companions, her undead audience following her until they realized there was meat in the pen with them.

Dr. Dragoon avoided the zombies for almost an hour, but eventually the heat and constant running wore him out and he collapsed. Jana hoped he was still conscious when they bit into him.

"I think we've earned a swim," Ken said.

"I think so," Jana agreed. Later, as she floated on an air mattress beside Ken, she said, "I suppose you're going to say I told you so at some point."

"About what?"

"Human nature. Everyone's greedy. Maybe Dragoon wasn't going to kill us all like you said, but he was a sham. He was robbing us."

"I suppose I could say it," Ken said. "But hell, thanks to you bringing him here, we got us a mighty fine piece of transportation. We'll be able to scavenge a lot further now, bring in more food from further away, and that Gatlin gun ..." He whistled. "That'll make the morning work go a lot faster."

"You know how to fly that thing?" Jana asked.

"Not yet, but I'll learn. First, though, I think we should go inside. You had some other delusion about me needing to be in control and I think we can fix that."

"Bullshit, man!" Lamar yelled from his own air mattress. "G, we're taking that chopper out and finding me my own woman as soon as one of us can fly it. Shit!"

"The world has ended," Tom mused. "We're feeding people to zombies, have no idea if civilization will ever be reestablished, and all you people can think about is sex. Makes me glad my pecker hasn't been hard in ten years."

255

GOOD NEIGHBOR SAM

SAM

by Mark Onspaugh

Sam's Day

It was a pleasant May morning and birds were singing when Samuel Petersen stepped out onto his front porch. He took a big breath and smiled, happy for another beautiful day on Pine Street.

Larry the paperboy rode by on his bike. The very same bike that Sam had fixed when the boy had ridden right into his new Buick.

Good neighbor Sam. That's what everyone on Pine Street called him, and he was proud of the nickname. His wife Esther used to tease him about it, but he knew she was secretly proud he was held in such high regard.

The paper was laying perfectly centered in the first square of the front walk.

Larry was getting better. At first, Sam would find his paper in the rose bushes or getting soaked on the dewy front lawn. Rather than yell at the boy, he had shown him how to throw a paper, something he himself had done as a boy.

Larry waved and called to him, and Sam grinned and waved back.

The paper was, as always, a source of information and comfort. Sam didn't go in much for television, preferring the

257

old fashioned ways of the Mayfield *Courier*.

"Paper's here," he called to Esther. She was busy in the kitchen preparing a roast for supper. He had told her he was going down to Skilly's Skillet Café on Emerson for breakfast, something he treated himself to once a week. He had promised to bring her one of the big jelly donuts that George "Skilly" Skilassky made with the deep fryer that Sam had helped him install.

Good neighbor Sam.

Sam left the paper in the front porch glider. Unlike him, Esther preferred to learn about the world on a morning news magazine show before settling in to watch the soaps, what she called "her stories."

Sam caught his reflection in the front window. He was tall and lanky, with a careless grace of a practiced athlete. At sixty-five he was still quite fit, having stuck to a regimen of exercise and healthy eating since his basketball days at Mayfield High. He still had a full head of hair, but most of it had gone silver-gray since he turned fifty. His blue eyes still had no need for corrective lenses and he kept hair short and clean shaven. Sideburns are for beatniks, his father used to say.

"Don't forget my donut!" Esther called from inside, and Sam chuckled.

"You think I'd risk getting locked out of my own house?" he called back, and heard her laugh. After forty-five years he could still make her laugh.

Sam ambled down the front walk, listening to the birds and the pleasant whish-whish of lawn sprinklers. He loved all seasons in his town, but spring just might be his favorite.

Hattie McCullough was muttering over her roses, her large straw hat obscuring the prominent chin and hook nose that had encouraged all her students at Ryerson Elementary to call her "Witch Hattie" behind her back. Many of those same name-callers were now prominent doctors, lawyers and artists, their first endeavors in their chosen professions nurtured by the old "witch."

"Looks like aphids, Hattie," Sam said, seeing the tiny pale green insects clustered on many of the more delicate leaves and shoots.

Hattie looked at him and nodded. Her eyes were moist under the veil of her sun hat.

"Tell you what," Sam offered, "I'm going to Skilly's, then I'll have Randy run over with a sprayer of Neep Oil to get rid of those little rascals." Randy was his new part-timer at the hardware store. The boy was a daydreamer but worked hard enough if you kept an eye on him.

"You're such a kind young man, Samuel."

Sam laughed. Not many on Pine Street were old enough to call him a "young man."

"No problem. You taught me to read, the least I can do is save your roses."

Sam continued on his way, thinking of what he might order for breakfast. Several folks called to him and he waved, pausing once to throw a ball back to some kids in the park. They laughed and went about their game, and Sam marveled at their boundless energy.

At Skilly's, everyone looked up from their meals or papers and called to him.

Good neighbor Sam.

Abby's Day

Four shamblers were feeding on an Australian shepherd, and Abby winced when she heard the animal cry out. Dogs were an invaluable ally, good at sniffing out any pus-bag before it got within a hundred yards.

Dr. Davis had assured everyone that zoms would only eat humans, but the pretentious asshole never left his lab. He kept putting forth this motivational fairy tale BS that the undead would eventually rot away, leaving the survivors a pristine Eden rich in flora and fauna.

259

Abby had told him she had seen shamblers feeding on livestock, and had once seen a zip catch a rabbit. Hell, she even saw a slode feeding on cow, at least that's what she thought it was doing. Davis told her that these were anomalies, "exceptions that proved the rule," an expression which had always sounded like bullshit to her. The way she figured it, the pus-bags craved living human flesh. In the absence of that, their misfiring brains would compel them to feed on anything living, like an addict.

Although she had seen animals bitten by zombies, the Zed-17 virus didn't seem to affect them. That was one of the small blessings in this world. She wasn't sure how they could have coped with zombified house pets.

The birds were another matter. Carrion feeders like turkey vultures and crows had spread one of the earlier strains of the virus throughout the avian population. Abby had often thought one of the sadder aspects of this whole shit-storm was the absence of birdsong.

Though the dog-eaters were in range, she was loath to use four or more shots to take them down. It was true there were lots of bullets available, for now. Unless someone got off their post-apocalyptic ass and started learning how to manufacture gunpowder and bullets, they'd end up fighting off the pus-bags at close quarters, not a good idea when your opponent can infect you with a bite or some of its copious oozings getting into a open wound.

Abby compromised by putting a bullet in the dog's skull, ending its suffering. The shamblers kept feeding, but would stop once the carcass cooled to 80°F.

While the shamblers continued their meal, she checked her map.

She was in Grid 37-E on the outskirts of Mayfield, Ohio. Her primary job was to locate caches of supplies, weapons, food and medicine. If she found any uninfected survivors, she was to assess whether they would be an asset to the Compound and, if so, bring them back.

She had once asked what she was to do with anyone who would not be an asset. Her superiors had looked away, all except Tyler. He had pantomimed putting a gun to his head and pulling the trigger.

She understood. Put them out of their misery, eliminate one more potential pus-bag.

It was Tyler she was searching for now. He had come to this area two months ago and not returned. Abby would have gone looking for him right away, but she had been on a B&B (Bag & Burn) at Wright Patterson Air Force Base near Dayton. The base had been crawling with a high percentage of zips, and they had lost several good people, including her best friend Trang. It had taken their team more than six weeks to clear out the base, but now it served as their fully secured base of operations.

Something caught her peripheral vision, and she saw a figure standing in the street about a quarter of a mile away. It began to run, becoming almost a blur as it reached the feeding shamblers.

Freaking zip. Her orders on these were clear. Kill zips at all costs.

It took four rounds, as the creature seemed to anticipate where the bullet was headed and avoid it. The techs couldn't figure how the zips moved so fast; hell, they couldn't figure how any person with no respiration or circulation continued to move, vocalize and eat.

Freaking techs.

She finally nailed the zip by shooting counter-intuitively, aiming at a point opposite of what "felt right." The zip's head exploded, and peppered the dog-eaters with gore.

Abby reloaded. The shamblers had finally registered she was there, and were moving toward her tree. She dropped all four with an efficiency that belied her sixteen years and then was on the ground and moving toward Grid 37-F.

There were two slodes in her path. Ever cautious, she gave them a wide berth. Slodes (as in "slowed down") were the opposite of zips. They could be mistaken for statues or mannequins from a distance. You could watch one for an hour and never discern any movement. This pair would probably take a good two weeks to reach the tree she had just vacated. Davis figured they would eventually rot and fall apart without hurting anyone, and Abby agreed with him on that. Still, she never wanted to get complacent where pus-bags were concerned. She wasn't so young she didn't remember the term "playing possum." Who was to say some zoms hadn't figured out that staying still might draw in an unsuspecting hot meal?

There was a short alley up ahead on her right. According to the map, this would lead to a cul-de-sac called Pine Street, which then would communicate with the town's main drag Emerson. She checked behind her and noted the only zoms visible were the two slodes.

A zom in a patrolman's uniform was seated in front of a dumpster, staring at the wall opposite. At this distance it was impossible to tell what type he was.

Further on were four zombies in bridesmaid dresses, their pink taffeta dresses in tatters and stained rust with dried blood and bits of gore. They were gathered at a chain link fence that blocked off the alley. The fence was secured both to the brick walls of the alley and to the asphalt. Topped with razor wire, the only thing visible beyond it was a large jasmine bush, its tendrils and white flowers slowly filling the gaps in the chain link.

Abby eased back and quietly checked her map. She could backtrack a block and reach Emerson via Oak Street, provided no one had fenced that area off, as well. The fence was encouraging, it meant a possible enclave of survivors.

She was ready to move off when she saw it, a white circle with three characters inside it: a pine tree, a date and the initials TK.

Tyler Kennedy.

Even without the initials she would have recognized his handwriting, his marking a route with a bit of white spray paint and a laundry marker.

The pine was obviously Pine Street, the date about the time he had disappeared.

Tyler had come this way, and had decided to see what lay beyond the galvanized steel and jasmine. Whatever he had found, he hadn't come back.

Abby checked her weapon. Two left in the mag. She eased around the corner and plugged the sitting cop and one of the pink ladies. The cop had turned toward her unbelievably fast as she had pulled the trigger, but he hadn't been able to dodge the bullet.

A zip... Playing possum. Son of a bitch.

Abby reloaded as the three remaining bridesmaids started shuffling her way. One dragged a foot behind it that was hanging by a frayed length of tendon. One was missing her lips, her yellowed and chipped teeth bared in a grimace of unending fury. More often than not, the pus-bag ate their own lips in some zom equivalent of nail-biting.

Abby took out each girl with a well-placed headshot. Some of her colleagues preferred the "double-up," one in the chest to take it down, one in the brain to shut it down. Abby was the best shot in all of Columbus, and preferred not to use more bullets than necessary.

She waited, and the alley seemed clear, but she knew better. She walked slowly toward the dumpster at the end, and a legless horror wormed out from under it, teeth gnashing as it trailed intestines like ragged purple and pink sausages.

Abby dispatched it with a clean shot into one cataract-glazed eye. She instinctively leaned to the left and a spray of yellow fluid narrowly missed splashing across her chest. That eye-ooze was what Tyler used to call "matter-custard," after some old song about a walrus. She loved Tyler but his taste in music was weird.

Music made her think of lullabies, but this was not the time for those kinds of thoughts.

Focus, Abby, focus, she admonished herself.

There was a scratching sound above her and Abby instinctively rolled out of the way. She narrowly missed getting squashed by an enormous zom that had fallen from the rooftop. Still, the big boy had knocked the Russian Kalashnikov from her grasp and now covered it with his undead bulk, his head pulped like a rotted cantaloupe. Abby wanted to retrieve her gun but two more pus-bags jumped from the roof, their hunger for her flesh causing them to leap like lemmings. They landed on the fat boy, who broke their fall.

Abby still had an Army issue Colt .45 and a machete on her belt. The first of the pus-bags to recover, a former grease monkey in bloodstained coveralls, moved so fast sitting up he had to be a zip. She fired the entire clip at his freaking head, and he managed to dodge every bullet like some graveyard Shaolin. She'd never reload in time, and finding a place to hide was out of the question. Zips had heightened senses, like sharks they could home in on the smallest cut, the tiniest drop of blood.

When in doubt, do the unexpected.

The zip's instincts told it she would run back the way she came.

Instead, she ran toward him, delivering a vicious blow to the side of his head with her steel-toed hiking boots. The instant he went down she was scrambling up the chain link like a monkey with his tail ablaze, trying to put vital distance between herself and the hyperspeed pus-bag.

It is one of God's graces in this world that zips, like their slower brethren, were unable to climb. They could navigate stairs, but ropes, fences and ladders were beyond their ability.

But zips could jump, often higher than an accomplished high school athlete. The zip leaped, and managed to grab her pant leg and boot. It began to pull itself up, its teeth clacking together as spittle sprayed from its shredded lips.

Tyler had been merciless with Abby's physical training, making her do one-handed pull-ups once she had mastered the usual sort. She had cursed him with each painful rep, but that suffering stood her in good stead now.

Holding on to the fence with her left hand, she pulled the machete from its scabbard. As the zip was scrambling to get to her abdomen, she took off the top of his head and left eye. The zip fell back on the remaining pus-bag, who was a shambler, thank God.

Abby wiped the blade quickly on her pants and re-sheathed the machete. Though her left hand and arm were throbbing in agony, she forced herself to the top of the fence. She perched there to reload. With luck, there was a gun shop in town where she could at least find a serviceable semi-auto.

Several new pus-bags appeared at the entrance to the alley, two men in suits, a nun and a man naked except for a lobster bib. Abby would have to tell Tyler about that one.

She ejected the Colt's clip into a side bag as she rammed home the full one with practiced ease. She nicked her forearm on an errant strand of barbwire, and the small trickle of blood sent all of the zoms into a frenzy. Lobster Bib turned out to be a zip. In a move she had never before seen he ran toward her, vaulted up the dumpster and was flying up toward her, a rotting gargoyle with taloned fingers and bare toes slashing the air, his eyes fever-bright with unending hunger, the plastic bib rustled and was emblazoned with a lobster and the words "I got mine at Cray's Fish House!"

Abby brought up the .45 in a fluid motion. The zip's head disappeared in an explosion of red spray and skull fragments, and then his headless body was slamming into her, knocking her off the fence. She shut her eyes and covered her nose and mouth with her free hand, not wanting to chance taking a gulp of contaminated blood and fluid. She forgot all about her cut, but thankfully no viral ooze touched her wound.

As she came down on the opposite side of the fence, her pants snagged on the upper twists of the chain link, which bit into her calf. Abby's head connected with one of the fence poles as the pus-bag fell to the ground. Hanging upside-down she lost consciousness, and willed herself to keep a grip on the .45.

Sam's Day

It was a slow day at the hardware store. Randy had finished his deliveries early and was anxious to be off playing baseball. Sam tried once again to interest the boy in learning some more of the fundamentals of plumbing, painting or electrical, but all the kid could think of was joining his buddies.

Sam sighed. He decided to put some time in on the pocket watch and then call it a day.

The watch was a beauty, owned by his great-grandfather Lucas when he was a conductor on the Chesapeake and Ohio Railroad. The watch had been brought over from the old country by Lucas's grandfather Meistridge and had been passed down to each eldest son until it fell to Sam. He was sorry that he had no one to pass the watch to. He and Esther had had several arguments about children, and she would wail and cry if he pressed the issue.

Now they were too old, anyway.

Sam sighed and tried to concentrate on the far simpler problems of worn gears and dust buildup.

At noon, no one had so much as stopped in to chew the fat, so Sam closed up. In his exuberance, Randy had forgotten Hattie's Neep Oil, so Sam took it himself.

He thought of getting a grilled cheese at Skilly's but the place was dark. Skilly had talked about becoming a breakfast-only establishment, and Sam hoped that would not be the case. They needed some new blood in town, it was true, but surely with a little advertising Skilly could make lunch cost-effective again.

He'd help Skilly with the signs.

Good neighbor Sam.

Sam walked down the street, enjoying his town and the lazy afternoon. Esther was probably watching her soaps or gossiping over tea with her friends. He wasn't about to go home and get underfoot.

As he reached Pine Street, the sweet song of birds was nearly drowned out by an awful racket.

Fearing dogs had gotten into Hattie's garden, Sam hurried down the street.

Abby's Day

The searing pain in Abby's calf woke her up. She had been dreaming of Tyler, of the time they had gone swimming in a real pond. They had actually had nearly an hour of peace before the zoms showed up, and it was enough time for him to profess that he had been in love with her since the day they had found her holed up in the First Methodist of Gannville steeple. That had been four years ago. He was nineteen now and she sixteen, and he wanted to ask her something important. Abby knew that conversation could take place anywhere, but a chance at privacy under an Indian Summer sky was a real rarity. She had shushed him, gently, and the two had made love under an old oak. It was the first time for both of them, and she thought that there still must be a God somewhere if such sweetness could still exist.

She shook off the last vestiges of sleep and dreamy afterglow, her view of the world inverted. The zip that had landed her in this fix was lying in a puddle of goo in the middle of the street. Abby could hear a half dozen pus-bags on the other side of the fence wailing for the blood that trickled down her leg, but their odor was masked by the sweet scent of jasmine.

She was proud to see she had kept a hold of her firearm,

though that hand was now beginning to cramp. She transferred it to her left and tried to assess her situation.

If she could do a sort of half-assed handstand she might get her leg free without tearing a sizeable gash in her leg, but that would mean holstering the firearm.

Command had insisted she travel with someone, but she didn't trust anyone but Trang (now dead) and Tyler (missing). So she snuck off before morning chow, figuring that finding Tyler was worth a few demerits and a cut in rations.

Hell, she'd be on light duty before long, anyway.

She was taking one last look at her surroundings when she saw something impossible, something insane.

It was a kid on a bicycle.

A zombie kid on a bicycle.

She had no time to reconcile this craziness, he was moving toward her at the speed of a zip.

Abby took a deep breath and banished all thoughts of pain and loss and fear. She sighted in, and just as he got within ten feet she fired, taking off his head and most of his neck. Amazingly enough, the kid-corpse stayed upright and veered away from her, legs pedaling furiously.

Abby quickly holstered the Colt, gripped the fence pole and pushed upward, like a gymnast in some bizarre floor exercise.

The pain in her leg burned and throbbed, but she kept from doing too much damage. When her pants proved too entangled to free easily, she did a painful sit-up and cut away the cloth with her knife. As the final tatters ripped free she pushed off from the fence and twisted like a diver, landing solidly on her feet on a grassy parkway bordering the sidewalk.

She could see the kid pedaling away, his headless body swaying with the motion of the bike. She saw now that the bike was mounted on some sort of track.

What the hell?

Abby moved cautiously down the street, and heard

something she hadn't heard since she was in Lancaster Elementary.

Birdsong.

Warbling, chirping, trilling, it was so lovely she stood transfixed for a moment. Her breath caught and her eyes teared up at the sheer beauty of it, this gift of carefree exuberance.

Abby looked up, trying to spot at least one of the tiny creatures that survived here despite the sure presence of Zed-17 and its predecessors.

Cunningly hidden in the tree was a small speaker.

As she began to curse her gullibility, something moved toward her from the right.

It looked to be a rosy-cheeked old woman in a sun hat and garden gloves, but Abby could see beneath the veil the skin stretched taut over the skull, the mouth in a permanent scarecrow rictus. And, masked by bath salts, deodorant and perfume, the repugnant odor of decay.

The old woman was wailing at her, lidless eyes bulging from their sockets, her movements too smooth to be a shambler.

Some new kind of zip.

The old woman's hand came up, and Abby was alarmed to see gleaming pruning shears clutched in the gnarled fist.

Pus-bags...using weapons?

Even as Abby was trying to process this impossibility and correlate it with the headless bike rider, her training was taking over. She raised the Colt and shot the old woman square in her large nose, blowing away most of the face and the improbable sunhat.

The old woman's body stayed upright, and Abby thought of chickens on her granny's farm running headless after being decapitated. Despite her training she whimpered as the headless body stopped just short of the white picket fence and rose bushes.

The hand bearing the shears moved up and down and side

to side, but there was a mechanical quality to its rhythm and repetition. Abby peered closer, ready to expend a clip in the gaunt torso, if necessary.

The old woman's body was bolted to an articulated framework. This framework was partially hidden by clothing and, in some cases, seemed have been in embedded in the arms and legs. The whole, corpse and armature, was bolted to a circular base that was mounted on a track running from the bushes to the front door.

Abby listened, and could hear the clockwork whirring of gears and pulleys as the headless corpse continued to gesticulate with the gleaming shears.

Peripheral movement caught her eye, and she saw an older man running toward her, waving wildly.

Abby sighted in on him, and then he cried out.

"You! What have you done?"

Though he was clearly alive, he seemed crazy. Abby kept her weapon on him.

He ignored her and went to the fence. When he saw the headless gardener he began to weep.

"Hattie! Oh God, no! Hattie!"

He began to cry, and she actually felt pangs of guilt.

"She… she was a zom…"

"She was my neighbor and my friend!" he yelled, his face tear-streaked and red.

Abby stepped back at this sudden display of hostility.

The man walked toward her, his face filled with sadness and fury.

"She never hurt anyone! Why would you do that?"

Abby stepped off the curb into the street. She wasn't keen on shooting him, but she wasn't going to let him hurt her, either.

"Answer me! Why did you do that?" He pointed at the gun as if it were some sacrilegious object he was forbidden to name.

"Don't come any closer, old man, or I'll have to put you down."

He looked at her, and nodded. "You're one of those troublemakers from the bad side of town."

"Bad... bad side of town? What the hell are you talking about? This shit is worldwide, man."

The old man frowned. "Please don't curse, we have families on this block." He softened a bit at that, and held out his hand. "My name is Samuel Petersen, but my neighbors call me Sam."

"Abby. And if it's all the same to you, Sam, I think I'll pass on the handshake."

"I understand. I overreacted about Hattie. You probably had her as a teacher and thought of her as a witch."

"Mister, you're not helping your case."

"Look, Hattie will be fine. I represent the Pine Street Neighborhood Watch and I have been a terrible host. Please come to my house, my wife probably has a fresh batch of cookies and some lemonade made."

Abby's stomach rumbled, and she realized she hadn't eaten since dawn. He started up the street and made a "come on" gesture, looking for all the world like everyone's favorite uncle.

She followed him, keeping a safe distance. Two more clockwork zoms gibbered and a gestured at her, but she did not shoot. Now that she could see they were no threat, she wasn't about to waste ammo.

She was still trying to figure out what it meant. Some kind of shooting gallery or training facility? If that were the case, why did he bawl over a target? Maybe they only used paint rounds or something. A mech who had tricked out this whole thing might be a bit loopy about damage to his gizmo.

A small dog, obviously stuffed, whirred out to the front of an unfenced lawn and barked tinnily. She saw it had only been a puppy when it had been transformed into an automaton and

271

wondered if it had been dead first. Surely…

The dog was following by a tall zom with unruly brown hair, plaid shirt and jeans. The thing waved at her and wailed, its mouth already bearing the telltale marks of a lip-eater.

Abby felt the world around her pitch and roll like a funhouse ride, and she vomited bits of protein bar and bitter yellow bile onto the clean sidewalk.

It was Tyler.

Like the others, he was bolted to an armature that dictated his motion. His eyes peered at her without recognition, and his teeth clicked and clacked together as he strained against his prison of steel and wire to get at her, to feed on flesh he had once touched with gentleness.

His skin, once the nut brown of his Cherokee and Creek heritage, was now pale white tinged with gray. His tongue, a grotesque slug-like thing of black and purple, lolled in his mouth, and she could see with awful clarity he had eaten part of it.

She felt a tiny movement in her belly, and thought it might be her terrible, wonderful secret, but knew deep down it was just cramps of nausea.

She turned toward Sam, intent on blowing his head off, but then felt the sting of a needle in her arm.

Abby fell, but Sam caught her.

Good neighbor Sam.

Sam's Day

It was a pleasant November morning and birds were singing when Samuel Petersen stepped out onto his front porch. He took a big breath and smiled, happy for another beautiful day on Pine Street.

Larry the paperboy rode by. He was getting too big for the bike, and Sam figured another boy would be taking his place. Perhaps he would need Sam to help him learn how to ride a bike, and throw papers with accuracy. Sam would enjoy that.

Good neighbor Sam.

Sam hurried down to check on the newlyweds that had moved into the old Amberson house. Abby and Tyler were two of his favorite neighbors, although he wouldn't tell the others that. He could remember when Abby came to him, crying some nonsense about not wanting to stay on Pine Street with Tyler, that she was carrying a secret that might change everything.

Shoot, Sam had been around, he knew not every child was conceived in wedlock, especially these days. He had had a good talk with Abby, and she had since become a model wife and neighbor.

Their puppy Snoop rushed out to meet him, and then the lovebirds came out, doing a little impromptu twirl before striding out to meet him.

As they talked about the coming holidays and neighborhood gossip, Sam thought he saw a little bit of worry in Abby's blue eyes.

Probably worried about that baby.

Shoot, if the Doc wasn't up to it, Sam could help Maybe he'd start reading up on birthing and obstetrics tonight after supper.

Good neighbor Sam.

AND TO THE DUST RETURNETH

THAT, WHICH SURVIVES

by Morgan Ashe

Titanium bars crisscrossed to form the front and top of the cage. Acrylic panels on the outside provided a somewhat effective barrier from any liquid contaminates sprayed or flung. A sliding security door set on guide rails was the only way in or out. Poured concrete completed the sides and far wall of the structure. Overhead floodlights illuminated every corner ensuring there were no shadows.

I knew every square inch of it, every corner and crevice, but I had ceased seeing the cell long ago. My full attention was focused on its occupant. Watery pale-blue eyes were set in a face I saw in my sleep, in my nightmares. Those eyes stared at me. Fixed, unblinking. No recognition, no emotion, no thought was communicated by that gaze. Well, one thought. It wanted out. It wanted me. It wanted to feed on my flesh.

Even after all these months, I couldn't contain the chills as I observed it with a near morbid fascination. It tore at the flesh it held in its hands with yellowed teeth behind ragged lips. Shredded tendons and sinew hung from the limb. Blood dripped from severed veins to pool on the cement floor – fresh red splatters to join the dried remains of previous meals.

I needed to begin my day's work, continue my studies to understand the genetic makeup of the zombies. In an effort to

277

stay calm and collect my thoughts, I paced back and forth. Still, its gaze never wavered, and it panned its head back and forth to follow my every move as it ate.

It must have been one of the millions of tourists that had been stranded and died in China when countries around the world had shut down their borders. It had probably been buried in one of the hundreds of deep trenches outside of Beijing. Before we knew better. Before we knew to shoot each in the forehead and then burn the body. This one had smears of grave dirt on its clothes from when it had dug itself up and out of its mound to begin feasting on the living.

Fresh human flesh.

Zombies wouldn't eat anything else – neither fish, nor fowl, nor good red herring as the old saying goes. China's political prisons and detention centers had an inexhaustible supply of fresh flesh to provide my lab. For now. No one was sure if those prisoners would turn. At least they were behind bars. Like this one. This zombie was Australian. I couldn't quite tell the nationality of its supper.

Jiang Shi.

To the rest of the world, and here at the lab in Beijing, they were zombies. The population of this country and the local news reporters called them by the other term. It literally meant stiff corpse, but the words themselves were imbued with a magical power I knew the rabid creature in front of me didn't deserve.

It was an old myth, and one that didn't apply. How could it? These were not the combination vampire and zombie of legend. These zombies did not attack their victim to drain it of its chi or life force. It was nothing that romantic. No, these were the mindless, flesh-eating dead whose sole purpose was to find their next victims and consume them. Simple. Pointless. Unstoppable.

I didn't know which was worse – the sight, the stench or the unceasing moans and groans that emanated from it. The sounds never stopped, morning and night.

The smell was just as horrifying. The fetid, rancid smell of decayed and putrescent tissue. Even though I tried to breathe through my mouth, I had a copper, metallic taste on my tongue.

The technicians bleached and sanitized the cage when one zombie had outlived its usefulness and another was brought in for testing. But, no matter how many times I had washed my face or showered, the smell remained.

I turned my back on the caged zombie and searched for a distraction, praying I could turn off the sounds of flesh being pulled away from the bone and eaten, the sounds that meant that thing would torment me for yet another day.

Scattered across the top of my desk, another type of horror awaited me. I looked at the constant reminders of what had happened around the world. Photos of slaughter and destruction intermixed with newspaper clippings. Families found dead and mutilated in their homes. Terrifying, the stuff of nightmares. Except they weren't dreams. They were all too real.

What, at first, were isolated killings had become widespread, reported in city after city. Headlines from a year ago, which had announced the carnage and mass killings had changed to the unthinkable, the unbelievable. It was a nightmare no one could quite comprehend or explain. There on top of the pile, lay the proof-laden article that had made the world's population sit up and fear their future as a species: "The Walking Dead."

Was it only two years ago that the first zombie had been found? Police who'd been responding to a report of a missing family had entered the family's residence, only to find an adult male hunched over the body of a child.

From the man's moaning, the officers had at first thought they'd found the father. That perhaps he had been holding the child to his chest in grief over her murder.

Then it had raised its head.

Bloodied lips had been curled back over bared teeth. Multiple bites and rips from the flesh had made it clear what had been happening.

The child's body had been thrown aside as the zombie lurched to its feet and shuffled toward the police. The police had commenced firing, but it had continued towards them, heedless of the bullets...until one struck the man between the eyes.

The autopsy had revealed that the man had already been dead when the police had shot him. The results were irrefutable. The man's blood had solidified throughout his body. From the tests that had been run, it had hardened days before the police found him. It had made no sense. It was impossible. Yet there was the body.

As one of the world's leading geneticist, I had received the autopsy results when they had been published. I had thought at the time this was an isolated incident, some type of mutation or virus. But even I, with all my knowledge could not believe the man had truly been dead. There had to have been some other explanation.

Then the next one had been found and captured alive. And that was when we had confirmation – the dead were walking.

As more were found in every corner of the world, the Chinese government had built this lab and provided one zombie after another for me to study. I was focused on studying the DNA. Testing samples. Trying to determine if a virus or bacteria was responsible for creating these monsters. Other labs were established across the country and every continent as the world's scientists concentrated their efforts on finding a cure. A global database was created to document test results. The information was almost overwhelming.

It had taken us a little longer to discover how to kill them permanently. Too long. The world–

A rustle behind me caused me to still in abject terror. My heart stopped and sweat formed across my brow. It was behind me. The hairs on the back of my neck stood at attention, and the smell of rot and mold increased until my olfactory glands shut down in protest. I didn't want to see it. I didn't want to see its hands reaching for me with those bloodstained fingers, those long sharp nails with pieces of human flesh trapped beneath them.

I turned, the need to meet my fate overcoming my fear.

Nothing.

Nothing was there.

It sat in its cell staring at me, gnawing on another limb. The first one lay at his feet, chewed clean to the bone.

I slumped and fell onto my chair. The rush of adrenaline subsided, leaving me weak. It took several minutes for me to regain my composure. Each noise caused me to swivel around again and again, sure that this time the zombie would be behind me. Finally, in desperation, I took a small mirror and propped it against my lamp so I could see the zombie in its cage.

I tried to eat some of my breakfast of rice and water chestnut cakes. It was too much. The taste in my mouth and the smell of the zombie made swallowing impossible. I set the ceramic bowl aside in disgust. As I did, an image on the small TV on a side table captured my attention. It was the daily report of known deaths. I turned up the volume to listen to a well-known news anchor from the U.S.

"...continued today as the number of deaths has risen to over two billion. Reports are continuing to come into the Associated Press regarding the decimation of entire villages, towns and cities in many third world countries. Governments are proactively organizing groups from state and federal prisons to dig up those buried in the past year, shoot each corpse in the head and burn the bodies."

"Dr. Steven Ruellins of the World Health Organization, or WHO, has stated that if a vaccine is found, he is hopeful it will work for those that have just been bitten by zombies as well as those infected by the unknown source. To date, there are no clues on how the dead reanimate within twenty-four hours of death. Zombies have been reported in almost every corner of the world, but no virus or bacteria has been found that provides a common denominator as to the cause. Ruellins has…"

The news anchor paused for a moment to listen to his headpiece. The hardened news anchor, who I had seen report from multiple war fronts around the world, looked shaken. "We interrupt this report to go live to a situation unfolding at Lanzhou Village in China's Gansu Province. Army troops were dispatched there early this morning as reports of mass carnage were disclosed. Our own Roger Grant is there at the scene. Roger." The TV signal flickered for a moment, and a new scene appeared. It took me a moment to comprehend what I was seeing.

Dawn was breaking. The first rays of the sun were shining over the peaks of the Gaolan Mountain Range, revealing a silhouetted mass of zombies advancing from the plain. There were hundreds, thousands – men, women, children. Their gait never varied from a slow walk. Although the sunlight was dim, from the few spotlights the army had aimed at the plains I could see their vacant stares.

There was only silence from the army. The camera captured the profile of the reporter, Roger Grant, as he stood staring, unable to pull himself together for the report. Who could blame him?

Only the moans and groans from the zombies could be heard. The noise grew in intensity as they stumbled closer. My heart pounded. I had never seen so many in one location.

The zombies crossed the scrub brush that dotted the sandy earth, and the soldiers opened fire, hopelessly outnumbered. Zombie after zombie struck the dirt, skulls split open by the bullets. Others kept advancing. They walked, no… make that shuffled over their dead.

Several zombies reached the line of soldiers, their sheer number overwhelming those in front, biting whatever body part was closest. I knew the moment groans turned to howls that the zombies had smelled the warm human blood. Some tore the arms from the living with their inhuman strength as others fell on soldiers and began to feed on their living flesh. Even if an airstrike had been called up, it would be too late to save these men.

A howl pierced the air behind me.

I jumped up and whirled around in one move. The lab zombie was at the bars of its cage, probably brought forward by its wailing brethren. Its hands were clawing at the bars trying to get out. All the while, its gaze never left mine.

And then it opened that dead mouth and keened. I clutched my ears trying to escape the sound. How could something dead be so…alive? I turned my back on that monster, but the others were still there in front of me as the carnage continued at Lanzhou. Monsters on the TV and in my mirror. The living dead surrounded me, and there was no escape.

I watched as one of the soldiers used his own pistol, bringing it to his head and killing himself rather than face the horror that was in front of him. I watched as those bitten realized there was no future. A bite from a zombie was a death sentence. Soldiers now had two targets – the zombies and their bitten comrades. For the bitten it was a mercy killing.

The slaughter continued. Mercifully, within minutes, the signal was lost as the cameraman, and, presumably, the reporter went down. The TV blared static for a minute until the station cut back to the main newsroom and a stunned and silent news anchor.

I wept. My father had served in the army as a doctor. He had fought the Japanese in World War II.

Then we had known the enemy. We had understood their motives. But zombies didn't have and didn't need a motive to justify their actions. How do you fight an enemy when they have no worlds to conquer, when their only want is to keep eating? This was becoming a war, not of "Will we win?" but one of "How long will we last?" There was no hope for peace. No hope at all.

A soft ping alerted me. It was almost time for the daily samples. I tried to erase the morning events from my expression. I knew it was a hopeless gesture. I bent and looked at myself in the mirror and saw a face I hardly recognized. Dark shadows lay under my eyes. Wrinkles creased my brow, and my hair was pure white. It was a face that wore every horror it had seen over the past two years. I straightened, and the face in the mirror was replaced by that of the zombie's.

I glanced at the clock. It was time.

The door hissed open. A group of soldiers, heavily padded in protective gear, the same used by divers against shark attack, arrived. Black metal helmets and face shields completed their outfits. They hardly looked at each other let alone me. This was one of the most dangerous jobs in the lab. It was no secret their mortality rate was tenfold that of the regular army.

The need for daily samples tested everyone's mettle. But it was a necessary task to discover the cure. Drugs had no effect on the zombies.

In several labs, a new method was being used. A mechanized, inner titanium wall was placed into the cage. When it was time for samples, the wall would be activated and slowly push the zombie against one of the side walls, immobilizing it. It was a much safer method than what was employed here. This lab wasn't on the schedule for such an improvement. Sheer brute force was the only method we had to subdue the zombie.

Today's draw of samples began as they all did. Five soldiers stormed the zombie and had it face down on the spattered ground within seconds. The lab technician, dressed in as much protection as possible, came forward and began drawing samples. A swab here, a small slice of dead gray flesh there.

Without warning the zombie screeched and jerked away

from the soldiers holding it down. It grabbed the tech by the arm and, before anyone could stop it, bit and tore a piece of flesh out of his hand.

The technician's high pitch scream was cut short as one soldier drew his sidearm and shot him between the eyes. The zombie was dispatched with the same method before the sound of the first shot had finished echoing around the lab. Blood and brains splattered the concrete walls.

There was no longer a need to take precautions, but the soldiers took no chances. They backed away from the bodies. The soldier that had fired the shots took careful aim and discharged more bullets into both heads.

The bodies of both the technician and zombie were placed in a steel mesh cage and wheeled out of the lab. I knew they were being taken to a fire pit where the bodies would be doused with gasoline and set on fire until they were reduced to ashes. No one could afford to take any chances these days.

Technicians came in and soon the smell of bleach pervaded the room. It didn't matter how well they scrubbed, the concrete continued to show bloodstains, and the stench of the zombie never left my nostrils. A fresh and bloody foot was placed in the far corner of the cell.

A new zombie, baying with its desire for flesh and blood was brought in. I could only guess how many had died capturing this one. But the details of their capture had never been shared with me.

The soldiers performed a series of elaborate steps and safety measures in preparation of releasing the zombie into the cage. Finally, the smaller cage was secured into the opening of the cell and unlatched. The zombie, smelling the blood, lurched and shuffled its way over to the limb in the corner and proceeded to chew and gnaw at it. The cell's security door was slid into place, and the cage removed.

Several technicians processed and ran a variety of tests the rest of the day, analyzing the samples the lab technician had taken prior to his untimely demise. I carefully reviewed each result as it came in, but, like every one that had gone before, it was another day of failure. The technicians left at the end of their shift, looking as haggard and disappointed as they felt, and keeping their distance from the cage.

I sat at my desk with the test reports in front of me. My eyes grew weary of looking at numbers, at sequences of DNA. The patterns blurred before me, but I pressed on. The answer was here. It had to be. Perhaps I was too close to the problem. I knew there was something familiar here that I had seen before, but my brain couldn't make sense of it.

I finally pushed the papers aside in frustration, upending my forgotten bowl of rice and shifting the mirror. The image in it changed. Now, instead of seeing the zombie, I saw the reflection of the patterns of DNA with grains of rice scattered across the papers. I reached to adjust the mirror and froze.

The horror I had just seen at Lanzhou was nothing compared to the feeling I experienced at that moment. Rice. I recognized that pattern in the mirror. I had seen it hundreds of times. It was the DNA sequence I had introduced into my rice. My genetically modified rice.

I checked and double-checked, frantic to prove it wasn't true. But after minutes of comparing dozens of lab tests, there was no doubt. The DNA strand I had used to increase the yield of the rice had somehow reversed its sequence and created a mirror image of itself in the zombie's DNA.

The words on the monitor faded to black as my vision narrowed to a white pinpoint of light. At that moment, I knew. The deaths of over two billion people cast their shadows upon my soul. It was all because of me, and the rice they had eaten.

This explained why no virus or bacteria could be found. It was much worse. It was in the very fabric of our flesh and blood. It was in our DNA.

Four years ago, I had created an experimental strain of genetically modified rice. When planted, a field that had originally produced a hundred bushels in return now yielded a thousand bushels.

My rice had been distributed around the world. China's export of rice had risen from forty percent of the world's supply to almost seventy.

The Chinese government had immediately seized my discovery and planted its first crop. Within six months of that harvest, they had begun exporting rice at prices that even third world countries could afford. The rice output was hailed as a miracle. The ingenuity and superiority of its Chinese growers acclaimed.

The genetic engineering was kept secret. The world had long demanded years of testing before introducing any genetically modified food. But my government didn't want to wait. They needed the income. I was heavily monitored and warned to remain silent. My work had been redirected to other areas.

Then, two years ago, the zombies had begun appearing. The attention of every scientist and lab in China had centered on understanding the problem. I had been given no choice. It was my duty to analyze the zombies and determine what, if anything, could be done. Find their weakness. Determine a method to destroy them faster than a bullet to the head. They knew I would do as I was asked; the safety of my family was guarantee enough.

I looked around. The new zombie stared at me. Fixed, unblinking. No recognition, no emotion, no thought was communicated by that gaze.

Titanium bars crisscrossed to form the front and top of the cage. Poured concrete completed the sides and far wall of the structure. Overhead floodlights illuminated every corner ensuring there were no shadows.

I had ceased seeing my cell long ago – my cell with the zombie's cell inside of it. I looked up. Security guards looked down from the metal walkways that lined the ceiling of the concrete bunker we were housed in. Guns were always aimed at the zombie. In time, I knew they would be turned on me, someday, when I had outlived my usefulness. I had been thrown into this cell when my wife had died a year ago. The government had been afraid I would defect with no hostage to keep me quiet.

My heart stuttered. My wife. Had my rice killed her also? Had she risen from her grave to join the walking dead?

Why hadn't I died? I had eaten the same meals as she had. Yet here I was, and she was dead.

I turned to stare at the zombie. It still chewed at the foot. Blood dripped down the side of its mouth. Then it did something that made me catch my breath. Its dead tongue slid out of its mouth, rotted and spotted with festering sores, and it licked away the blood. Finally, it all became clear.

The blood.

That was it.

Proteins. I had wanted to test a specific protein found in human blood. By using recombinant DNA technology, I had succeeded in isolating the code for this protein and joined it to the genetic material in one of the many species of oryza sativa – rice. I had wanted to strengthen the rice's outer hull for protection against disease. Somehow the DNA had created a mirror image of itself, multiplied in the human eating it and, after a time, solidified the blood. What happened afterward to create the zombie? I couldn't begin to understand.

Was this why the zombies craved human flesh? Was it really trying to get at the blood?

But why did some people die and others seem immune? In fact, the majority of people died. Yet I showed no signs. What was the key? I'd had the same vaccinations as the rest of the Chinese population. Had never had a disease other than chicken pox and measles as a young boy. I gave blood regularly because my blood type was so rare.

It was–

Wait. Could that be it? I had one of the rarest blood types in the world, AB negative. Could it be that the blood, which helped create the zombies, made me and others like me immune?

I searched the global database of test results. Tests had catalogued blood type along with a variety of other diagnostics. There it was, right in front of me. No zombie had ever had AB negative.

My mind began to shut down in protest. The ramifications were clear. I, singlehandedly, had presented almost every man, woman and child in the world with a death sentence.

It did not matter that I had wanted to test the rice before it was distributed. That I had started my modifications with the best of intentions. I had not sounded the alarm four years ago. I had kept quiet when the rice was distributed.

This was all my doing. A death that was created from my own body.

I broke at that point. Broke down and cried. Tears of remorse. Tears of self-pity.

I looked around. The zombie continued to stare at me. And in those cold eyes I saw my future.

This cage, this zombie, this would be my penance. From this day forward, every minute of every day that I am still alive, I will be reminded of what my work has done to this earth. Regardless of whether or not I can find a cure with the cause now known, I will have over two billion deaths on my soul. Two billion souls and unimaginable grief.

I looked at the mirror in front of me. I stared at the monster I saw in it. The destroyer of humanity. It wasn't the zombie I saw reflected there. It was me.

I am the true monster.

AUTHOR BIOS

Morgan Ashe fell in love with the macabre and bizarre years ago at the knee of her grandmother watching *The Twilight Zone*, *Night Gallery* and *Ghost Story*. Her library consists of many fiction and non-fiction works on post-apocalyptic events, conspiracy theories, mythology, plagues and forensic science. She lives on the East Passage of the Narragansett Bay with her wonderful and ever-patient husband and their cats. Based on the cats[1] behavior, she suspects they are demonic imps from another dimension running tests on humans. You can find out more about her writing and the devilish cats at: morganashe.com.

Steven W. Booth still doesn't know what he wants to be when he grows up. To date he has been a fundraiser, a taxi driver, an alarm service technician, a marketing consultant, a computer technician, a grocery store cashier, a synagogue facilities manager, a web developer, a short video producer, a teacher, and a writer. The last four activities have occupied his attention reasonably well, so he hopes to continue with them far into the future. Steven lives in the Los Angeles area with his wife and too many cats. Visit him at www.stevenwbooth.com and www.gosmultimedia.com.

J. L. (Judy) Comeau is an award-winning author whose short stories have appeared in major horror anthologies including *Best New Horror*, *The Years' Best Horror*, with multiple publications in the *Borderlands* series, the *Dark Visions* series, the *Hot Blood* series and many others. You are invited to share her enthusiasm for the horror genre at her book review web page, The Tomb (www.countgore.com), where her reading recommendations and interviews with horror luminaries are

291

posted every Saturday night. Her official website is located at www.HorrorWriter.com, and you may also befriend her at www.facebook.com/jlcomeau.

David Dunwoody is the author of the zombie novel *Empire*, as well as the collections *Dark Entities* and *Unbound & Other Tales*. Upcoming projects include the Lovecraftian post-apocalyptic novel *The Harvest Cycle*. Dave lives in Utah, and can be visited on the Web at daviddunwoody.com.

Rob Fox lives in Mableton, GA (Just outside of Atlanta) with his wife, Darcy, their dogs Tweek and Otis, and two cats Lasia, and Sticky. Rob is Author of the *Z Day is Here* blog (located at www.zdayishere.blogspot.com), as well as the author of the zombie novel also entitled *Z Day is Here*. Rob has written a number of zombie and horror related short stories, movie scripts, and is currently working on the follow up to the *Z Day* novel. You can also check out his webpage for all things Rob Fox at www.zdayishere.com.

Boyd E. Harris is the publisher of and an editor for *Cutting Block Press* (www.cuttingblock.net) a company specializing in horror anthologies. His book, *+Horror Library+ Volume 3*, earned a nomination for a *Bram Stoker award* for best anthology in 2008. He is also the publisher of and an editor for *Dark Recesses Enterprise*, (www.darkrecesses.com) a *Black Quill Award* winning onine horror magazine. A writer at heart, Boyd soon hopes to spend more time exploring the horrific through his own pen.

Richard Jeter is the itinerant gypsy type, currently residing in Macon, Georgia. For a few more minutes anyway. During his travels, he has stopped long enough to type up tales which have been featured in independent short story anthologies in America, Canada, and the United Kingdom. With one book having completed a small press run and another looking for a good home, there's plenty of activity to keep up with, all the details on which can be found at either his Facebook fan page or blog, richardjeter.wordpress.com!

Stephanie Kincaid is a freelance editor and writer who lives with one foot in the deliciously grotesque landscape of her imagination and the other in Oklahoma. Her work can be found in *Book of the Dead 3: Dead and Rotting* from Living Dead Press, as well as in upcoming anthologies from Library of the Living Dead Press and Lame Goat Press.

Matthew Louis edits and publishes the seedy pulp fiction journal, *Out of the Gutter*, and is co-founder of the independent press, Gutter Books.

Lisa Mannetti is the author of *The Gentling Box* (Dark Hart Press, 2008), which won a Bram Stoker Award, and *51 Fiendish Ways to Leave Your Lover*, (Dad Moon Books, February 2010). Her stories have appeared in numerous anthologies; "Everybody Wins," was translated into a short film by director Paul Leyden entitled *Bye-Bye Sally*. At present she is working on several pieces to be published in 2010, a longer tale called *Spy Glass Hill*, and a paranormal novel – *The Everest Hauntings*. Lisa resides in New York with demonic twin cats, Harry and Theo Houdini. Visit Lisa on the web at www.lisamannetti.com.

Michelle McCrary is an emerging writer in the horror genre. She has several short stories in the *Zombology* series from Library of the Living Dead Press, as well as a short story in the *Ladies of Horror Anthology*, coming soon from the Library of Horror Press. When not continuously making sure her loved ones have a zombie plan, she is thinking of ideas for new stories. Mrs. McCrary lives in Shreveport, Louisiana with her husband, two sons, and their many pets. Read her blog at deadmama30.blogspot.com

Joe McKinney is a homicide detective for the San Antonio Police Department who has been writing professionally since 2006. He is the author of several novels, including *Dead City*, *Quarantined*, *Apocalypse of the Dead*, and *Lost Girl of the Lake*, and more than thirty horror, crime, and science fiction short stories. As a police officer, he's received extensive professional training in disaster mitigation, forensics, and homicide investigation techniques, some of which finds its way into his stories. He lives in the Texas Hill Country north of San Antonio. Visit him at http://joemckinney.wordpress.com for news and updates.

Bob Nailor is an author and editor who resides with his wife on a quaint country acre in NW Ohio. When not in the RV traveling the country visiting friends and doing research, he spends his time writing and editing. He is a contributing author and co-editor of *Nights of Blood 2* plus a contributing author to *A Firestorm of Dragons*, *The Fantasy Writer's Companion* and *The Guide to Writing Science Fiction*, for which he won an Eppie in 2008. He is also published in *The Archives of Arrissia, 13 Nights of Blood* and *Spirits of Blue and Gray*.

Mark Onspaugh grew up on a steady diet of horror, science fiction and DC Comics. He wrote the upcoming film *Kill Katie Malone* and co-wrote *Flight of the Living Dead*. Some of his stories appear in *OZ: Shadows of the Emerald City* (JW Schnarr, ed.), *The Book of Exodi* (Michael K. Eidson, ed.), *The World is Dead* (Kim Paffenroth, ed.), and *Footprints* (Jay Lake & Eric T. Reynolds, ed.). His essay on monsters appears in *Butcher Knives and Body Counts* (Dark Scribe Press). He lives in Los Osos, CA with wife, author/artist Dr. Tobey Crockett and three enigmatic cats. www.markonspaugh.com.

Harry Shannon has been an actor, an Emmy-nominated songwriter, a recording artist, music publisher, a VP at Carolco Pictures and worked as a Music Supervisor on *Basic Instinct* and *Universal Soldier*. His novels include *Night of the Beast*, *Night of the Werewolf*, *Daemon*, *Dead and Gone* and *The Pressure of Darkness*, as well as the Mick Callahan suspense novels *Memorial Day*, *Eye of the Burning Man*, and *One of the Wicked*. His new collection *A Host of Shadows* is from Dark Region Press. Shannon has won the Tombstone Award, the Black Quill, and has been nominated for the Stoker. Contact him at www.harryshannon.com.

Marge Ballif Simon's works have appeared in *Chizine*, *The Pedestal Magazine*, *Strange Horizons*, *Dreams & Nightmares*, and more. In 2008, she won the Stoker for Best Poetry Collection for *VECTORS: A Week in the Death of a Planet*. Marge is former president of the Science Fiction Poetry Association and serves as editor of Star*Line. Her next collection, *In the Garden of Unearthly Delights* is pending from Sam's Dot Publications. Marge and her amazing husband, Bruce Boston, reside in Ocala, Florida. For more information, go to www.margesimon.com.

Nate Southard is the writer of *Just Like Hell*, *Broken Skin*, *He Stepped Through*, and the graphic novels *Drive* and *A Trip to Rundberg*. His short stories have appeared in such venues as *Cemetery Dance*, *Thuglit*, and numerous anthologies. *Focus*, a novella he wrote with Lee Thomas, will be available later this year. Nate lives in Austin with his girlfriend and a quartet of lazy pets. He is currently hard at work on his next novel. Nate's a friendly kinda guy, and he welcomes communication with readers. You can learn more at natesouthard.com.

Lee Thomas is the Bram Stoker Award and Lambda Literary Award-winning author of *Stained*, *Parish Damned*, and *The*

Dust of Wonderland. His short story collection *In the Closet, Under the Bed* was released in 2010 by Dark Scribe Press. In addition to numerous magazines, his short fiction has appeared in the anthologies *A Walk on the Darkside* (Roc), *Unspeakable Horror* (Dark Scribe), *Darkness on the Edge* (PS Publishing), and *Inferno* (Tor), among others. You can find him on the web at www.leethomasauthor.com.

Bev Vincent is the author of *The Road to the Dark Tower* and *The Stephen King Illustrated Companion*, along with numerous interviews, essays and nearly sixty short stories, which have appeared in places like *Ellery Queen's Mystery Magazine, Cemetery Dance, Tesseracts Thirteen, The Blue Religion* and *When the Night Comes Down*. He has been nominated for the Bram Stoker Award twice and once for an Edgar. He is a contributing editor with *Cemetery Dance* and blogs about writing for *Storytellers Unplugged*. He writes reviews for *Onyx Reviews* (onyxreviews.com) and his website is bevvincent.com. He lives in Texas.

Calie Voorhis is a life-long fan of the fantastic. An alumnus of the Odyssey Fantasy Writing Workshop, she is currently completing a MFA degree in Writing Popular Fiction at Seton Hill University.

Steven E. Wedel is a life-long Oklahoman best known for The Werewolf Saga books: *Murdered by Human Wolves, Shara, Ulrik* and *Call to the Hunt* (Scrybe Press). His other books include *Darkscapes* (Fine Tooth Press), *Seven Days in Benevolence* (Scrybe Press) and *Little Graveyard on the Prairie* (Bad Moon Books). Steve has held many jobs but is currently a high school English teacher. He holds a master's degree from the University of Oklahoma and a bachelor's degree from the University of Central Oklahoma. Steve lives in central Oklahoma with his wife and four children. Visit him online at www.stevenewedel.com.

Mitchel Whitington has authored twelve books, contributed to ten anthologies, and has a total of over one hundred credits to his name across all platforms of publication: books, magazines, newspapers, etc. While he enjoys writing fiction – especially horror fiction – his favorite topic is dealing with the realities of the supernatural… which works well, since he lives in an 1861 home with his wife, basset hounds, and more than a few resident ghosts.

CPSIA information can be obtained at www.ICGtesting.com
Printed in the USA
LVOW011618130313

324130LV00015B/611/P